THUNDER ON SUNDAY

The sound of hail on the Perspex was deafening. Caught in an aerial whirlpool, Tango Foxtrot slipped and sank, juddering in all her plates, her engines whining and screaming.

'Have to get down soon, sir!' Barrett called from the panel. 'Losing fuel fast!'

'Mayday!' Spence called into the microphone. '*Mayday*!'

'I'm taking her right to the sea, Mr Spence. First sign of fire, I'll have to put her down.' Lampeter pushed the control column forward. 'Here we go!'

Peter Spence felt a sick wrench in his stomach, as they pitched and rolled in the heavy turbulence. A watery bitter fluid welled up in his mouth. He was still calling into his microphone:

'Mayday . . . Mayday . . . Lightning strike . . . losing fuel . . . May have to put down in sea . . . *Mayday . . . Mayday . . .*'

KAREN CAMPBELL

Thunder on Sunday

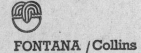

FONTANA / Collins

First published in 1972 by William Collins Sons & Co Ltd
First issued in Fontana Books 1976

© Karen Campbell, 1972

Made and printed in Great Britain by
William Collins Sons & Co Ltd Glasgow

CONTENTS

To Catherine Campbell McNeill
of Kilchoman

27th October   SUNNANDÆG

The Day of the Sun

'Queer!' said Lampeter.

With his left hand, he shielded his eyes against the late October sun dazzling the windscreen, and gazed down eighteen thousand feet at the sea below. His thick black brows drew together over the high-bridged nose, reputed on Celtic Airways to be able to smell a storm before the parent clouds were within striking distance. But there were no clouds this afternoon. An hour out from Keflavik on the 106 weekend flight to Glasgow, the day remained gin clear and glassy calm. On the other side of the fuselage, Tango Foxtrot's jets whistled their muted, perfectly tuned duet. The sun streamed in through the Perspex, bringing to the flight deck, despite the Captain's rather gritty presence, something of the atmosphere of a south coast solarium. An atmosphere intensified by the Sunday smell of roast beef slices and brussels sprouts, and the decorous flower perfume of the stewardess as she moved deftly behind the pilots' seats.

'Queer!'

Lampeter said it again, staring at the needle on a small round instrument tucked away in the bottom left-hand corner of the panel. The air temperature gauge was reading plus 2° Centigrade – very warm for this height at this time of year.

Reaching across the throttle box, he picked up the blue weather folder that the Met Officer at Keflavik had given him and opened it up. He studied the cross section first of their route, Iceland to Glasgow – a picture in zones of the expected weather. The forecaster had drawn a fanciful curl of cloud over Reykjavik that had proved to be a puff of fair weather cumulus, no more, but for the rest of the route just sunshine all the way.

'And the winds?' he had asked.

'Light easterlies,' the forecaster had said. 'Nothing to worry about.'

Out of the corner of his right eye, Lampeter saw his First Officer, Peter Spence, blinking his eyes in the sunlight, pick up the microphone and report, 'Oceanic Control, this is Tango Foxtrot, position 12.00 is 61 north, 1432 west, cruising in the clear at Flight Level 180. Estimate Glasgow 13.43.'

'Sir?'

At the sound of the female voice, Lampeter turned round impatiently. They had brought only cargo up from Scotland last night, and had picked up the stewardess along with the passengers this morning. The girl proffering the tray was new, but she had obviously heard of him. Large hazel-brown eyes set slightly aslant like a fawn's beneath a wide, delicately sweeping brow, regarded him warily. A delicate face altogether, Lampeter thought, under the smooth centre-parted hair – nicely chiselled nose, cheekbones and pointed chin. But he was not so sure of the mouth. Full lips curving into a slightly lopsided smile contradicted the demureness of the rest of the face. From eight years' flying as a captain, Lampeter had acquired the habit of instantaneously diagnosing weather, engines, people.

'You're new?'

'No, sir.'

Lampeter frowned at the bald contradiction.

'I've been on the line three months.'

'What's your name?'

'Claire Masefield.'

'You haven't flown with me before.'

'I haven't had that –' a slight smile quickly swallowed – 'pleasure, sir.'

Lampeter gave her a sharp glance and, satisfied that no pertness had been intended, looked down to the sea again.

'Where shall I put your tray, sir?'

'Here!' He thumped the flat surface of the throttle box. Irritably he found himself staring at her profile spotlit by an undiminished sun. Then as she straightened he saw a sudden glitter in the lapel of her jacket.

'What's that you're wearing?'

'Sir?' She turned her head, flushing slightly. 'This?'

'Yes, that.'

'Oh, it's just a sort of Icelandic St Christopher.' She turned her lapel and brought it near so that he could see the squat figure fashioned out of some silver metal. 'There's a German couple . . . the Hagedorns . . . he's a historian . . . they gave it to me.'

'Take it off.'

'Sir?'

'You heard me . . .' He watched her hesitate, flush deeper, then shrug slightly, unfasten the pin, and drop the brooch into her pocket. 'For one thing jewellery isn't allowed with uniform. You know that. And for another, Celtic Airways doesn't fly on luck.'

For some stupid reason he wished he hadn't said that. He stared down again at the surface of the sea. Now tiny arrowheads of white caps pointed the unmistakable way the sea was running.

'That position,' Lampeter said suddenly, 'was it the flight plan position?'

'Yes, sir.' Peter Spence had just dug his fork into his roast beef. He swallowed nervously. 'Dead reckoning.'

'Dead is probably right,' Lampeter said drily. 'Get a Loran fix.'

Deftly Miss Masefield leaned forward, replaced the fork, scooped up Spence's tray. Lampeter watched them both. They were both young and inexperienced. They had both felt the sharp edge of his well-known tongue. Even so, they didn't exchange sympathetic glances, and Lampeter warmed to the pair of them.

And then as she passed him to move back to the engineer's console, Miss Masefield said softly but very clearly in his ear, 'Then why don't they ever have a seat thirteen, sir?' There was no mistaking now the glint in the deceptively innocent eyes.

Lampeter stared after her for a moment in disbelief. Then he grinned and said, 'Touché.' But she was already talking to the engineer.

Beside Lampeter, Peter Spence had his face glued into the rubber eyepiece of the Loran. There were little beads of sweat on his forehead. He counted the jumping electric lines and the long number blips chanting out loud, 'Thirty-three, thirty-four, thirty-five,' as though to reassure an unnecessarily irascible schoolmaster, '. . . thirty-six seventy-one, sir.'

He then transferred his eyes to the Loran map swirling with curved lines and began following the red one numbered L1 till it crossed the green one.

In the quietness, Lampeter could hear the enthusiastic squeak of Bill Barrett's knife and fork on the plastic lunch tray.

'What's for pud, Claire?'

Miss Masefield's voice answered, 'Your favourite, apple pie.'

'Hope you let the knife slip. Ah yes, indeed. You girls spoil me.'

'Us girls have to.'

Little Bill Barrett's comfortable laugh, in keeping with the sun and the calmness of the day. Why should it irritate Lampeter now?

'Ah, you just don't stand a chance. Competition's too great.'

Still grinning, the engineer was waving a fond hand at the real love of his life. His twins. Known throughout Celtic as bachelor Bill's birds.

'How are they?'

'Spot on. Doing what all you girls should do. Keeping quiet and burning hot.'

Close now to retiring age, Bill Barrett remained as he always said, a bachelor like his father, in love with his red-hot gassy girls. Irritably Lampeter sighed and scanned the sky. The blue was paling as if the dome of the sky was swathed in gauze. Dead ahead a faint serrated line of cloud stretched like a distant landfall.

'Haven't you got that position yet, Mr Spence?'

'Sir? I've got *a* position report. But it can't be right. I must have made a mistake. I'm taking another now.' The sweat ran down Spence's pink cheeks and dribbled off the end of his chin. He wiped it off like a schoolboy with the back of his hand.

'What position was it?'

'Sir . . . twelve ten west . . . fifty miles east of track.'

10

Lampeter said nothing for a second. Then he grunted. 'Just what I thought. There's a hell of a wind down there. Damn Met! Light easterlies, eh? Westerly, ninety knots more like . . . and dead on our beam. Give me a new course.'

'One-eighty magnetic.'

'Altering to one-eighty.' Lampeter swung the aircraft round to the right. 'Mr Barrett . . . give me climb power.'

Immediately and obediently the twins roared up. 'Climb power, sir!' Noisily Bill Barrett shoved aside his tray.

'And now, Mr Spence, call up Control. Give them the right position this time. And get clearance to FL three-six-oh.' Lampeter reached up and switched on the seat-belt sign. 'I'll have them strapped in, Miss Masefield. Collect this clobber and then go back and see they do as they're told.'

Claire Masefield glanced out of the window as she picked up the trays. The sun still shone but the sky seemed to be closing in. Below as they climbed the tiny waves shrank smaller still, till they were no more than white lacy threads on green georgette crepe. But it was a crepe that moved steadily towards the east as if an invisible hand inexorably pulled a carpet from under their feet. And now coming up from the south to meet them was a white net of cloud.

'Reported that position yet, Mr Spence?'

'Sir . . . sir . . .' Peter Spence was clicking his microphone and shaking it. 'Oceanic Control . . . Glasgow . . . Reykjavik . . . nobody's answering, sir . . . Hell of a lot of static and nothing else. Can't raise a peep out of anybody.'

Claire stood for a second under the glowing seat-belt sign, assembling a momentarily fractured smile. Two of the passengers were having an after lunch sleep. The rest gave her what stewardesses christen the 'Moses look'. She had just come down from communion with the Almighty. Now they waited for her to tell them what the hell it was all about.

She tackled the sleeping passengers first. Four rows back on the starboard side, Signor Borghese, the wine salesman from Lombardy, slept with his head against the porthole window. Some small vibrations had wiped his hair like a rag over the Perspex, leaving a greasy print. Claire leaned over him and pulled the straps shut over his knees. Painfully thin

11

knees, she noticed sadly, the suiting worn and shabby but carefully pressed. There were dark circles under his eyes, and in repose, his face had a defeated look.

Not so the other sleeper, two seats back and on the other side of the aisle. Mr Jerry (and no rude cracks about that) Ainsworth, photographer to his companion, the model Miss Dawn Playfair.

'Don't wake him.' Miss Playfair leaned across the occupant of the middle seat, a large, white, woolly lamb, and pressed a Chinese-purple fingernail to matching lips. 'I like him best that way.' She patted the woolly lamb. 'When I need intelligent conversation, I talk to Larry.'

'Is he your mascot?'

'Which one?' Miss Playfair's violet eyes drooped under their inch-long mascaraed lashes. 'Larry? Sure.' And in the same breath, 'Do I really have to put this cigarette out?'

'Please.'

'I thought that sign just meant the pilot was going to have his Sunday sleep.'

'So it does,' Claire said, smiling briskly, glancing over her shoulder to see how many others looked as if they were going to argue the toss. 'But the smell of smoke disturbs him.'

'In that case,' Miss Playfair smiled, 'why didn't you say so before?' She leaned forward towards the ashtray. A sudden spiral of turbulence twisted Tango Foxtrot's frame. The ash spattered over the model's immaculate black suit. She looked from her skirt to the sky. As Claire moved quickly down the aisle, she was thumping Mr Ainsworth's arm, and telling him to wake.

'Either I've got DT's, *or there's water in the carburettor.*' With a bright, I'm-not-nervous, exaggerated smile, Mrs Ewart, the Canadian widow, threw up her pretty, beringed hands to indicate her inability to cope with the buckle of her strap.

'It's a bit of turbulence, that's all,' Claire said, flicking it shut for her.

'I promised my married daughter I'd write her one of your postcards, but the table was quivering like a ouija board.'

'You'll get it done all right before we get to Glasgow,' Claire said, folding the offending table back against the seat

12

in front, and recognizing the passenger's need to talk. 'Is this the daughter you've been visiting?'

'Correct. My one and only. The American Air Force grass widow. She tells me storms blow up faster than Procter and Gamble bubbles.'

'And blow out just as fast,' Claire said. 'Her husband's based in Reykjavik, is he?'

'Well, he hangs his hat there. She's like me, homesick for little old Montreal.'

'Aren't you going the wrong way?' Claire prepared to move back. Beyond the starboard wing tip the sun burnt feebly like a dying candle flame in a whitening waxy sky. They had levelled out. The same white cloud stretched below their feet. She wondered what the sea was doing.

'No, honey, I'm not going the wrong way. I'm on a sentimental journey.' Her pretty hazel eyes filled with tears. She stared out of the window. Abruptly the sun went out as if dipped in water. Mrs Ewart didn't appear to notice. Claire moved back towards the Hagedorns. In the minute she had been talking to Mrs Ewart, the aisle had turned into a fairground cake walk.

But Herr and Frau Hagedorn appeared not to notice. They were sitting bolt upright with their belts fastened, riding the now marked turbulence as if in a Mercedes on an autobahn. He was very tall with sloping shoulders and a pear-shaped figure. His long-nosed profile resembled General de Gaulle's, and in fact he exuded something of the General's aloof authority. His wife was small and round and apparently boneless, with very fine grey hair, and round blue myopic eyes. She wore a tight blue dress stretched inadequately over plump middle-aged thighs. Herr Hagedorn was engrossed in some technical journal. Frau Hagedorn was knitting as if she had so many yards to do before landing.

'We are both with the seat-belts correctly fastened.' Herr Hagedorn spoke for the pair of them. His wife's English was limited.

'Are you quite comfortable?'

'Yes, thank you indeed. My wife had just remarked on the smoothness of the flight.'

'Not for much longer, I'm afraid. It's stormy ahead.'

'Stormy?' Herr Hagedorn leaned forward, looking at the jagged cumulus-nimbus tops that now punctured the line of the southern horizon. Not with trepidation but with interest. When he had given her the brooch before take-off, he had told her he had been lecturing on the Icelandic myth and folk tales and their common origins with the Celtic and German. As a lightning flash zigzagged across the sky, he said in a gleeful, guttural way, rolling the r, 'Thor-rr.'

'Sir?'

He pointed through the Perspex. 'Thor's chariot, drawn by two he-goats . . . cannot you see it?'

Claire saw a thunderhead ripped by lightning.

'Regularly Thor-rr brings back his goats to life with his hammer. The hammer has the same shape as the cross. Interesting, yes?'

'Very.'

'Thor-rr, god of thunder and lightning, also the sun god. Worshipped by the Druids as Eochaid, the great father, propagator of all life. Thor-rr, son of Odin, or in Anglo-Saxon, Woden, in German Wotan –'

'Wotan.' His wife at last recognized a word she could understand and beamed.

The southern horizon was now alive with lightning. 'Thor-rr,' Herr Hagedorn said with satisfaction. 'God of the Vikings who called this the sea of storms. History is continuous. Yesterday and tomorrow, they are here today. And so are the thunderstorms.'

'Damned thunderstorm!'

The last three seats on the starboard side were fully occupied by the passenger Claire Masefield had already pigeon-holed as the one who was bound to give trouble. He lay with his back against the window, and his scruffy suède boots on the upholstery, cradling a guitar. Naturally his seat-belt was unfastened, and he looked as if he wasn't going to do it up. He was a pale young man of twenty-one, with a thin, prematurely lined face, red-rimmed angry brown eyes, and a rusty red beard that contrived to grow at right angles to his chin.

Herr Hagedorn became concerned.

'Young man, you blaspheme. The gods are not strange, only the way they are worshipped. And the weather does not change. Only the means of overcoming it.'

'And let's hope ours are better.'

'Oh, I think they're a bit better.' Claire was maintaining her balance with difficulty.

'What have we got that Vikings haven't got?' His beard tipped towards her interrogatively.

'Passengers, for one thing.'

'That's a debit, marm.'

Claire grinned and nodded. 'There's Loran. Radar. Automatic navigation. And now, sir — ' she indicated the sign — 'would you, please?'

'It's the thin end of the wedge.'

'What is?'

'That sort of automation. Fasten your belt. Unfasten your belt. Go to the toilet. Return from the toilet. Eat. Stop eating. Open the door. Bale out. Just do what the machine says. Come to that, how do we know you've got a pilot at all?'

'Mr Philby — ' Claire smiled grimly — 'if you don't fasten your belt, you'll soon find out we've got a pilot.'

'Of course.' Mr Philby swung his legs to the floor. 'When I'm asked nicely like that.' He dragged the belt shut, and lifted his guitar on to his knee. A colonnade of cumulus clouds stretched now on either side of them. Silently, distantly, the thunder lost behind them, lightning flickered between the towers like some weird Morse code.

'Thunder on Sunday brings death on Monday,' Mr Philby intoned, pulling at the strings of his guitar.

Immediately Mrs Crowther's permanently waved head appeared from behind the seat in front. The lights of the cabin twinkled on round horn-rimmed spectacles, too big for the little crinkled Pekinese face.

'It's all right, Mrs Crowther, my old dear, not heavenly music. Not yet.'

'Eeh, come forward an' talk to us. He's a real narky chap!' Mrs Crowther included them both in a wide, piano-keyed grin. 'I never heard such a load of rubbish as that young bloke talks, not in all my born days. Here, lass, there's a spare seat. Strap yourself in. You can get yoursen knocked around same ast' rest of us. And we haven't had a chat with you yet.'

Thankfully, Claire moved forward and perched herself on the third seat beside the Crowthers. She put her hand in her pocket and touched the little charm the Hagedorns had given her. She could see enough of the sky now to know it was going to be one hell of a storm.

> 'Thunder on Sunday,
> Dead on Monday,
> Who is it going to be,
> The butcher, the baker, the candlestick-maker,
> Or why not say all three?'

At first Mr Philby went on strumming his guitar, extemporizing the words to the endless variations of what rhymed with be. 'Philbee. Poor little me, the black-eyed ladee, the pair from Germanee.'

Then lightning and thunder coming almost simultaneously drowned the song. The aircraft was buffeted from side to side. Claire watched the port wing dip into a waste of water, and rise up again dripping like the prow of a sinking ship. Hail rattled on the metal skin. Icy fragments slithered down the portholes. The aircraft seemed to fall flat on its belly in the turbulence, drag itself up, skeeter sideways. Mr Barrett's birds roared and screamed. But nothing quenched Mrs Crowther, the lady from Halifax.

'By gum, lad, they're giving us a ride for our money.'

And when a white magnesium flare of lightning exploded in their eyes, 'Look, love, someone up there's taking us photos.'

'Reckon you should be used to that all right, lass.' Mr Crowther spoke for the first time. Despite the nervous cries from the rest of the passengers, novelty kept them unmoved.

'How's that?' Claire asked, thankful for the pair of them.

'Tell her, lass.'

'Nay, lad, she don't want to know.' And turning her huge thick spectacles to Claire, 'Did you never scratch your head how working folk like us could come on a trip like this?' And in the same breath, 'Dost eat cod, lass?'

Claire shook her head to the first and said, 'Sometimes.'

'Ah, but not much, eh?'

'No.'

'Then that's how, lass. Neither does nobody else.'

'She won a competition.' Mr Crowther's big Teddy-bear head was spotlit in lightning. 'The missis won a competition for t'best sauce recipe for Icelandic cod. One hundred pounds, and a free trip to Iceland. It's been a real education. Marvellous. Mind, she's a marvellous cook. And not just sauce, though she's got plenty of that.' He dug his elbow into her skinny ribs. 'You should sup a bit of her trifle. Cake and red jelly and you could serve it the Queen with no disgrace.'

'I'll give you the sauce recipe, lass. It'll come in handy. Now you tek a nice knob of best butter and warm it over t'stove. Then flour. I allus use Co-op flour and a nice pinch of . . .'

But the rest of the ingredients were lost. A sudden crack of sound seemed to open up the sky, like an atom bomb exploding above them. A magnesium glow burned momentarily dazzling and white hot. Then all the lights went out. The aisle tilted crazily. In pitch darkness and pouring rain Tango Foxtrot plunged towards the sea.

'Damn this bloody weather!'

Barrett had picked up his torch and was out of his seat before Lampeter had righted the aircraft. Steadying himself on the engineer's console, he sent its powerful beam out into the black.

Over the flight deck, there was darkness broken only by the lights on the panel flickering on and off like a fruit machine gone mad. As the two pilots wrestled with the controls, Barrett stood transfixed, staring out at the starboard wing. Out there was a sight that made his round face break out in a sweat, and the hairs on the back of his neck prick up like a hound's.

'Christ, sir!'

'What's up?'

'Starboard fuel tank's holed.' Barrett transferred the spotlight to the left. 'And the port!' He watched the yellow exhaust of the engine – and, just above the flames, a twisting translucent rope, an oily, spiralling, liquid trail. 'Leaking kerosene like mad!'

'Mr Spence, haven't you got Control *yet*?'

'No joy, sir.'

There was a moment's pause. Hail sheeted down on the windscreen. Deep inside the dark cave of cloud came flashes of wet lightning.

'Where's the nearest land, Mr Spence?'

The map shook in the First Officer's hand. 'Just checking, sir.'

The wavering circle of Spence's torch flitted on the crumpled chart on his knees.

'What about the Hebrides?'

'Too far, sir.'

'Where, then?'

Half the First Officer's attention was fixed on raising Control.

'Just trying to see.'

The sound of hail on the Perspex was deafening. Caught in an aerial whirlpool, Tango Foxtrot slipped and sank, juddering in all her plates, her engines whining and screaming.

'Have to get down soon, sir!' Barrett called from the panel. 'Losing fuel fast!'

'Send out Mayday, Mr Spence! And come on, *quickly*!'

'Sir, I'm –'

'Don't worry about an airfield.'

'I'm not, sir.'

'Just a piece of dry ground –'

The round yellow disc of illumination stopped. Ringed round with light, right at the centre of the chart, was a tiny spiderlike mark with jagged edges.

'What's *that*?'

'It's –' Spence lowered his head, peering at the now illuminated blob dancing madly on the chart in the heavy turbulence. 'Can't see, sir!'

'An island?'

'Yes, sir. A . . . R ; . D , ; . Can't read it, sir.' He steadied the vibrating paper. '*Ardnabegh.*'

'Ardnabegh.'

'Heard of it, sir?'

'Yes. Somewhere or other. Give me a course to steer.'

'Hundred and ten.'

'Turning on to hundred and ten.' Lampeter eased the aircraft round. 'How far away?'

'Ninety miles, sir.'

'But we'll have the wind behind us. Barrett,' he yelled. 'How long have we got?'

'Fifteen . . . twenty minutes, sir. If we don't go up like a Roman candle first.'

'Spence, give them our right position.'

'Still trying, sir – '

'And call Mayday!'

'Mayday!' Spence called into the microphone immediately. *M'aidez* – help me, the radio telephone distress signal. '*Mayday!*'

Lampeter leaned across the console, looked at the chart, crumpling and rustling on Spence's lap, and saw hachures and the spotheight 2956. 'Mountain to the north. High cliffs to the south.'

'Hospitable sort of place, sir.'

'Better than the Atlantic . . .'

Behind them the engineer was swearing away at the weather. In thirty years' flying, no one had ever been in trouble because of his engines or his fuel. He regarded the storm as a personal affront. His thick stubby fingers delicately touched the throttle controls, trying to conserve every teaspoonful of fuel, as he cursed the storm and the lightning with one breath, and prayed there would be enough to get them to that tiny little dot. Mixed in with the ominous sharpness of kerosene, he could smell his own sweat. From time to time, he pressed his face against the side window. The cloud was thinner now. But the new light served only to show that perilous hangman's rope, swaying near to the flame and away again. One extra strong current of air, one over-sharp movement of the control column . . .

'I'm taking her right to the sea, Mr Spence. First sign of fire, I'll have to put her down.' Lampeter pushed the control

19

column forward. 'Here we go!'

Peter Spence felt a sick wrench in his stomach, as they pitched and rolled in the heavy turbulence. A watery bitter fluid welled up in his mouth. He was still calling into his microphone:

'Mayday, Mayday . . . Oceanic Control . . . Tango Foxtrot . . . Mayday . . . Mayday . . . Lightning strike . . . losing fuel . . . Turned easterly for Ardnabegh. May have to put down in sea . . . Mayday . . . Mayday – '

That monotonous desperate chant was what Claire Masefield heard as she came back to the flight deck. She closed the door behind her and steadied herself against it, catching her breath momentarily, even though she had expected this. She had seen the fuel leak. So had half the passengers.

As she came forward, Barrett glanced up at her, face illuminated now only by the phosphorescent light of the instruments. His rage increased. 'If I ever have a daughter,' he said furiously, 'I won't let her be a stewardess.'

'When elephants fly, eh, Bill?'

'Yep.' He sighed, and lapsed into his favourite expression. 'Nights like this, I'm glad I'm not married.'

He looked outside. The silk rope was thinner and more dangerous, wavering and dangling just above the flames.

Lampeter turned his head, and saw the girl standing there. He said, 'Prepare the passengers for ditching, just in case. We're depressurized, so open all emergency exits. See they put their life-jackets on.' And then more gently, 'And mind you're strapped in, and braced for landing.'

'I will be, sir,' she said, but already he had turned his attention back to the black wet world outside.

Only Barrett watched her leave the flight deck. A sudden irrational thought pierced his anger that he would have been rather proud of a daughter like her. For the first time he regretted his lifetime's obsession with aero engines.

'About seven minutes' fuel left, sir!'

'Thank you, Mr Barrett.'

'Mayday, Mayday.' With a gulp, Spence stopped his transmission. Now his whole face was puckered up with the effort of listening.

'Hear anything?'

'Dead as a dodo.'

'What's the matter?'

'Burned out, I reckon.'

They were low now. Drifts of torn cloud fled past the windows, giving glimpses of a boiling sea below.

'See anything, Mr Spence?'

The First Officer leaned forward and pressed his face against the Perspex, more for the reassuring feel of its solidity than for any help with vision.

'No, sir.'

'When I do put her down at Ardnabegh there'll be a jolt. But at least we'll be almost out of fuel, so there'll be no fire risk.'

Why the hell does he talk like this, Barrett asked himself. Ardnabegh . . . he repeated the name over and over again like a swear word. It had a baleful, ominous sound. He was pierced with the sudden cold truth that even if they found it, they wouldn't all get out of the aircraft alive. Aloud he said, 'Fuel tanks all reading dry, sir.'

And simultaneously, Spence shouted, 'Something ahead, sir!'

The slanting rain parted like a bead curtain. The mist suddenly solidified into a wet grey cliff of rock. Lampeter turned the aircraft on its starboard wing, and skidded round just above a shingle of grey pebbles fringed by white foam.

'See the coastline, sir?'

'Yes.'

'Any sign of life?'

'A hill.'

'Beach below us, sir.'

'Look for a field.'

'Looking.'

Another burst of rain exploded over them, turning the windscreen into opaque crystal. Fierce upcurrents were bouncing them up into the trailing skirts of the cloud as they went round the southern tip of the island. And then, as they started to emerge, suddenly the port Perspex was dyed brown, then green.

'Fields, sir!' And then, unbelievably, 'And sir . . . sir, a *runway!*'

Barrett had seen it, too – poking its wet elephant trunk out of the mist. Not only a runway, either. A huddle of old dispersal huts, a broken-down hangar, the square box of a control tower.

'D'you see it, sir?' Spence was bouncing up and down with excitement.

'I see it.'

'We're in luck!'

'Yes. Old wartime station.' Lampeter eased Tango Foxtrot round in line with the runway direction. 'Give me the wheels!'

Barrett heard the undercarriage grind down, but still the certainty of doom hung over him. The starboard engine had started coughing.

'Hell of a cross-wind, sir!'

The starboard engine backfired. Barrett watched the altimeter slowly unwind. Five hundred, four hundred . . .

'Twenty flap.'

There was another terrific bang.

'Losing the starboard engine, sir.'

Stuttering, jolting, zigzagging an uneven glide-path, battered by the wind and the sheeting rain, Tango Foxtrot descended. The altimeter was reading two hundred feet, but now below their wings, Barrett could see bracken and heather. The next moment there was a jolt and a bang.

Now grass was rushing past his window. The wheels were running fast along an old grey potholed runway.

They were down!

In the right-hand seat, Spence let out his breath in a long sigh, and blinked disbelieving eyes at the sodden island scenery that moved rapidly round them on either side. Grass and reeds, crumbling concrete and rusted corrugated iron. A flowering gorse bush thrust up through what had once been a hard-standing. Beyond that, there was simply a shroud of mist and rain.

The brakes squealed. The engines faltered. Tango Foxtrot came to a halt beside a pile of pebbly scree. An eerie silence, broken only by the uneven drumming of the rain, and the moan of the wind outside, descended on the flight deck.

Peter Spence slid back his window. Salty sea-laden air

blew in. There was a smell of crushed grass and heather. Far away, he thought he heard the bleating of sheep. A pair of gulls rose squawking from the flats beside the runway. Something in their mournful tone made him want to cry with relief.

'After landing check!'

Spence began automatically touching and checking the levers and switches, chanting aloud his mechanical litany just as though this was Glasgow and not a ghost airfield that had suddenly materialized out of the grey limbo of the storm.

'Ardnabegh,' Lampeter said softly. 'Well, at least we've arrived. And all in one piece.' He unstrapped himself and stretched. 'I'll go to the back and have a word with the passengers. Peter, go and rustle up some of the locals.'

Eagerly, Spence got out of his seat. His limbs felt unnaturally stiff, the result of holding his muscles so tense. His hands on the handle of the side door felt as if they had frostbite. His feet were clumsy as he let himself down the rope ladder. Once on terra firma, he stamped them up and down, not just to get the circulation going, but for the sheer exquisite joy of being alive.

All around the mist was thickening again. A fine soft spray of drizzle wet his cheeks. He drew in great gulps of scented air. He felt blissfully, dizzily happy.

Now his mind was slowly coming to life again like his body, he pondered for a moment which way he should start walking. He screwed up his eyes, trying to revisualize the terrain they had glimpsed under their approach. He decided to walk forward down the runway in the direction Tango Foxtrot's nose was pointing.

As he walked, peewits disturbed by his footfall rose from the rough grass. One with a nest nearby came very close, flapping its coarse black and white wings, dive-bombing him. From far away, up perhaps on the lower slopes of the mountainside, he heard again the bleating of sheep. A vision of Scots hospitality – a warm hearth, hot soup, oatcakes and farm-churned butter filled his mind, completing his sense of well-being. He quickened his pace. The runway surface was pitted with holes, and the tarmac was scored with blisters where bracken and nettles and willow herb and thistles had thrust themselves up. There was a curious sound effect, too — an echo — that must be his own footsteps bouncing back off the mist.

He slowed down. The echo did not. He stopped. The echo went on.

Then he laughed out loud. Someone of course would have heard the aircraft. Spotted her descent, perhaps. Help did not have to be sought. Help was coming.

He cupped his hands to his mouth and yelled. 'Hello there! Can you help us?'

The footsteps stopped behind the curtain of mist.

'Hello! We've made an emergency landing. Celtic Airways.'

There was no reply. Then it dawned on Spence that whoever it was probably only spoke Gaelic. 'SOS,' he shouted, the universal cry for help. 'SOS. Save our souls.'

He heard the footsteps start up again. He sighed with thankfulness, and waited.

The footsteps now were brisker and faster. Only this time they were not coming any nearer.

They were going away.

Lampeter was just finishing explaining the situation to the passengers when Peter Spence returned. As might have been expected, Claire thought, busy taking round soft drinks and brandy, he was pulling no punches. Bill Barrett had investigated the damage, and his report to the Captain simply underlined the fact that they were all lucky to be alive. With both port and starboard wing fuel tanks holed by lightning, only a cupful of kerosene remaining, and the radios burned out, they had made this island, which was the nearest land, but a hundred and ten miles from their track. What there was on Ardnabegh and whether it was inhabited, was unknown. They had been lucky not to blow up in mid-air. They had been lucky to find this old wartime station. If their luck still held there would be people here, even a telephone to the mainland.

'Any luck, Peter?' Lampeter looked behind him as the First Officer came through the flight deck door into the cabin.

Spence shook his head. 'I walked as far as the old guard-room. There's a road of sorts.'

'Any sign of life at all, Peter?'

'No, sir. I thought I heard footsteps. I called. But nobody answered.'

'Echoes, boy,' Ainsworth said. 'The acoustics of an empty stage.'

'There's lots of birds. And I certainly heard sheep.'

'There is a saying,' Signor Borghese said with his sad, defeated, salesman's smile, 'that the good shepherd is never far from his sheep.'

'If there's sheep,' Mrs Crowther piped up, 'we won't go hungry. Have you ever done a bit o' scrag and lemon stuffing? Done slow it eats like chicken.'

She was doing her best, Lampeter noticed, to hang on to the brief euphoria of danger passed. But it was evaporating fast. In a little while, he thought, eyeing them reflectively, a reaction would set in. Other problems now loomed. Not so dangerous perhaps as those in the air. But for which he had no book of rules, no blueprints except his own common sense.

Already cold was pressing in through the metal skin. Rain deluged down. All around they could hear the moan and sigh of a wind. Low cloud formed, dissolved, re-formed. Beyond the curtain of the rain they could see only the brown tarmac, and the heathery turf between the runways, broken with bracken and rank with weeds. Even the derelict buildings, the mountain they had glimpsed coming in, were hidden. Soon this grey formless no-man's-land terrain would give them all a feeling as dangerous as cut-off.

'Someone must have heard us,' Lampeter said, punching the fist of one hand into the palm of the other. 'We made enough racket getting in. They can't be used to aircraft way up here.'

'Always supposing there's anyone to hear us.' Philby was being irritating again. 'I remember reading many of these islands can't support a population. The young won't stay.' His red-rimmed eyes travelled the group as if to say, and without the young like me where the hell would you all be? He touched his guitar. The note echoed. 'Maybe this island is deserted. They all just upped and went. Or they got the plague and they had no medicine man. Or maybe St Whatsit

came along and turned them all into sheep. Or maybe—
I know—' his hands caressed his guitar. The opening bars of
the Dead March vibrated eerily down the cabin as if the
fuselage were a conch shell. 'Maybe we really crashed back
there. That's it! We're all dead and we don't know it. Owch!'

His voice ended in an outraged squawk as Mrs Crowther
leaned round her seat and smartly cuffed him on the ear.

'You're alive all right, you haven't cocked your clog, you
bad lad. Any more of that an' I will warm your jacket.'

'All right,' Lampeter said, coming to his decision, 'you've
had your joke, Mr Philby. Let's get down to something
constructive. The odds are the island *is* inhabited. From the
bit we could see in the air, there looked like a village to the
south-west. Now though you, Mr Philby, might not agree,
we're a pretty agile bunch. The sooner we all get to an inn or a
farmhouse, the more comfortable it's going to be.' He took
the beaker from Miss Masefield, and said irritably, 'I thought
you girls were supposed to wear sensible shoes.'

'I've got some boots in my overnight bag.'

'Then put them on. And stow some flasks and food in a
bag.'

'Yes, sir.'

'And all of you. Wrap up warm. Put on coats, scarves,
extra jumpers. Fill your pockets but don't weigh yourselves
down. I don't know how long the walk will be. I'll give you
ten minutes. Then come up to the flight deck exit.'

The deliberately easy, relaxed smile left his face as he
walked up to the flight deck. 'Well, Bill?'

The engineer was wiping his hands on his handkerchief
and shaking his head. 'We *could* fix it if we had the equipment.'

'Which we haven't.' Lampeter had already taken off his
jacket and was pulling a thick sweater over his shirt.

'I always carry extra tools, but they may not be up to this
lot.'

'Glasgow will have to send a relief aircraft.'

'D'you reckon they'd get in?'

'Sure. If the cloud lifts a bit.' Lampeter began stuffing the
emergency kit into his pocket. 'After all, *we* got in.'

'There's not many pilots that could have,' Bill Barrett said simply.

'Marvellous what you can do when you have to,' Lampeter grinned.

'Which made me think, sir. Might not be a bad idea if I took a dekko round. I remember it was bloody amazing what was left in some of these airfields, specially with all this ocean between them and the Maintenance Unit.'

'Could be. But it'd be pretty decrepit, I'd've thought by now. Anyway, first things first. A message. And get the customers comfortable.'

'Customers on their way up now, sir.' Miss Masefield appeared briskly on the flight deck dressed in obvious souvenirs from Iceland, a white suède jacket and matching high-heeled boots. Captain Lampeter raised one eyebrow, frowned, but made no comment.

'Do they teach you girls anything about this sort of emergency?'

'Well, they send us on survival courses, sir.'

'It's us men that need survival courses,' Bill Barrett said reluctantly, setting his console to rights and getting out of his chair.

'And anyway, sir, it's just the two extremes they give. Survival in the desert, and survival on the open sea.'

'This,' Barrett said, shaking his head, 'is bloody both.'

'Come on.' Lampeter walked over to the exit and lowered the ladder. 'Wait till you're eating bannocks or whatever by some blazing hot fire.' And to Claire, 'I'll get down first and help them. Careful with the older ones.'

'Meaning who, eh, might I ask?' Mrs Crowther was the first passenger, wearing a heavy tweed coat and a cloche hat covered in blue petals. 'If they can all keep up wi' me they'll not be doing so dusty.'

She climbed down the ladder like a monkey, scorned Lampeter's helping hand, and said, 'Eeey, but I feel like kissing t'ground, wet an' all as it is.'

'It sure is good to feel terra firma.' Mrs Ewart shuddered. 'There were times back there . . .'

'It is refreshing the legs to stretch.' Herr Hagedorn followed his wife down, breathed deeply of the wet heather-scented air, stamped his feet and then took his wife's arm protectively. They hugged each other close, watching the rest of the passengers descend.

Philby was the last. He came bumping down the ladder with Spence helping from behind to steady the guitar, and murmuring, 'You'll really have to ask the skipper, you know.'

'May I, Captain? Bring it along?' For the first time Philby looked the right age.

'So long, sir, as you belt up when you're told. Now is that everyone? Come on, Bill. Hurry up.' Lampeter began counting heads. Then he glanced at Philby quellingly.

The guitar did not draw attention to the fact that they numbered thirteen.

For a moment while Lampeter brought out his compass they stood in a silence capped rather than broken by the low sob of the wind and the thrash of the gusting rain. Stamping her feet in the inadequately soled boots, Claire wished to hell Philby had kept his mouth shut. There was a kind of 'this is the way the world ends' desolation about the place. Everything sodden, dead, decayed.

If there were people living on the island, why by now did no one come? The driving rain whipped their coats against their legs, but the cloud curtain remained low. A peewit rose squawking from the heathery grass between the runways as if terrified at the strange sight of them. A white gull hovered just below the overcast. Far away something that sounded like an old tin roof flapped and rattled.

'Right then,' Lampeter said, dropping the compass in his pocket. 'Peter and I will lead the way. Claire, you and Bill bring up the rear. No straggling now. No wandering off the tarmac. There'll be peat bogs.'

He began walking briskly down the runway, trying to piece together in his mind the fragments of terrain he had glimpsed from the air. The village on the coast had seemed to lie towards the south-west. Then there was the big mountain somewhere to the right of them.

'I can smell the sea.' Lampeter stopped suddenly. 'And listen. That booming?'

'Is that not the roar of the wind, Signor Capitano?'

'No. Not strong enough. Besides it reverberates. Breakers. Careful, everyone. Some of these airfields were built for take-off over the sea.'

'We don't want to do a lemming act,' Philby said. 'Though, Christ, if we're stranded in this godforsaken place long, I'm liable to change my mind.'

'Always supposing –' Ainsworth, shivering in a very short, very thin coat, mimicked Philby – 'that there's a mind to change.' He made a bleating noise.

'Signor Capitano,' the wine salesman interposed quickly. 'Should we not shout? To call the attention of the good shepherd?'

'Not a bad idea. Give the youngsters something to do.' Lampeter turned and glowered at Ainsworth and Philby. 'All together every twenty paces. Mind your steps, though. There are a lot of deep puddles here. One, two, three, shout!'

Nothing but the faint echoes of their own voices came back to them, the bleating of sheep, and the rhythmic roar of the sea.

At the end of the runway where it joined the perimeter track, Lampeter paused. Couch grass and heather and stunted gorse bushes had narrowed the track. Fronds of bracken sprouted in the holes and cracks. Visibility was still down to about fifty yards. But he could feel in his face a mizzling of salt spray mixed with the rain.

'Guard-room's to the right, sir.'

'I know. Just having a look-see.' Lampeter walked a few paces and bent down, staring at a little iridescent star on the tarmac of the perimeter.

'Petrol, sir?' Spence stood beside him.

Lampeter touched it with his finger. 'And fairly recently spilled by the look of it.'

'Then we're all right!' Peter Spence shouted, putting up his thumb. 'Come on. Petrol means vehicles. Eureka!'

Most of the passengers began walking more briskly now towards the guard-room. Suddenly, thirty yards on, there was a flash of soft white light. Lampeter and Spence whirled round.

'It's OK, folks. Relax, everyone. Don't get jumpy. Just

29

keeping the old masterly hand in.' Mr Ainsworth lowered his camera. 'Dawn Playfair in mink in the middle of the ocean. Really Sunday supp. stuff!'

'It won't be the Sunday supplement,' Lampeter said grittily. 'The back page of *The Times*, if you don't do as you're told. Keep up.'

'The obituary column,' Philby said. 'Consider yourself told off, Ainsworth.'

'Guard-room coming up now, sir,' Spence said.

'Well, there's not much left of *that*,' Lampeter said. 'Down like a pack of cards.'

A couple of sheep were huddled in the shelter of the caved-in walls. A gull was perched on what had once been the chimney-breast.

'Eey, lad,' Mrs Crowther sighed nostalgically, 'it looks like one of them souvenirs from Blackpool. A lump of rock with a white gull stuck on t'top.'

Mr Crowther had walked a few yards away. Now he shouted as if he'd panned gold. 'There's a dog's turd on this end o' t'road!'

'Going west-south-west. Mmm. Not *quite* the way we want. But the road's less overgrown that way. Let's try it.'

'Where there's a dog turd might there be the good shepherd?' Signor Borghese said wistfully.

'All right, everyone,' Lampeter called. 'Let's shout again. And watch out. We're close to the cliff. One, two, three, yell!'

But no good shepherd and no dog appeared to answer their call. Just their own voices echoing back at them from the sea or the cloud or the mountain. It made it all the more strange when, fifty yards or so on, Mrs Crowther sniffed. 'Eey, I can smell coffee. I fancy a cup of coffee and a slice of long-bun.'

'You are smelling what you wish to smell,' Philby said. 'Medical fact.'

'Medical rubbish.'

Ten yards further on, well within hailing distance, a shadow solidified out of the mist to the left of the road. A pile of stones built into a sheep shelter. And within it, bending over a pan on a little paraffin stove, an old bearded shepherd with his dog beside him. The dog pricked his ears and whined but remained where he was. They might have been miles away or in a different dimension. The whole scene was close, yet distant and dissociated as if contained in a glass shell.

'Crowther's turd-dropper,' Ainsworth said, breaking the eerie spell and thumping Mr Crowther on the back.

'Hello, there,' Lampeter called, leaving the road and picking his way cautiously over the sodden heather.

The shepherd glanced over his shoulder at him, and quickly averted his eyes again. He said something softly and soothingly to the dog. Then he leaned forward and extinguished the stove. Perhaps with age, his hand trembled. When he turned back to them again, his whole body registered a kind of stoical apprehension. Only Signor Borghese noticed that before the old man came forward reluctantly to greet them, surreptitiously he crossed himself.

Close to, the shepherd was not so old as Lampeter had at first thought. The untidy beard, the pale hooded eyes, the scooped-out pallid cheeks, gave an impression of great age. But the man could not have been more than sixty, if that. He regarded them as they approached with something less than fear but more than astonishment. Something, Lampeter thought, like disbelief. He kept screwing up his eyes as if he doubted their message. He half raised his hand and said something in Gaelic. Then he appeared to notice the women. Apprehension gave way to relief. He bowed deeply in a manner that should have been ridiculous but which was not.

'My name's Richard Lampeter. We need help. I'm a Celtic Airways pilot. We've just made a forced landing at the old airfield back there.'

'Duncan McDermott it is. Good afternoon to you.' He spoke very slowly in a high, sing-song voice. As they shook hands, he stared intently into Lampeter's face. His eyes were a very pale, translucent grey, the pupils pin-head size, giving the milky appearance of blindness.

'We were flying from Iceland,' Lampeter said, thinking he still does not quite believe me. The hand that held on to his trembled slightly.

'And where would you be after going, sir?'

'Glasgow. These are my crew.' Lampeter waved a blanket

introduction. 'And the passengers. Luckily we hadn't many.'

The shepherd with the dog now at his heels walked down the line extending a hand to each in turn, murmuring his own name, repeating theirs, giving each this same intent, searching stare, not content just to shake hands either, but covering theirs too with his left. As if, Claire thought, he really is blind.

'Mrs Ewart ma'am.' The old man nodded his head approvingly. 'There was a Ewart on the island, that iss so.'

'Well, land's sakes, that is good to hear. And is there still a Ewart now?'

The old man shook his head. 'Rory Ewart was changed these many years, God rest his soul. He's in the kirkyard wi' a fine sight of the sea.'

'So there's a kirk and a minister, then?' Lampeter interrupted.

'Only once in a wee while. They're not over fond of the Kirk. He's an old man, that iss so. He lives away beyond from here.'

'Is the church in a village?'

'Aye.'

'In that direction?' Lampeter pointed the way he remembered the huddle of cottages.

'Aye.'

'How many miles?'

The old man shrugged, and returned to his greetings, bowing low in front of Mrs Crowther, and with apparently mounting confidence, giving her the first, faint, frugal smile.

'Eeey, now I know what t'Queen herself feels like. Happen that's what the old chap teks me for. Queen Mother come down on one of her trips to that Scotch castle.'

'There iss also, aye, a castle. And now a laird.'

'What about a telephone? Are there telephones on the island?' Lampeter said, glancing at his watch impatiently. 'Does your boss have one?' The white mist was turning grey as daylight dwindled.

The old man stared at him. 'I have not over much, sir, of the English tongue.'

Lampeter put one hand to his mouth and ear. He thought,

but was not sure that he saw a gleam of something like amused malice in the pale grey eyes.

'Aye, Mr Fraser, I am his man, sir, he has that sometimes, sir.'

'How about with the mainland? Over there? We need spares. We need our aircraft mending. We need to let the families of these people know they're safe.'

'Safe.' The old man repeated the word with a curious doubting emphasis. He closed his eyes for a second and opened them again very wide.

'Aye, there was to the mainland, that iss so. But there iss not now.' He sighed. 'This great storm. Mr Fraser was after telling me he could not get a sound from herself.'

'Herself being the telephone?'

'Aye.'

Lampeter frowned. 'Does the village have an inn?'

'Aye. A poor place, Angus Menzies has, but an inn it is after being.'

'And is there a road to the village?'

'This same road.' The old man spread his hands. 'She goes all round the side of Begh.'

'The mountain?'

'Aye. She is a fine road. She was made when the air force field was made.' The old man sighed.

'Were you here then?'

'Aye, that iss so. Then it was I was learning the English tongue.'

'What sort of aeroplanes did they fly? Four engines? Two?'

The shepherd held up four fingers. 'Very fat in the belly as if in lamb.'

'Shackletons by the sound, sir,' Bill Barrett said. 'Well, if they could get off, we could.'

Lampeter nodded. Under his breath he said to Barrett, 'I hope to hell he's wrong about the telephone.'

'Could be. He looks as nutty as a fruit cake.'

'Interbreeding, sir.' Peter Spence tapped his head.

'Well, let's get to the village and find out,' Lampeter murmured, and, raising his voice, 'Could you direct us to the inn? We follow this road, do we? For how many miles?'

'Too many, sir. She winds like a river. She has many pitfalls . . .'

'Like a woman,' young Philby said.

'Aye.' The old man nodded seriously. 'And it would be
night.'

Unhurriedly he began to stow away the little stove,
emptied the dregs in the pan, wiped it round, put everything
in the shelter.

'I will be after taking you, sir. I know a path that will make
the journey shorter.'

'But how much shorter?' Ainsworth whispered to Claire as
Spence beckoned them all to follow. 'Better arrive late in this
world than early in the next.'

'Notice those pin-point pupils?' Philby murmured. 'Sure sign
of . . .'

'Sure sign of what?' Ainsworth's voice squeaked nervously.

'I forget now.' Philby eluded Ainsworth's upraised hand.

'Now then, you lads, ye'll get a thick ear apiece.' Mrs
Crowther shook her little fist.

Herr Hagedorn looked at his watch, murmured something
to his wife. Apparently satisfied that he had left everything
tidy, the shepherd raised a finger to his lips commanding
silence. Far away behind the steady roar of the sea, they
could hear the thin bleat of sheep. Then he nodded, and,
beckoning them to follow, began to walk up a rough sheep
track behind the shelter.

'You've got sharp ears,' Lampeter said, falling into step
beside him.

'Aye.'

'I'm surprised you didn't hear us overhead then?'

'Ah yes, that iss so, I heard you.'

Courteously with his stick the shepherd turned back the
fronds of sodden bracken that grew on either side of the track.

'Didn't you wonder what had happened?'

'No, no. I am not of an enquiring disposition.'

'And you didn't think you'd come and see?'

'No . . . no.' In a strangely theatrical gesture the old man
closed his eyes and laid his gracefully spread fingertips over
them. 'I see many things. Sometimes I see clearer –' he

opened them dramatically – 'without these.' They walked for a moment in silence with only the sound of their feet on the moist track and the subdued murmur of the passengers behind. 'Do you understand, sir?'

Lampeter thought it best to nod. The sea sound had changed. At a guess he would say they were cutting across the rocky headland he had glimpsed from the air. A spumy breaking sea was very close on the right. He licked his lips, feeling the salt spray on his face. An uncomfortable doubt of the sanity of their guide reasserted itself. Now he kept his eyes on the ground to the right. The bushes thinned to a few wind-bitten gorse clumps, bent stiffly away from where he was sure was the cliff and the sea. He held his head on one side to catch the altered note of the breakers. He thought he heard the rattle of pebbles dragged back by the undertow. Then the bushes disappeared altogether, the wiry grass was strewn with small boulders. Just to the right of the sheep track there was what looked like a narrow fissure. Lampeter tossed a pebble into the crack. It disappeared. He heard it bouncing down, striking first one side of the crevasse, then the other.

'Mind where you're treading back there.'

'Aye, aye, Captain.'

'And I will tell you,' the old man said as if sensing Lampeter's withdrawal of confidence, 'it is a foolishness to venture yon when the sounds come.'

'Sounds? Which sounds?'

'Like yours. And lights also.'

'D'you mean engine sounds? Aircraft engines?'

Lampeter glanced sharply sideways at the shepherd.

'Aye. Like yours, but not like yours.' He paused a moment to chivvy a stray sheep away from the path to the left. Then in the same sing-song, matter-of-fact voice, 'They are not of this world, you understand?'

'No,' Lampeter said. 'I don't think I do. You're not telling me there are ghostly aeroplanes?'

With thankfulness he saw the path was taking a left sweep. They were descending again. The roar of the sea lessened. There were gorse bushes again. The shepherd paused to break away a branch that trailed over the path.

'That I do not know. The folk believe that iss so. For myself I know it is an evil place. What has been and what is to be and what is now can mingle like the waters.'

'What's evil about it?' Lampeter laughed shortly. 'Apart from that mountain a bit too close.'

The old man fixed his eyes on Lampeter's face for a moment. He seemed about to say something, then shrugged his shoulders. 'It is unlucky, so 'tis said.'

'Did they have trouble with it when it was an airfield?'

'Aye. And when they were building it. And after. It should not have been built there. The ground wouldnae rest quiet. After it came the island began to die. The young folk went.'

'The young folk,' Lampeter said gently, 'are going from all these islands.'

'Aye,' the shepherd said politely.

'And these sounds –' Lampeter glanced around at the gathering misty darkness – 'will be some mountain echo from aircraft miles away.'

'Aye.' A gleam of pity showed in the strange eyes. 'We are simple people. We do not understand these things.'

'Next time –' Lampeter switched on his torch – 'some of you should go up there and take a look. You'll find nothing there but the wind.'

'No one will be after doing that,' the shepherd said with finality. 'Unlucky enough it is to hear the ground sounding. But to see the shapes themselves . . .' He leaned closer to Lampeter. 'That, sir, is *death*.'

Still bringing up the rear of the crocodile with the dog sniffing and snapping at her heels, Claire Masefield shared Lampeter's mistrust of the shepherd. Every step that they took through this weird half-hidden landscape seemed to contain an indefinable menace. She watched the shepherd's flowing hair and beard bobbing ahead, now a pale nimbus against the dark overcast, now merging with the white sea mist rolling in. From time to time he let out a low soft whistle to the dog, and the dog answered with a sharp immediate bark. Half a mile on, the shepherd and Lampeter disappeared from view, reappeared again as the wind parted the mist. The shepherd whistled again. And this time, behind, not just the dog, but another whistle or an echo answered him.

A silence had fallen on the passengers. They all walked, head down, with small careful steps. Like sheep, Claire thought. And as if he read her mind, Philby, pausing to free his trouser-leg from a thorn, whispered, 'Like lambs to the slaughter.' He grinned as Barrett gave an indignant snort. 'Well, for Chrissake, we don't know where the hell he's leading us.'

'To the inn,' Barrett said sharply. 'And now, sir, *please* get back to your place in front of Mrs Ewart. We don't want to lose anyone.'

'Land's sakes,' the Canadian lady shuddered. 'Just the *idea* of being left out here alone all night's enough to send you round the bend.'

'That's what's wrong with our guide,' Philby muttered. 'He's been left out too damned many nights.'

'Are you all right, Mrs Ewart?' Claire interposed. 'You seem to be limping.'

'Just these silly shoes, I guess. I didn't bring any sensible ones. I just didn't figure . . .' her voice trailed.

'If he is mad –' Ainsworth turned – 'the survivors could sell the story to the Sunday supps. Make a bomb.'

'We're coming to a steep part,' Lampeter shouted. 'Hang on to the person in front.'

They seemed now to have reached the summit of the path, and to be dropping down. There was a shaley slope bordered on one side by rounded granite boulders. They could hear the pebbles screeing off the slope as the leaders shuffled down. And once the echo of a big stone falling and bouncing, and then a plopping. Claire and Bill exchanged glances.

'Must be inlets.' And raising his voice, 'Some sort of water seems close, Skipper.'

'Yep. Mind how you go.' His voice still sounded relaxed and confident.

'You go in front just behind Mrs Ewart,' Claire whispered, stepping behind Bill Barrett. And as she did so, she had the sudden irrational feeling of being watched. She felt her hands sweat and her whole skin prickle. The dog butted the back of her legs with his head, whining. She shone her torch. Green eyes glinted out of the cracks in the boulders.

'Only sheep,' she said aloud.

'We're at the bottom of the slope now,' Lampeter called. 'Easier. But marshy. Don't step off the path.'

The path turned left again and the gradient eased. A smell of peat and something sweetish and vaguely nostalgic mingled with the tang of the sea.

Bill Barrett fell back beside her. The feeling of being watched receded, but did not quite disappear. She kept glancing over her shoulder at the total misty darkness behind. Bill Barrett shone his torch on either side. Nothing but wet brown bracken, growing straight down here, and heather. His torch hovered on what looked like a pile of boulders covered with rusty red bracken.

'Concrete and corrugated,' Barrett said. 'Part of a dispersal. Or mebbe a bomb dump. We're at the back of the field.'

'Told you he's mad,' Philby said in a low voice. 'We're moving in a circle.'

'Oh no,' Mrs Ewart wailed.

'So what?' Barrett said. 'Any island's round.'

'Didn't you hear all his mularkey about the field being haunted? Crazy as a coot. Certifiable.'

'Nonsense,' Bill Barrett said. 'He knows this place like the back of his hand. The cliff road's dangerous at night. That's why he's taking us this way.'

'Well, this isn't exactly highway nine.' Mrs Ewart tried to laugh but failed. 'Honey, are your feet soaking wet?'

'Yes. Tell your daughter not to buy any suède boots in Reykjavik.'

Claire caught her breath. Something – some animal or bird – rustled in the heather just beyond the reach of her torch. Sheep's wool caught in a thorn bush moved frighteningly in the breeze.

'I'll write her first thing. Soon as we get out of here tomorrow.' Mrs Ewart paused. She turned to Barrett. 'We *are* going to get out of here tomorrow aren't we?'

Bill Barrett drew in his breath sharply and stumped on in silence for a pace or two. Mrs Ewart had touched him on an acutely tender spot. The fact that Tango Foxtrot was unserviceable, her passengers stranded in such discomfort was bad enough. But the fact that he with all his experience could at present do nothing about it was an intolerable humiliation. No matter that even in this scientific age what had caused the trouble was classed an Act of God, and that he had managed to nurse those engines long enough for them to land safely. Tango Foxtrot was his charge and in its present unflyable state a slur on his professionalism.

'I'd give everything I've got *and* all my pension to be able to say yes to that.'

'But you can't?' Mrs Ewart whispered, a little taken aback by his vehemence.

Bill Barrett shook his head. 'If it's humanly possible, we'll repair it. But then we've still got to take on fuel.'

'The skipper'll get a message to Glasgow,' Claire said, glancing behind again.

'*If* the phone's working,' Philby said.

'Oh, give over, lad.'

'That's what we must keep our fingers crossed for, then.'

'Just a sane Ardnabeghian face would do me,' Philby said.

Lampeter's voice then called out. 'Not much longer now. There's a dyke. Then a stream. Wet as hell. Take it slowly. After that we're on the road.'

They heard the front people splashing through water. They saw the white disc of Lampeter's torch. His voice asking, 'Looks deep? Is it?' And the shepherd's answering, 'Aye.'

Just to the left of them where the airfield must be some strange bird cried out.

'Night-jar,' Bill Barrett said firmly, leaning forward to take Mrs Ewart's arm over the dyke.

'Don't think you get them this far north.' Philby was helping her down the other side. 'God, the Captain's right about it being wet. We'll all have pneumonia before we get there.'

There was the sucking sound of feet through mud and then Lampeter's voice edged with unmistakable relief. 'Here's the road now. Macadamed. Not bad. And another one. Looks like a track going back to the airfield.'

'Told you,' Philby said.

'No, I told *you*,' said Barrett, getting rattled.

'Mr McDermott says only another half mile or so. Come on everyone. No hanging back now.'

'Honey, I've just got to ease this shoe a bit.' Mrs Ewart hung on to Claire's arm. 'There's a blister on my heel like a balloon.' She kicked off her shoes, while Bill walked on. 'Now we're on the road, I'm going to walk without them. They're killing me.' She bent down to retrieve her shoes. 'Drat it. Lost them. Can I have your torch, honey?'

Claire wheeled round. Then she froze in absolute terror. The torch waved in her trembling hand. Caught in the turning beam was what looked like a headless man, standing motionless by a gorse bush. An orange jacket and baton reflected back her light. Then she saw a pale face and glittering eyes. She screamed. The torch fell from her hands.

'Bill, Bill. Bill, quickly. A man up that path.'

Bill Barrett came back and picked up her torch. 'Steady on, girl. Where?'

'Up there.' She grabbed her torch from him. The twin beams showed nothing but sodden gorse bushes, the farthest ones melting into the mist.

'But I tell you, I saw someone,' Claire said, less certain now. 'Didn't you see anything, Mrs Ewart?'

'No, thank heavens. Negative. I was turned round this way, looking down for those silly shoes. Drat them. Here they are. Found them.'

'He was wearing an orange jacket, Bill. And he was standing absolutely still. Just by that gorse bush. The one in flower.' Her voice wavered.

'That's it. Yellow flower. Orange. A trick of the light, girl. Amazing what you see in the mist.'

Ainsworth, hugging the model's arm, called out, 'Just back there *I* saw a smashing blonde. She wasn't wearing anything at all. She was beckoning me. But *I* didn't holler.'

'Come on.' Lampeter called from the front. 'What's up?'

'Nothing,' Claire answered.

'It's just the Canadian lady.' Mrs Crowther's voice. 'Her shoes are giving her gyp.'

'I'll stay behind you,' Bill grinned to Claire. 'If the man in the orange jacket comes he'll get me first.'

The crocodile moved forward again, briskly now that they

were on the home stretch. Claire kept her torch moving from side to side of the road. It was narrow and the surface worn and cracked, but once it had been well surfaced with a high camber for drainage. It was bordered by ditches thick with reeds and bulrushes. She could hear the faint tinkle of the everlasting rain water trickling into it, and somewhere the breaking of the waves again.

'Mist's thinning,' Bill Barrett said. 'Going out with the tide.'

'Civilization,' Lampeter called back. 'A pavement.'

'Are you eating your words, Mr Philby?' Barrett called past Claire. 'About the mad guide?'

'He's got too much respect for his stomach,' Ainsworth murmured.

A red-curtained light showed at a small cottage window. The curtains tweaked back as their steps echoed on the uneven black flagstones, and closed quickly again. Two more lighted windows. An alleyway opening up. A smell of fish. Then, in the middle of another line of mean-looking cottages, a swinging, clumsily painted sign of an oak tree, with the one word *Darag* underneath. A small fanlight glowed over a peeling door. Thin chinks of light shone out from between close-shuttered windows, illuminating the drizzling rain.

'The Ardnabegh Hilton,' Philby said. 'Bet it's full of sheep.'

'Not to worry, sonny,' Ainsworth said. 'There's room for just one more.'

'Git-aht-of-it, lads.' Mrs Crowther raised her fist.

'It is best, yes, to knock first, that iss so,' the shepherd said as Lampeter made to grasp the handle of the door.

'Don't want to interrupt an orgy, Captain,' Ainsworth said. 'Call girls and all that,' as the old shepherd walked up and slowly rapped three times on the painted panel of the door.

For a full minute nothing happened. The rain gurgled down the open drain of the road. The sign creaked in the slight wind. The dog whined impatiently. Then steps slowly approached from within. A deep voice was raised in query. The shepherd answered at length. Another silence. The shepherd spoke again. Finally the door was flung open.

A large, heavily built man stood framed in the light of the doorway. He wore his shirt-sleeves rolled up and a leather apron. He looked more like a blacksmith than a landlord, with a low receding forehead and a dour fleshy face. A different type of man altogether from the shepherd. And yet they had one thing in common. The expression of awe and fear and astonishment was exactly that of the shepherd's a couple of hours before.

There was another, this time angry, exchange in Gaelic, both of them gesticulating up to the sky. Finally, the shepherd said, 'This is where I must leave you with Angus Menzies,' and turned away, while the innkeeper stepped back and beckoned them all in. As they passed him into the narrow hallway, he scrutinized the face of each and every one. Then he flung open the door of the bar, placed his hands on the shabby counter and shouted to someone in the rear. The tone was curiously triumphant.

'What is he saying?' Lampeter demanded of the shepherd, as the old man began walking away down the street.

'Just that you are here, sir, that iss so.'

'Not quite, sir,' Herr Hagedorn stepped forward. 'I a few words of the Gaelic have. He has just said, *he has come, like I told you he would.*'

Inside the inn there was a comfortless warmth. The bar was lit by an oil lamp on a thick wooden counter, and another hanging from the ceiling. The slamming of the door behind them rocked the light, sending a procession of their distorted shadows over the mildewed walls. First the bearlike shadow of the landlord, then the passengers, and the crew behind. Lastly Lampeter. There were half a dozen kitchen chairs arranged round a baize-topped table, ringed with glass stains, and against the far wall, to one side of the fire, an oak bench. Thankfully the passengers shuffled over the sawdust floor and flopped down on the seats. They produced handkerchiefs and began mopping the rain from their cheeks and hair. The smouldering peat fire hissed as they shook their caps and coats. The place smelled nostalgically of burning paraffin, but the room had a queer arranged look like a stage set hastily assembled for their entrance. There was a feel about it that wasn't right, Lampeter thought, watching the landlord lift the bar flap and, taking up his stand behind the bar, regard them with a look of gathering hostility. As if they, to his thinking, were not quite right either.

'They've got a radio,' Bill Barrett said, making a beeline for a battered set standing on a corner shelf by the window.

Mr Ainsworth, finding an empty tankard, began banging on the counter, 'Service, please, waiter.'

'See what they all want, will you, Claire.' Lampeter caught her arm. And then to the landlord, 'Before anything else, let's get everyone a drink, eh?'

For a moment the landlord remained as he was, arms akimbo, staring all the way round the room, briefly at Mrs Crowther polishing the rain off her round spectacles, and Mrs Ewart twisting the little grey side curls of her coiffure into place, then lingering on Bill Barrett coaxing nothing out of the radio set but a few harsh bars of music half drowned in static. A long sombre gaze at Peter Spence squeezing the water from the crown of his uniform cap. Then all round the room again.

'There iss too many of you, that iss so,' the landlord said finally.

'That's all right,' Lampeter said. 'We'll be paying. We don't want it on the house.'

'No, no, that iss not the concern, you understand.' The landlord's frown deepened. 'The islanders are well known for their hospitality, indeed, yes. But . . .' He paused, groped for the right words, gave up the struggle and then mumbled stubbornly again. 'There is too many, aye.'

'Seven double whiskies, a port and lemon, and a pint of mild and bitter,' Claire said, coming up to the bar behind Lampeter. 'And Captain, please, something to eat. Crisps. Sausages. Chocolate. Anything. Everyone's so hungry they'll eat the sawdust off the floor.'

'At this rate,' Lampeter said, watching the landlord reluctantly reach for a bottle of whisky, 'they may have to.'

But there he was immediately proved wrong. A door behind the bar was suddenly thrust open and in a cloud of harsh perfume a large black-haired girl of about seventeen came in carrying a tray with bowls of soup and a pile of baps.

'Aye, my daughter will see to ye.' Menzies nodded at the sighs of satisfaction from the passengers. 'The islanders are well known for their grand hospitality. And – ' he raised a half-filled glass of colourless liquid to the lamplight – 'for their whisky. Ardnabegh whisky made here at the distillery.'

'The real McCoy, a hundred and thirty proof by the look of it.' Lampeter turned to the passengers. 'So watch how you drink it.'

'Hits the spot all right.' Ainsworth downed his at a gulp and then began choking.

'You'll rot your gut doing that,' Philby said, rolling his slowly round his tongue. 'Medical fact.'

'Baps is fresh any road,' Mrs Crowther said, pinching them expertly. 'Baked today. Must've known we was coming. But I don't reckon much to t'soup. Meat cube an' a drop o' water.'

'Eeeh, lass, don't luik a gift horse in t'mouth.'

'Horse is right,' Dawn Playfair huddled herself in her mink coat.

'Horse something else.' Ainsworth took a mouthful and grimaced.

'Who does t'cuiking, lass?' Mrs Crowther called over to the big girl as she handed out her last bowl and prepared to linger beside First Officer Spence. 'Your mum, love?'

The girl shook her head and pointed to herself. 'Thought so,' Mrs Crowther said triumphantly. 'You can't put an old head on young shoulders. You need a bit of teaching, that's all. What's your name, love?'

'Maiyrat.'

'Fancy that! Well, that's a pretty name,' and, sturdily ignoring the puffy plain features, the ungainly figure, 'for a pretty lass.'

'The islanders,' Miss Playfair said, 'are well known for their beauty.'

'And what does your mum do, love?'

'She's been changed these many years, God rest her soul.'

'Anything for afters?' Bill Barrett asked, fiddling with the radio. 'I'm ravenous.'

The young girl eyed him speculatively for a moment, seemed undecided, and then she turned suddenly to Peter Spence. 'Would ye like a candy bar?' she asked, her plump cheeks colouring.

'We'd all like a candy bar,' Ainsworth said, raising his brows. 'What has this lad got that we haven't?'

'A candy bar,' Philby said, watching the girl extract something from her apron pocket and hand it to the First Officer. 'A genuine American candy bar. How in the world did that get here?'

'The Icelandic people,' Herr Hagedorn said, finishing his bowl of soup, 'used to call this island the joining of the world.'

'Then by gad, sir,' Ainsworth said, striking his music hall pose, 'stop the world. We all bloody well want to get off.'

Standing at the bar, still trying to get some sense out of the landlord, Lampeter heard the words and silently concurred. For the sixth time he tried to find out what material help there might be on this godforsaken island. What was there besides sheep and ghosts and whisky and rain? Surely the distillery had machinery? There must be vehicles because they had seen fuel stains. But where were they? In all probability, as Bill Barrett said, the RAF left some spares and tools behind. These lamps in the bar, their feathers of black smoke curling away, burned paraffin, didn't they? Well, his engines burned paraffin too. So how did they get it and where was it kept? Reluctantly interspersing his slow speech with Gaelic, the landlord replied that he had no knowledge of such things. Paraffin, aye, they had paraffin, the boat came from the mainland about every two months. There would likely be another before Christmas, that was so, weather being favourable, did he understand? And then, fixing his black eyes on Lampeter, 'So it was the lightning then, Captain, that sent ye here, ye say?'

'Yes.'

'Took ye awa' frae where ye were going, ye say? Against yer ain will?'

'Yes.'

It was, Lampeter thought, like going back a hundred years in time. The smouldering peat, the smell of the oil lamps, and the sawdust, the flickering shadows against the walls, the creeping sense of mental as well as physical isolation. Behind him Philby was strumming irritatingly at the guitar again.

'Here we sit like birds in a wilderness . . .'

Most of the others were silent.

'Well we'll jest have to get usselves summat to do,' Mrs Crowther said in answer to some whispered remark from the model. Even Ainsworth didn't seem able to think up a reply. 'There'll happen be places we could go and see,' Mrs Crowther went on. 'Castles and suchlike. You could tek another of them photos, Jerry lad.'

Herr Hagedorn had abandoned his journal and was pacing up and down the room. His wife was staring listlessly into the glowing fibres of the fire.

'Not Sunday supp. stuff.' Ainsworth thrust out his legs and stared gloomily at his sodden shoes.

'Oh, give over! There'll be summat else. Hey, landlord! Is there owt to see? Fisheries? Suchlike?'

'The distillery, aye. The island is well known for its fine whisky.'

'Then us'll go there. Tek a white horse anywhere. There then, there's a title for your picture an' all.'

'I suppose you can put us all up, can you?' Lampeter asked the landlord, abandoning for the present anything more technic....

'Aye. Though I wasnae prepared for sech numbers, you understand. It is a wee place, that iss so.'

'You might see what accommodation you can sort out, Claire. Are you getting anything out of the radio, Bill?'

'This and that. Comes and goes. Got a spot of wrestling just now. Couldn't tell if it was the crowd or the screeching static. Talk on gardening. Anyone interested? Not very clear.'

'Leave it on. We might get something.'

Now even Mrs Crowther had fallen silent. Lampeter watched Claire talking to Maiyrat about the rooms. The stewardess looked oddly diminished by the bulk of the younger girl. They were all diminished, come to that, he thought, looking around.

The horizontals and verticals of their life had been shifted. In this strange primitive environment of poverty and superstition, Lampeter was beginning to despair of communicating adequately with anyone on this island, or of ever making contact with the mainland. A grim picture of them staying here for months on end in this gloomy inn flitted through his mind, when suddenly there was a quick draught of air behind him. Before he had time to turn, a quiet English voice said, 'Having trouble?'

Lampeter spun round and met intelligent golden-brown eyes set in a middle-aged but cherubic face, rosy with the cold. A man of middle height inclined to a comfortable plumpness, wearing an obviously expensive brown tweed suit under a riding mackintosh, had just come into the bar.

'Let me introduce myself, Captain.' The man smiled warmly and extended his hand. 'Frank Dundas . . . laird for my sins of this godforsaken island!' He waved aside the chair that the landlord obsequiously put out for him, and contemplated Lampeter with a quizzical smile.

As Lampeter shook the man's hand a wave of relief washed over him. He felt as if order had at last returned to his world. Civilization was not, after all, so far away. He could explain to this newcomer exactly what their situation was. In fact it seemed hardly necessary. He knew most of it already.

'Heard from my ghillie you were here. Gave him the fright of his life! Real orphans from the storm, eh? Mainland know you're here?'

'That's the trouble. Radio's burned out.'

The man shrugged sympathetically and then said briskly, 'Wouldn't have been much good, though, anyway. Our damned mountain, low be it spoken. Have you seen the brute? That's why I've never gone in for a radio telephone. Damned awkward, though, the telephone going. It'll be weeks before they get round to mending it. Well, we'll just have to get you off pretty pronto. Anyone got any idea where you are?'

'Most unlikely.'

'Well, if you like to put me in the picture, we'll see what we can rustle up for you.' He became suddenly aware of the large whisky that the landlord had set at his elbow, 'Well, *slainte*.' He raised his glass and smiled around. 'Gaelic for good health.'

'We could use a spot of good luck too, I guess,' Mrs Ewart said.

'You've had a portion so far, just getting here,' Dundas said, then smiling again. 'But meeting up straight away with poor old McDermott, the teller of tales, the seer of visions, *that* wasn't so lucky.'

'Oh, I don't know,' Lampeter said, 'he got us here.'

'He should've brought you to my place. Except, of course, my housekeeper would probably have left on the spot. Sure you wouldn't like to?'

'Thanks. But we've just fixed up here. What I really want are tools. Bill can probably do the repairs if he's got some tools. Then we'd need kerosene. I don't suppose . . .'

'Just leave all this with me. We have to be pretty self-supporting, you know.' He downed his drink and hastily the landlord refilled his glass. 'Steady on, Angus Menzies.' And lowering his voice, 'He's an odd character, too. But then they *all* are. How did you make out with poor old McDermott?' He shook his head.

'The shepherd? All right.'

'Didn't he keep you entertained with his stories?'

'Not very much.'

'Not even about the airfield? Didn't he take you all the way round instead of cutting across it?'

'He might have done, yes.'

'They're all the same. Won't go near the place at certain times. They think their hair'll fall out or they'll get warts, or I don't know what.' He shook his head, the bright brown eyes brimming with laughter. 'What was he seeing this time, old McDermott?'

'Hearing,' Lampeter corrected. 'Aircraft.'

'Oh, *that*. The ground shaking. This was all before my time, but in the war the airfield was none too lucky. It had its crashes. What airfield didn't? But they, bless 'em, said it had been built on sacred ground. The damned mountain was angry. And since the war things haven't been too clever here. The airfield's their kick-it. You'll know what that means.' He smiled at Mrs Ewart. 'Don't they say in America every home should have a kick-it?'

'Some of the villagers have seen people,' Claire said firmly.

'And others besides.' Dundas grinned mischievously at

48

Claire. 'When you shone your torch on poor old Jamie Walker I don't know which of you was the more scared!' He took a sip of his drink, still smiling. 'I've got some grouse up near there. Walker was having a look at them. Know anything about grouse? No, well take it from me they're damned silly birds. Weather like this disorientates them.'

'Why didn't he call out?' Claire asked.

'Because it's my belief he ran like a rabbit! That's the trouble with these stories about the airfield. Not many really believe them. But they all *half* believe them. Even Walker. Well, they've got no one else to listen to, except old McDermott. No tele. Not much radio.' He smiled over at Barrett.

'Funny thing was,' Barrett said, 'there was a runway heading on control tower when we came in.'

'Was it the right one?'

'Yes.'

'There you see! Proves my point. It's my belief it's hardly been touched up there since the war.'

'When did you come, sir?'

'Nearly five years ago. I made a bob or two in the city and bought the place.' He smiled. 'Ghosts thrown in.' He downed his drink. 'Courting couples more likely, I tell them.'

'There's gey little courting these days,' the landlord who had been ostensibly polishing the surface of the bar with the flat of his hand broke in. 'The island's finished. There's no' enough sun.'

'There's no sun, period,' Philby said, pulling the opening chords of 'Oh, island in the sun'.

'Gerraway, it's no worse than Manchester.'

The landlord ignored the interruptions. 'And the young folk are awa'. A fine lassie like Maiyrat cannae find a man . . .' He glanced thoughtfully at Peter Spence.

'Quite true, alas,' Dundas said. 'And when they do a bit of courting, it's their cousins. Or worse. That's how you get . . .' He tapped his head again.

'Mind, he's a fine laird, Mr Dundas, that iss so . . . . He does what iss right.' The landlord nodded his big head obsequiously.

'Oh, I don't know about that. I've done my best to stimulate a bit of work. Well, there's practically nothing. Only small fishing boats. Bit of weaving. The distillery's the main thing. I've sunk a bob or two there. And not much return so far.'

'I was after telling them about the fine distillery,' the landlord murmured ingratiatingly. 'The strange folk are wishing to see the place.'

'It's no tourist place, I assure you . . . I'm rather ashamed of it . . .' Mr Dundas held up his hands in horror.

'It'd mek a nice change, though,' Mrs Crowther sighed.

'You'd be bored rigid . . .'

'It would keep them out of mischief,' Lampeter said, 'while we get cracking on the aircraft.'

'Well, if that's what you really want, I'll have a word with Todd. He's the manager.' Dundas looked at his watch and whistled. 'Nearly nine. Must get cracking if we're to get you off tomorrow. I'll send you a Land-Rover in the morning. First thing. Now all of you get a good rest.' He raised his hand and walked towards the door, and paused to smile at Barrett still turning the knobs on the set. The familiar chimes of Big Ben surged, rattling the bottles behind the bar and sank in the static. Dundas checked his watch. 'Half a minute slow.'

'Ssh,' Lampeter held up his finger.

In a sudden devastating surge of sound, the BBC announcer's voice filled the bar-room, the tone ponderous with bad tidings.

'It is feared that there are no survivors from the Celtic Airways jetliner Tango Foxtrot, now seven hours overdue into Glasgow. It is now known that there were adverse unforecast weather conditions in the area at the time. An Icelandic trawler has just reported hearing a faint Mayday signal and then silence. Search aircraft have found no trace of rafts or survivors. We have in our studio the flight superintendent . . .' The announcer's voice faded, and when a minute later it returned to strength again, it was to report armed guerrilla activity on the Israeli border. For several seconds there was heavy silence in the room. The cultured British voice struggled distantly with the static. The rain rattled on the windows. The fire hissed softly.

Mrs Crowther broke the oppressive silence. In a cracked

little voice she said, 'Eeeh well, that's it then! Now us knows what it feels like to be ghosts.'

She winked jauntily at Claire. But the stewardess said nothing. She was watching the landlord. He was leaning with his chin cupped in his hand and his elbow on the counter. From where she stood she could just see the gloating smile that curved his lips.

'Bill,' Lampeter said, when Dundas had gone, 'leave that damned radio. We don't want to hear any more news. You and I will start on the aircraft at first light. We'll get to hell out of here somehow.'

'What about me, sir?'

'Yes, you come along as well, Peter. Claire, you can manage the passengers. Take them around the distillery, for God's sake.' Dropping his voice, 'Find them something to do, otherwise they'll be as nutty as the locals. They can't hang around in this dump, twiddling their thumbs . . .' And, raising his voice, 'An early night for everyone. I know how you're all feeling. And I know how your families'll be feeling. But with *luck* we might be off tomorrow evening.'

'Well, I guess I need my beauty sleep if no one else does.' Mrs Ewart was the first to rise, blushing becomingly as Signor Borghese vehemently shook his head at her remark. 'Who am I sharing with, honey?'

'Frau Hagedorn and Mrs Crowther. Miss Playfair's in the top room with me.'

'Let's get weaving then before the lads start snoring.' Mrs Crowther got up, placed a quick conjugal kiss on her husband's forehead, and reminded him severely to take a bismuth tablet. 'His stomach allus gives him gyp when he's not on home cuiking.'

'Remind me,' Mrs Ewart said, slipping her hand through Mrs Crowther's arm, 'to get that cod sauce recipe from you. I'll trade it for mine on baked clams.'

'If you hear a cry for help in the night,' Bill Barrett whispered to Claire as he went upstairs, 'don't worry. Maiyrat'll have got young Pete or me.'

'That's everyone now. You going to turn in, Claire?'

Lampeter watched her set the last of the glasses on the bar counter. 'You'll need your sleep. It might be another long day tomorrow.'

'And a disappointing one?'

'Could be.'

The landlord was behind them raking out the ashes of the peat fire but listening carefully to every word. Then he straightened and pulled the cord of the hanging lamp, dimming its light to a wheezy blue incandescence. The room was suddenly very cold and full of shadows.

'Stop the world, we really have got off.' Claire tried to grin jauntily at Lampeter.

Now the landlord was bending over the counter lamp, his big red hands clumsily dimming it. For a moment his heavy-jowled, thick-browed face was spotlit in its yellow glow. It still wore that only half concealed expression of savage triumph. Claire shivered. We are in his power for some reason, she thought, and was immediately ashamed of her own nervous fantasy.

'Good night, Mr Menzies,' she said.

'A good night to you.' The landlord turned. Out of the light his face resumed its natural dour but harmless expression. 'I hope you will pass a quiet night. Maiyrat's room is very douce and comfortable, that iss so.'

'It was awfully kind of her to give it up.'

The landlord glanced at the now empty staircase, then he took a step towards her and licked his lips as if he might be going to say something else. Automatically she backed away. She felt touched by some emanation of evil as powerful as the thick black smoke of the dulled lamps. Then he obviously changed his mind. In his sing-song voice he said, 'The islanders are well known . . .' nodded his head several times leaving her to complete the text for herself.

She climbed the stairs that led from the back of the bar. There was a good deal of murmuring and creaking going on behind the three closed doors on the landing as the passengers sorted themselves out.

She tapped on the female passengers' door. 'Everything all right?'

'Jest fine. You get yourself some sleep, honey.'

Claire left the landing and climbed a wooden ladder to the room above. 'Maiyrat's wee room aloft –' Dawn did a fair imitation of the landlord – 'is exactly that. A loft.'

Claire had to duck her head to cross over to the tiny window cut out of the top of the front wall a few feet above the swinging inn sign. A faint illumination sifted into the loft from the light below it. There was a skylight in the unlined roof, and a small bedside oil lamp which sent long shadows over the whitewashed walls.

Dawn was wearing a filmy nightdress and her mink hat. 'The rain's coming in through the fanlight. And there's all sorts of wildlife in the tiles.' She sat up clasping her knees. 'There are spiders' webs and the place hasn't been cleaned out since last Christmas. There's still a bit of mistletoe over the bed.'

'The islanders,' Claire said, laughing nervously as she assembled a mattress out of a pile of pillows, 'are well known for their Christmas festivities.'

'But what's she needing mistletoe for up here?'

'Bundling, maybe. The Hebridean custom of courting in bed.'

Dawn giggled, 'Hope it doesn't give Mr Jerry Ainsworth ideas above his station. Hey, are you going to be able to sleep in that?'

'Tonight –' Claire pulled her uniform blouse over her head – 'I could sleep in a gorse bush.' She crept in under the hairy blankets. 'Come to that, I think I am sleeping in a gorse bush.' She stared up at the thick muzzy darkness pressing in through the skylight. The inn settled down to quietness. There was no sound from the rooms below. Once she thought she heard the creak of a stair tread. A door at the back of the inn opened and shut. A night-jar called, its cry uncannily close through the thin tiles.

'Dawn, are you awake?'

There was no answer but the other girl's regular breathing. Claire huddled down under the protective layer of the blankets. She must have drifted off to sleep. She remembered waking suddenly and staring at the fanlight window which now showed a clear indigo rectangle of sky. A single star shone in it. She had the curious certainty that some sound had wakened her. She strained her ears. There was no noise at all except the distant turning of the waves.

Then she heard it, soft at first, rising, strengthening, reverberating. The sound of an aircraft. A heavy-laden aircraft, like the shepherd had described, heavy in the belly as if in lamb.

28th October   MONNANDÆG

The Day of the Moon

Lampeter woke at first light and immediately got out of the ramshackle truckle-bed. He stepped over Spence sleeping like a babe on a mattress on the floor, and, easing himself between the camp beds of Borghese and Philby, walked to the window. It was still raining, and the cloud was down on the deck. The room faced west-south-west. There was a whiteness to the cloud that looked like sea mist, but the faint light disclosed only the lean-to of the kitchen quarters at right angles to the main building, a couple of dilapidated sheds and a flagged fenced yard. Beyond, just the curtain of rain. There was a light burning in the kitchen but no sound of anyone stirring. Lampeter with difficulty raised the sash of the window a few inches. It made an unused grating sound. Ainsworth turned over, mumbling. Peter Spence said in a high voice, 'Honestly, sir, can't raise a peep.' Down below across the lighted kitchen window a shadow flitted.

Lampeter closed the window, struck a match, lit the oil lamp, and shaved himself in cold water from a ewer on an old-fashioned marble-topped washstand. Then, once more in his uniform, freshened, and feeling slightly more in command of the situation, he woke Spence.

'Come on, Peter. You next. We'll let the passengers sleep a bit longer. Get dressed. I'll go next door and give Bill a nudge.'

He opened the door of the largest of the three bedrooms carefully. It faced the same way as the other. The heavy shutters were closed. He pulled his torch out of his pocket and shone it round, smiling to himself. The room had the appearance of an elderly boys' dormitory. The two beds had been awarded for seniority. Herr Hagedorn, still regal in sleep, lay in one with his head protected against the draught with a white silk scarf. Mr Crowther was in the other, his clothes neatly folded over the foot, his watch and his bismuth tablets beside him. Ainsworth had a mattress on the floor, and so obviously had Bill.

'Bill?'

Lampeter's torch flicked into the dark corners of the room. Bill was already up. His mattress bed was empty and neatly made. Lampeter walked over to the window and swung back the shutters. Cold grey half light filtered into the room. Lampeter looked around, frowning. The big down pillow and the hairy blankets had not been used, that he would swear.

'Eeeh, lad, is it clocking-in time already then?' Mr Crowther sat up guiltily and reached for his watch.

'Please yourself, sir. It's early yet. Actually I was looking for Bill Barrett.'

Mr Crowther wiped the sleep out of his eyes and looked around. 'Isn't he here, then?'

'No. Did you hear him get up?'

Mr Crowther shook his head. 'Didn't hear him come back neither.'

'Back? Back from where?'

'Oh, nowhere to fidget yoursen about. Lad were a bit peckish. Said he couldn't settle down for his belly rumbling, an' there was a light on in t'kitchen. So off he popped to see if he could get owt to eat like from t'big lass.'

'And you didn't hear him come back?'

'No, lad. But that don't mean he didn't. It were all that fresh air, or the hot soup. I were off snug as a bug. I didn't know a thing after I shut me eyes. 'Cept when I fastened up t'shutters 'cos our friend here –' he indicated Herr Hagedorn now slowly opening one eye – 'suffers with his neuralgia, I saw the two on 'em. Their shadows. The big lass and yon engineer. Downstairs. Larking around.'

'Larking?'

'Playing. Oh, nowt wrong. Just a bit o' horse play by t'luik.'

By this time the other two passengers were now wide awake. Herr Hagedorn was following the conversation with his lips silently.

'Don't tell me I missed out on something. Horsing around, by God.' Ainsworth sat up and rubbed his aching bones. 'What sort of horsing around?'

'Did *you* hear Bill come to bed, Mr Ainsworth?' Lampeter cut in.

'No.' Ainsworth scratched his head and yawned. 'Don't think he ever did. I went down for a leak or two. God, that's a primitive place . . . that loo is prehistoric, Hagedorn, you should – '

'And Bill wasn't in bed then?'

'No. Not a sign of him.'

'Did you hear him talking to Maiyrat?'

'Can't say I did. Maybe they'd got past talking by then.'

Lampeter stared at him forbiddingly and Ainsworth went on, 'After that I slept the sleep of the innocent.'

'Mmm,' Lampeter grunted. 'Anyway, thanks.'

He walked to the bedroom door and went slowly downstairs. The shutters had been opened in the bar, and the door through to the kitchen was ajar. He could hear the clatter of pans and Maiyrat humming to herself. He smelled the oil lamp burning in the kitchen and a softly etched beam of light leaked through into the bar. It fell on the square of white paper in the centre of the baize-topped table. Lampeter walked over. 'The Skipper' was written on it in large childish letters. He picked it up and unfolded it. The clatter of pans and the humming stopped in the kitchen.

The paper was a sheet out of Barrett's engineering pad. On it was written: 'Have thought up a quick way of fixing the tank. Have borrowed Maiyrat's bike, and gone up the field. See you there.'

Lampeter stared for a moment at the paper in his hand. His first reaction was one of intense irritation that Barrett should have gone back to the field without his permission. Followed by a wry understanding of the engineer's frustration.

Irritation that Barrett had gone off without permission

mingled with an affectionate understanding of Bill's itch to vindicate his aircraft.

'So you got your friend's message, did you now, sir?' The kitchen door was pushed wider. Maiyrat came in carrying a tin tray loaded with plates and cutlery. It was a new Maiyrat. The sulky face was powdered, the lank hair brushed.

'Yes, thank you, Maiyrat.' Irritation gave way to amusement. At his age, old Barrett still knew how to charm food from the stewardesses, and help for his engines.

He was aware that the girl was watching him closely. He looked again at the block capitals of the message. They were large and laboriously formed. Not Barrett's neat, meticulous writing.

'Who wrote this, Maiyrat?'

'Me, sir,' she said promptly. She flushed. 'He told me what he wanted me to put, while he was after pumping up the bicycle wheels.' And staring at Lampeter's face as an afterthought, 'His hands were dirty with the bike, you understand?'

Lampeter said nothing. The girl's blue puffy eyes remained fixed on his face. As far as he could tell with any female, their expression was guileless.

'He was after telling me I write it well, sir?' she prompted after a moment.

'Very well.' Lampeter smiled, mentally shaking himself. The words were Bill's. Why the hell should it worry him that she had written it? Yet an indefinable feeling persisted that something was just slightly out of true. A shifting of something under his feet not unlike the slow shift of the sea before the storm. Determinedly, he shrugged it off.

'Peter,' Lampeter called up the stairs, 'get a move on.'

'Just coming, sir.' Spence came padding down in his stockinged feet. 'Forgot to bring any shoe-cleaning stuff. Did you think to, sir?'

'Oh, never mind that.' Lampeter looked at his watch. 'Quarter to eight. What time did Dundas say he'd come round?'

'He didn't. I don't think.' It was Claire Masefield who

answered. 'At least I don't remember him saying specifically. He just said as soon as possible, when he'd collected whatever he could collect.'

'What time's he organized the distillery for?'

'Ten-thirty. He's got to confirm it with his manager. But if we don't hear differently we go then.' She walked over to the radio set. 'Thought Bill would be at this doing his stuff again.'

'Bill's gone up to the airfield.'

Partly at Lampeter's tone, partly because Bill wasn't the type to override his skipper, Claire's eyes widened. 'How?'

'Bike.'

'Don't tell me –' Miss Playfair wafted down the staircase in her black suit, her mink hat and a long flowing scarf, obviously refreshed by her sleep and obviously bent on making an entrance – 'that your little mechanical egg-head also carries a fold-up bike just in case.'

'No.' Lampeter smiled abstractly at her. 'Apparently he borrowed Maiyrat's.'

'She was only the landlord's daughter but her three speed . . . God, I get more like Ainsworth every day.' She glided into the bar and sat herself down in a chair by the window. 'Still raining, I see.' She wiped the glass and peered across the street at the straggle of tiny low-roofed cottages, their rough cement fronts dark with wet. Two had curtains and a thin blue curl of smoke rising from their chimneys. At the other three glassless windows gaped. Someone had boarded up the empty doorways. She sighed.

'You look as if you slept well anyway,' Lampeter said to her.

'Oh, I did. With a cold shower thrown in at the same time. It was Claire here who didn't.'

Lampeter raised his brows at her.

'I thought I heard aircraft engines,' Miss Masefield said diffidently, and coloured slightly.

Lampeter gave her a thoughtful stare. 'What time?'

'I don't know. But I'd been to sleep.'

'Didn't you look at your watch?'

'I didn't think to.'

He nodded but said nothing.

'Anyone else hear them?' He glanced round the bar.

Mr Crowther had come in now and Mrs Ewart. They all shook their heads.

'*Sure* you heard them, Claire?'

'No. I only ever did say I *thought* I heard them. I might have dreamed it. But I remember looking up at the skylight and it wasn't raining.'

'Then you did dream it, sweetie,' Dawn said. 'If it wasn't raining it was all a beautiful dream.'

'Mmm.' Lampeter frowned and then held up his hand. 'If you're getting any joy out of that radio, I'd like to hear the weather forecast.'

'Comes on after the eight o'clock news, sir.' Claire twisted the knobs.

'I think we can drop the sir,' Lampeter said gently.

She gave him her odd quirky smile and coloured slightly. But Mrs Crowther stumping determinedly down the stairs, her sparse hair still in metal curlers, said jauntily, 'What's up with calling you sir, Captain? I remember my mother allus called me father, sir. An' that after she'd had the ten of us. Now why's that lass blushing, eh? An' you, Captain, you've got a bit of colour. Did I say summat I didn't oughter?'

'You're allus saying summat you didn't oughter, lass. An' it's about time you started calling me sir.'

In the general laughter, the morning began with good spirits. Rested and in the light of day, their chances of getting away seemed bright. They were lucky to have Barrett, they were lucky to have the laird's co-operation. Lucky in a way that the island had to be self-supporting. With a bit of luck now in the weather they would shortly be away.

One by one the rest of the passengers descended. Maiyrat bustled in, laid a torn faded cloth on the baize-topped table, spread out her trayful of plates and cutlery, and then returned with bowls and a large soup tureen full of porridge.

'You've forgotten one place, lass,' Mrs Crowther said in her self-styled role as Maiyrat's food mentor. 'Look slippy and fetch t'other.' And over her shoulder to Mrs Ewart, 'That bloke last night said they was a superstitious lot. Happen they don't want thirteen on us sitting down at once.'

'Bill Barrett isnae here,' the girl said, not budging but setting herself at the head of the table. She appeared to have gained in confidence since last night. With a secret shielded smile she began, hostess-like, to dole out the porridge.

'He's gone up to the airfield,' Lampeter said shortly as he handed Mrs Crowther her bowl.

'How so?' On his way to wash himself at the kitchen sink the landlord paused, changed direction and came towards Lampeter. Unshaved and bleary-eyed, his crumpled, collarless shirt looking as if it had been slept in, the landlord was an even less prepossessing sight than on the night before. His black eyes were bloodshot, and they were ringed with dark puffy circles. He put his hand on the back of Lampeter's chair and thrust his face close to the Captain.

'How so?' he repeated.

'How so . . . what?' Lampeter asked grittily.

'How so iss he . . . yon wee red man . . . awa' to the airfield? How iss it that he got there? The laird hasnae come yet. I have seen he hasnae come.'

Lampeter glanced from the man's face to Maiyrat's and then back again. 'It's not your business,' he said coldly.

Then Maiyrat let out a spiel of Gaelic. The landlord spun round towards her as if she had hit him with a solid object. He clasped his forehead. Then he drew himself to his full height. Theatrically, Lampeter remembered thinking. He spat something back at her. There followed a long ferocious exchange between the pair of them carried on above the passengers' heads. Unabashed, the Crowthers finished their porridge, and helped themselves to a bap. Mrs Ewart played nervously with her spoon. Dawn and Ainsworth exchanged grins. Signor Borghese, a mournful frown on his forehead deep with pain, glanced from face to face like someone following a disastrous tennis match.

Finally, arms hanging loose like some great ape, head thrust forward, the landlord came ponderously round the table towards her. Maiyrat lifted the porridge ladle. The innkeeper raised his clenched fist. Lampeter sprang to his feet, and put a restraining hand on his shoulder.

'Let me be.' And in a softer but more venomous tone he spat out a single word at her, and jerked his head towards the kitchen. She looked for a moment as if she would refuse. Then, tossing her head, she preceded her father from the bar room. The landlord kicked the door shut behind them. Lampeter walked over ready to throw the door open. Everyone waited for the noise to begin. None came. Just a soft exchange in Gaelic. Once, a quickly stifled, half hysterical giggle. Then the landlord came in. His face was unshaved but he had hastily washed. His hair was slicked down.

'He'll take care, ye mind, yon wee red man,' he asked ingratiatingly, 'wi my wee lass's bicycle?'

'Of course.'

'The islanders,' Dawn whispered to Claire, 'are well known as bicycle-lovers . . .'

'It's just that I'm after being anxious about the road . . . she is full of pitfalls, ye understand. Duncan McDermott himself would be after telling you?'

Lampeter narrowed his eyes, and stared thoughtfully into the innkeeper's face. The full lips were smiling, turning it into a curiously unnerving mask. But the mask didn't reach to the thick neck. In it, he saw a pulse beat nervously. Nor did it cover the eyes. Deep in their darkness was a spark of unmistakable terror.

'Peter. Grab yourself some bread or something. Get your mac. I'm not hanging around for Dundas. We'll start walking.'

'Anyway,' Lampeter said, thinking aloud, 'we'll get a better idea of the island walking.'

In daylight, the outside of the inn was the same rain-darkened cement as the cottages opposite. A small gate at the far side led to the back door and the yard. There was a padlock on it but it was unlocked, presumably to wheel out Maiyrat's bicycle. In the doorway of the middle cottage opposite an old woman was sweeping the step. A gull wheeled overhead. There was no other sign of life. The cobblestones of the street were washed clean with the rain and black as iron. Half way along some worn stones led down, presumably to the shore. There were a couple of lobster creels at the top, and a smell of stale fish.

'We'll just follow the coast road, shall we, sir?' Peter Spence took a quick running step to keep up with Lampeter.

'Yep. I'm not going to try to find McDermott's short cut.

Should do it in just over an hour, if we hurry.'

Abruptly, on either side, the straggle of cottages gave out. Heathery grass and bracken edged the road on either side for about half a mile. Then, on the left, the road curved beside soft ground with clumps of reeds. Lampeter screwed up his eyes trying to pierce the mist. A cormorant flapped up from the rush banks with a fish in its mouth.

'Salt marshes,' Lampeter said. 'Sea sounds about fifty yards away, what d'you reckon, Peter?'

'About that, sir.'

'D'you suppose –' Spence wiped the rain off his face – 'that Bill's been able to get cracking?'

'Probably.'

'So all in all the situation's brighter?'

'I've known better.' Lampeter walked on about a hundred yards and then paused. The road was rising under their feet, and the sound of the sea was close at hand. A heavy swell turned on a pebbly shore just beyond the curtain of mist. 'It's being incommunicado I don't like,' Lampeter said, continuing at a brisk pace. 'I'd like someone to know where we are.' He frowned as he said that. It was as if somehow they were eroded, made less real and less living by everyone else supposing they were dead. More acutely, he felt a personal loneliness. In the end now only he could take decisions that had to be taken. No independent voice could even advise.

'But if we get the tank mended, and Mr Dundas gets hold of kerosene, and the weather clears a bit . . .' Peter Spence help up his face to the rain. His voice trailed.

'Things will look a whole lot better.' Lampeter smiled at Spence. If only, he thought, he could get a good clear look at everything. Mentally climb to the top of a mountain and see them in perspective. Instead of the feeling that he was fumbling in fog and superstition and half truth.

Most superstitions had their roots in physical truth. In this instance, was the airfield dangerously sited? Had all this nonsense grown up because in the war a large number of aircraft had been lost? Perhaps by mountain wave effect? Supposing they did get the aircraft mended, and the fuel, was it risking his passengers to take off with so little know-ledge of the place?

'Bike tracks,' Peter Spence said suddenly. 'My side. Over here.' He pointed to the soft spongy shoulder of the road. 'Loud and clear.'

'Keeping well away from the seaward side, I'm glad to see,' Lampeter said.

'I reckon Maiyrat must've warned him, sir.'

'Bloody silly thing to do, really,' Lampeter said not unkindly. 'Feel the road rising?'

'Yes. Quite steep.' Spence puffed a bit at their speed, his pink cheeks glowing with the cold. 'Sea's further away too.'

'Further down,' Lampeter corrected. 'We're close to it.'

On the left-hand side the heather was sparse and strewn with stones, too regular to be natural. 'Been a wall here at some time,' Lampeter said.

'Solid rock this side.'

'See Bill's tracks?'

'No. Road's pretty clean.'

'Gets the wind here. Feel it?'

'I can feel the spray too, sir. Gulls' nests by the look of them in the ledges.'

'One of the island's industries, so Dundas said.'

'Good type, him, sir.'

'Very.'

'Wonder what makes someone settle in a place like this?'

'Away from the rat race, I suppose, Peter. A lot to be said for it.'

'Can't think of anything myself.' Schoolboy-like, Spence caught the drops cascading off the peak of his cap with his tongue.

'Bill's tracks again.'

'Lord, sir, slap through the sheepshit. Hope he cleans it up before Menzies sees it.'

'After her father's performance at breakfast, I'll see he damn well French polishes it!' Lampeter glanced on either side of him. The cliff above the road on the landward side was now diminishing to granite boulders. On the seaward side, there were the remnants of the old wall.

'I reckon this is the headland all right, Peter. I remember seeing it as we were coming in.'

'Me too, vaguely, sir. Wouldn't like to come bombing round here with Scotch in my tank.'

Here, too, they could feel the crash of the waves tremble the ground under their feet. Were there, Lampeter wondered, inlets, subterranean caves that the flood tide found? Could this make the shaking noise at the airfield?

Lampeter picked up a large pebble, tossed it in his hand, and pitched it over the sea wall. It disappeared. But there was no sound of it making contact with anything.

Now the road looped to the right. Lampeter pulled out his compass again. 'Thought so. Due east. Feel that wind, though.'

A vicious spiral of wind caught at their mackintoshes. It tore at the curtain of mist and rain. They could momentarily glimpse, sheer below, the grey sea swinging against the headland. And landward, a sweep of boulders, a patch of plangent marshy green, and further away, the granite flanks of Begh, its upper heights thick in cloud.

'Not all that far now, Peter. Road's descending.'

Out of the sea cliff below the road, a gull rose and hung level with them on motionless wings before sweeping down and skimming the surface of the sea.

'Never thought I'd envy a gull, sir,' Spence said.

Lampeter smiled. 'We'll be airborne like that soon. There's the bike again over that sandy patch.'

'Good show, sir.'

A sheep emerged out of a crevasse between the boulders, shook itself and went careering off to the right. 'Maybe there's a path up there.'

'We'll stick to the road. Guard-room will be coming up before long.'

A quarter of a mile on, the road levelled altogether. They passed a pile of concrete rubble that looked like an old airfield boundary post. The turf that bordered the road was greener and flat.

'Not all that bad a place for an airfield,' Lampeter said. 'They could take off over the sea and into wind.'

'Shall *we* do that, sir? If and when?' Spence held up his crossed fingers.

'We'll see. Here's the guard-room now,' Lampeter said, wishing the visibility would lengthen. But here over the spongy flat ground the mist hung thick, holding in the smell of peat and marsh gas, and echoing their footsteps on the tarmac of the road.

A startled sheep lumbered from the shelter of the derelict guard-room and jumped over the rotted roots of what had once been a swing gate. Out in the white misty distance of the airfield, that same bird sounded its high harsh call.

'Bill's night-jar,' Peter said cheerfully. 'As an ornithologist, Bill's a jolly good engineer. Mist's thickening, eh? D'you know, I can still smell *our* kerosene!'

As the road forked, one part turning in past the guard-room, the other overgrown and rutted, continuing north-east, Lampeter grinned. 'Well, we made it.' He wiped the mizzling rain off his face. 'Sharp right here for twenty-eight.'

'Yes, sir. Shall I give Bill a whistle?'

'No,' Lampeter said shortly. He had a mental note to first tear Bill off a strip. Then, by God, they were going to roll up their sleeves and get cracking off this place.

Three minutes' sharp walk brought them to the beginning of the long 28 runway. 'About three hundred yards up, weren't we?'

'Three hundred to three-fifty, sir,' Spence said tactfully. 'I think we had a bit more to spare than three hundred.'

Swinging his arms cheerfully, Peter Spence marched forward. Then the cheerful smile gradually faded. His pace quickened till he was walking about three paces ahead of Lampeter. He shaded his eyes as if he were walking in strong sunlight instead of mist and rain.

'It's a long three hundred yards,' Lampeter murmured softly. 'A long *four* hundred, come to that.'

'I suppose,' Spence said, feeling a sudden panic, 'that we couldn't have come up on to the wrong runway?'

'No,' Lampeter said shortly.

'Well, she must be further back.' He broke into a run. He began calling, 'Bill. Bill.' He felt the sweat mixing with the rain on his forehead. Suddenly he was aware that Lampeter wasn't following him.

'Peter. Come back here,' Lampeter called as Spence's figure was almost swallowed up in the mist.

Lampeter stood with his arms folded over his chest, staring down at a muddy weed-grown part of the old runway. 'Look there, Peter,' he said softly.

'Tango Foxtrot's tracks.' Peter Spence gulped. 'But . . .' He looked wildly around.

'But,' Lampeter finished for him, 'no Tango Foxtrot.'

Back at the inn the day continued slightly out of true. Dundas arrived at half past nine. They were all in the bar grouped around the radio trying to disentangle an intelligible phrase out of a shipping forecast mangled in static.

'It's going to be like this all day, I'm afraid,' Dundas said, shaking the drops off his deerstalker hat and smiling ruefully. 'I know *this* weather better than any forecaster can tell you. When Begh's in that sort of cloud . . .' He shook his head and turned up the collar of his windcheater and shuddered. 'Still, not to worry. You might get off at night. Get a clear spot sometimes in the wee hours. Or maybe you could get off in this?' His merry amber eyes travelled the room as if searching for Lampeter and the other two. Not finding them, slightly disconcerted, he addressed his remarks to Claire. 'You don't need so much visibility for take-off as for landing.' He laughed. 'Or so they tell me.'

'You don't usually.' Claire smiled. 'But it'd be nice to have it.'

Mr Dundas laughed with flattering heartiness. 'Well – ' he rubbed his hands together – 'I think your skipper's going to be quite pleased with my efforts. The kerosene is definitely laid on. And I've a load of spares out there in the Land-Rover that should gladden his eye.' Mr Dundas cocked his head on one side, bright eyes questioning like a plump sleek robin. 'Where is he? Don't tell me he's not surfaced yet?' The smile deepened. 'These feather-bedded pilots.'

'No.' Claire shook her head, 'He's started walking.'

The smile faded. 'Where on earth *to*?'

'The airfield.'

'*Both* of them?'

'Yes.' She spread her hands apologetically as surprise, concern and a hint of irritation conspired to set the laird's chubby face into a stiff, offended expression. 'They thought it was just as easy as hanging around here . . .'

'It takes time,' Dundas said huffily, 'to gather together the stuff Captain Lampeter wanted. I don't *think* I have been tardy. I was up at the crack of dawn.' He looked at his wrist-watch. 'When . . .'

'It was just,' Claire interposed swiftly, 'that Bill, the engineer had already gone up to the airfield and . . .'

'Not when it was dark?' Now concern wiped all trace of huffiness from the laird's face. 'Good grief! Don't tell me *he* started to walk too. These young fellows have no idea. That road is desperately dangerous at night. What on earth got into everyone?'

'He went by bike,' Claire said, but Dundas seemed not to hear. He blinked his amber eyes at her, now solemn as stones. 'There have been more accidents on that road than . . .'

'I wouldn't have thought there were enough vehicles to have many accidents.' Philby wagged his beard as if to indicate he, anyway, was game for an argument.

'You're a townsman,' the laird said crushingly and turned away. 'You can have accidents just walking. *And* cycling.'

Philby, about to say something, caught Mrs Crowther's eye and contented himself with pulling a chord on his guitar.

'When did they set out?'

'About eight.'

The irritation flickered back. 'They certainly didn't give me long. I'll simply have to go on up there. It was hoping to hand over this little lot.' Dundas pursed his lips as if deliberately and with effort swallowing his irritation. 'Well – ' he forced a polite host's smile – 'I'll nip up to the field and find them. They'll be at the aircraft?'

Claire nodded. 'They'll have got there by now. It's almost at the end of what seems to be the main runway. How can I explain it . . .?'

'It's all right. I think I know the one.'

Dundas smiled forgivingly at Claire. 'Well,' he said drily,

'I mustn't hold *you* all up as well. I can see that airline travel makes you all very time-conscious. Mr Todd is expecting you at the distillery. It's just round the corner and down to the harbour. On the left. The only big building. You can't miss it.' He opened the door. Singling out Philby for his parting shot, he said, 'That road is no joke, you know. McDermott the old shepherd doesn't even like his sheep getting up on it at night.'

He bowed to the ladies, clapped his deerstalker back on his head, and departed into the rain.

It was the cue Philby had been wanting. He fingered his guitar, and sang, 'I'm a poor little lamb that has lost its way, yah yah yah, bound from here to eternity . . . Lord hae pity on such as me . . .'

Till this time Claire told him to shut up before Dundas heard. She had a sudden acute understanding of how dependent they all were on the laird. Without him, Philby's silly song had an uncanny application to their own situation.

Apart from Mrs Crowther's injunction, 'Now think on, you lads, we're not luiking for any more bother than we've got already, so behave thissens,' the walk to the distillery was conducted almost in silence – the only sounds the breaking of the waves, the wild sob of the wind between the meagre buildings, and their own feet echoing on the wet cobblestones.

Down the main street as far as the little circular church, the wind came sideways, smelling of the sea and stale fish and peat smoke from the cottage chimneys. Then they turned right at the church past the solitary village store, down a steep slope that led like a slipway to the sea. The wind blustered straight in their faces, wet and salt on their lips and tossing curds of spume like snowflakes on the stones.

The row between Maiyrat and her father, followed by Dundas's ill-concealed irritation, had produced a curiously chilling effect. An effect deepened by this inhospitable, hopeless place around them. No inquisitive face appeared at any cottage window, no one came to a door to greet them. It was as if, like the outside world, the islanders didn't believe they were alive. A fleeting irrational idea assailed Claire's mind that for some reason they would never be able to leave this place, and that they would spend the rest of their days wandering around this grey limbo land. And though she said nothing, she knew from the bleak expression on their faces that something of the same passing nonsensical idea had touched them all as they hurried forward.

Frau Hagedorn was huddling herself close on her husband's arm. Dawn was dabbing the wet off her face with a handkerchief, and trying to look as if being beautiful was all that really mattered. Philby and Ainsworth glanced around them, casting hopefully for some pungent comment – preferably about each other. Only Mrs Ewart was improving the shining hour. She had charmingly admitted that her dried-out shoes troubled her. And with the humble expression of a sad, overprivileged hound, Signor Borghese was supporting her hand.

'Cheer up, folks,' Mrs Crowther exclaimed, 'we're not dead yet. Not by a long chalk!'

A momentary break in the overcast showed them ahead a small dripping jetty with an iron lamp-standard at the end, a pram dinghy riding the waves on a tarred mooring-rope and a huge white sea running in.

'Luik t'other side of the road, that's it! That's t'distillery. We'll get a bit of cheer in 'ere!'

More sprightly now, they crossed the cobbled street to where a group of buildings loomed out of the mist. These were surrounded by a stout wall topped with broken bottle glass set in concrete. Entry was by a pair of high wooden gates which bore a painted notice 'Ardnabegh Distillery, Ltd', in fresh white lettering. A single lamp shone at a first-storey window, sending a blurred beam out into the rain.

Claire knocked. Almost immediately the gate was opened by a tall black-haired man of about thirty-five dressed in a brown corduroy suit. He had a tanned thin-lipped handsome face.

'The orphans of the storm, eh?'

The voice was deep and harsh, the accent faintly Scots but hard to place. After a quick narrow-eyed glance around them all, he addressed himself to the most authoritative-looking among them, Herr Hagedorn.

'I'm Todd, the manager here.'

'Herr Manager,' Hagedorn shook the briefly outstretched hand.

'The outlook's beginning to improve,' Dawn whispered to Claire. 'He's rather a dish.'

'Well, come on in.' Todd stepped aside, with a curious catlike fluidity of movement. He turned up the collar of his jacket, folding his arms across his chest, glancing from side to side. Under his careless manner, there was a tension and excitement about him, like a wire coil not fully unwound.

'I'm afraid we haven't much to show you. But the laird tells me that you're at a loose end. And what the laird says in Ardnabegh goes.' He threw a thin-lipped angry little smile over his shoulder. He didn't actually say they were wasting his time and theirs, but it was implicit.

'Well, *I'm* glad we came,' Dawn said, as if in flat contradiction of Claire's unspoken thought. '*Anything's* better than hanging around at that inn. And he's a dish. That jet black hair! Wow!'

'Bet it's a wig,' Ainsworth said sourly.

'The balder, the sexier. Medical fact.' Philby brought up the rear as they all trooped in through the gateway into a large concrete yard, thick with sand stamped by tyres and stained with petrol and oil. Dark small-windowed buildings loomed on three sides. Open sheds covered stacks of planks, barrels of diesel oil and paraffin, mounds of peat and coils of hoop-iron. There was the sound of a chugging engine, and a thin metal pipe chimney sent a plume of white smoke to merge with the mist and cloud.

'As you know, there's no electricity on the island. We have our own generator,' Todd said. And then over his shoulder to a middle-aged man sweeping out a shed, 'See to the gate!'

'Looks more like a prison,' Dawn said skittishly, catching up with Mr Todd and fluttering her lashes.

'To keep people out. Not in.' Todd said curtly. 'Pilfering.'

Unabashed by the slatey blue stare, Dawn did a fair imitation of the landlord. 'The islanders, then, are not well known for their honesty?'

Todd snorted. 'That maniac! Menzies! What's he been telling you? No, they're not! Far from it.'

'For their poverty,' Herr Hagedorn said earnestly, 'for their poverty the islanders here will be well known.'

'Tha' doesn't have to be rich to be honest, think on!' Mrs Crowther pursed her lips severely. 'I know some rich folk that'd steal the cross off an ass's back.'

In a thin crocodile they followed their guide, descending into a large dark semi-basement. It smelled of dusty concrete and sour grain. It was full of large locked metal bins.

'Ali Baba's cave sans jewels,' Dawn murmured.

'Grain store,' Todd said tersely. 'Grinding mill beyond. Too dusty to go in. Get your clothes filthy.'

'Do you grow your own barley?' Signor Borghese asked politely, still gallantly assisting Mrs Ewart.

'Here? Not likely. Not enough sun. Don't tell me Menzies hasn't told you his theories on *that*.' He gave a dry bark of laughter.

'And how frequently, Herr Manager, the ships visit?'

'Like everything else here. As and when they feel like it. No, to be fair, weather permitting, about every two months.'

'And I guess,' Mrs Ewart sighed, 'one's just been?'

'' 'Fraid so. Ten days back.'

'I wonder,' Dawn said, for the moment giving up her attempt with Todd and joining Ainsworth, 'why *he* came? D'you suppose he's trying to forget some woman?'

Ainsworth made a rude noise with his lips.

'Trying to forget his bookmaker more likely,' Philby said. 'Notice those spatulate fingers . . . sure sign . . .' He began drumming his own fingers on the metal bins, drawing from them a hollow metallic rhythm, and causing Mrs Crowther to whisper fondly to her husband, 'Eeh! That lad'd mek music out of owt.'

'Stock up, do you, for the winter, Mr Todd?' Philby asked, trying to open one of the bins. 'When the ships come?'

'Naturally.' He gave Philby a curious cold stare. 'You won't be able to open that.'

'Pilfering?'

'Very much so.' Todd turned on his heel. 'Well, as you see, nothing very interesting here. Come upstairs.'

The stairs were a vertical wooden ladder leading up

through the roof to a low whitewashed room running the breadth of one building. It contained a huge soaking vat with an aluminium hopper leading down to it from the floor above. There was a small barred window at either end.

'This is where we soak the barley in the steeps,' Todd said, the slatey blue eyes still on Philby. 'Then it's spread out on the malting floors to germinate . . .' He was speaking in a bored expressionless voice, as if mechanically repeating what he knew by heart, getting it all over with as quickly as possible.

Claire walked to the seaward window. For the moment, the rain had stopped, but a fine spume frosted the glass of the window.

Down below a churn of grey water frothed and curdled around a new concrete slipway that led into a shuttered basement. There were bulkhead lamps set all the way down the slipway. And new steel ropes and pulleys.

'And how much, sir, do you export?' Signor Borghese asked.

'Very little. We're only just resurrecting this place. You can see for yourself.'

Claire walked to the landward window. From here she had a momentarily clear view of the village, the little huddle of rain-blackened cottages, the dark stain on the cloud that was Begh, and the queer round church on top of the harbour slope.

'Admiring the scenery, eh?' Mr Todd came over and stood beside her.

She smiled. 'It's a quaint church. Is it very old?'

'That I wouldn't know. The minister is, though.' He gave his short bark of laughter. 'And the church is falling apart at the seams. It's hardly ever used. The old man never comes. There's not the folk.' He paused, thrusting his hands in his trouser pockets, swinging himself backwards and forwards on his heels. He shot Claire a sudden sideways smile. 'Besides, the folks there have *other* comforts.'

'Like pilfering?' Philby suggested.

'Oh, much more colourful than that.'

'Well, tell us, lad. We got us ears pinned back.'

'No, I couldn't.' Todd shook his head. 'The laird's touchy

about these people. If he hasn't mentioned it, I can't.'

He began to move away from the window. 'The graveyard's very full,' Claire said, her eyes fascinated by the close ranks of wet black headstones, held back like prisoners by the low stone wall.

And then the cloud curtain dropped again. Begh, the church tower, and the huddle of cottages disappeared behind it, leaving only the cone of the church and the fretted skyline of the headstones. A torrent of rain swept down the harbour slope. Hail rattled on the black cobblestones. The scene subtly changed to a dark and deathly volcano, about to erupt, sweep down and engulf them all.

'Oh, aye,' Mr Todd said. 'The graveyard's full all right. Death at Ardnabegh doesnae wait for the minister.'

'Here, sir! Look!' Muffled by the fog, Spence's voice floated back down the runway. 'Tyre tracks. Tango Foxtrot's.'

Visibility was down to a few yards. All Lampeter could see of his First Officer was a muzzy figure bent down low over the tarmac.

He walked up and saw the thick fat rubber tread, printed on the mud of the runway.

'That's her all right, sir.'

Lampeter examined the marks and nodded, 'But why up here?'

'Search me, sir.'

'How far from where we left her?'

'Five hundred . . . maybe six hundred yards.' Spence stood up straight and frowned. 'D'you think Barrett taxied here?'

'Crazy thing to do . . . start up with fuel tanks leaking.' As Lampeter said it he was reminded that he had already used those words to describe Barrett's night ride on Maiyrat's bicycle.

'But Tango Foxtrot couldn't have moved by herself.' Peter Spence glanced nervously over his shoulder.

'No. On the other hand someone might have towed her.' Lampeter searched the ground for other tyre tracks. 'No sign of a tractor here.'

'Might have been washed away by the rain.'

'Possibly.'

'But who'd want to move her, sir? 'Cept us?'

'The sixty-four dollar question.'

'And where the hell could they have taken her?'

'The sixty-four-thousand dollar question.'

'Claire said, sir, that she heard engines . . .'

'*Thought* she heard.'

'Might've been Tango Foxtrot taxiing. Or – ' Spence paused, swallowed and added hollowly – 'taking off.'

'With that amount of fuel? And in that state? Come off it, Peter.' Lampeter began moving forward, his eyes on the ground. 'She's bound to be somewhere. We're wasting time theorizing. Find her and we'll find Barrett. He's got a lot of questions to answer.'

Together they walked forward, following the tracks to the end of the runway and then left on to the taxi track. They disappeared for a few paces on the clean rain-swept tarmac, reappeared where the big tyres had flattened a long clump of decaying willow herb, showed up clear in some sandy mud. Then fifty yards further on all tyre marks vanished, and there was a fork to the right.

'Which way, sir?'

Mist from the sea was pouring over them now like a white smokescreen. Lampeter could feel it on his face, taste it salty on his lips.

'This way.' Lampeter chose the track to the right. 'Remember where we're going. Otherwise we'll get lost.'

A hundred yards on, there were still no signs of any tracks. The surface of the taxi track was weathered and broken. Weeds had encroached on either side, narrowing the track. Heavy dark-winged birds rose squawking from the tangles.

And then, suddenly, Lampeter's heart-beat quickened. Looming ahead in the mist was a darker grey elephant shape with a tall tail.

'There she is, sir.'

The two of them ran towards it. Gradually the thing revealed itself. An aircraft all right, but smaller surely than Tango Foxtrot. Squat and fat, and no tricycle undercarriage.

'What the . . .?'

The mist billowed and reformed around them. A light sea wind momentarily parted it. A skeleton was revealed in front of them – an old Wellington bomber, its geodetic structure shown like a cage of ribs and bones with all its fabric picked away.

Behind it were other aircraft – a Liberator, two Halifaxes on their knees with broken undercarriages, a lop-sided York labelled RAF Transport Command indicated that the aerodrome had been used as a ferry station. An old petrol bowser spread its decaying hosepipe over the wings of a white Fortress. Further on, a bomb trolley, a broken-down tractor, three husks of khaki-camouflaged Hillman cars were abandoned outside a tumble-down motor transport section, its petrol pumps half eaten away by rust. And through all the gaps and the broken windows wreathed the wet salt mist blown in from the sea. Lampeter shivered. No wonder the villagers avoided the place.

'There's buildings and things up here, sir.'

Spence had disappeared ahead, and Lampeter had to follow the sound of his voice. Way beyond, there was the control tower with the huge letters 28 in peeling paint still displayed, and the ravelled remnants of an old wind-sock. There were the periscope fire-hydrants of underground fuel tanks. And then, three hundred yards or so further on, loomed up a big black metal hangar.

Spence's excited voice, 'Eureka, sir. Found her. She's in here.'

Coming up along the girdered side, Lampeter saw the sudden silver shape, this time unmistakably Tango Foxtrot. As they went inside, a whole flight of birds swooped down from the roof girders. A rat scurried across the dusty cement floor.

'Bill!' The noise echoed and bounced round the metal walls. There was no answer. The aircraft ladder had been run down from the entrance and they climbed up it into the cockpit. All the side windows had been opened. On top of the port wing was Barrett's open tool box, his soldering iron and the main fuel tank panel had been removed.

The fuel tank was integral with the metal wing, and the six holes made by the lightning had been plugged on the underside surface, and a fractured fuel pipe soldered.

Clearly the engineer had been at work. The fuel cock had

been turned on, and all remaining kerosene had been drained out and the tanks vented so that soldering could be effected safely. At the engineer's panel the two throttles had been pushed forward. The electric power was off, but on the instrument panel the clock ticked peacefully.

Half an hour and miles of dusty dark corridors later, they were all walking along a narrow gallery twenty feet above another concrete floor.

'Hold tight to the rail,' Mr Todd turned round to warn them. 'Nasty drop. These are the pot stills. Here the wash is being distilled, first in the wash still, then in the spirits still.' He pointed to two vats, one about twenty feet, the other half its size connected by a complication of glass and other tubes to one another.

'Looks like the fat lady on drip feed,' Philby said.

'Can we go down?' Mrs Ewart asked. 'Heights always bother me.'

'Certainly.' Todd nodded. 'But mind your feet on those metal steps. We don't want any accidents.'

'I shall make sure you come to no harm.' Signor Borghese skipped down ahead of Mrs Ewart and lifted her down over the last three rungs. One by one the others followed and stood staring up, dwarfed by the enormous vats, their lids shut down with stout brass hoops.

'Well I never did!' Mrs Crowther exclaimed. 'You could cuik all t'lot on us in there at a go.'

'The islanders are not yet known for their cannibalism,' Claire whispered to her.

'We hope, we hope! What did the dish mean by *other comforts,* then?'

'Sex,' Ainsworth said. 'What else?'

'They're too old.'

'Men are never too old.'

'I am reminded –' Signor Borghese pulled Mrs Ewart gently away from Ainsworth's contaminating presence – 'of a story about one of my country's vineyards. A family vineyard worked only by two brothers. One day they have themselves a quarrel. They draw knives. One brother kills the other.'

'Cain and Abel,' Philby said. 'Heard it somewhere before.'

'This brother very afraid.' Borghese coloured slightly, but ignored Philby. 'What to do with the body? Then idea! Into the vat of wine. And down – ' he pointed to the lid of the pot still and pretended to hammer – 'he fastens the lid.'

'Didn't it ruin the brew, then?' Mrs Crowther asked, trying to see the colour of the liquor inside the pot still.

'No, no. Not at all. *Bellissima. Dulcissima.*' Signor Borghese kissed his fingertips. 'Never was there such a wine. So bold. So clever. A trifle mischievous in flavour. But the bouquet out of this world.'

'Don't give Mr Todd any ideas about improving the flavour of Ardnabegh whisky.' Dawn shivered.

'And don't you give Mr Todd any ideas, period,' Ainsworth growled.

'If I had any ideas to give Mr Todd,' Borghese said, 'I would tell him that this chamber is inclined to chill his esters.'

'Please, please.' Ainsworth pretended to look shocked.

'You've a dirty little mind,' Philby said.

'Give over lads, stop fratching. Mr Borghese is right. It's as cold as charity in here. I could do with a sup out of that pot me'sen.'

'I was going to suggest – ' Todd turned, eagerly seizing on Mrs Crowther's remark – 'we adjourn now. There's very little else to see. We're not malting at the moment. You don't want to go round a lot of old warehouses. Come to my office and sample the stuff.'

'Some of us is only here for the beer.' Ainsworth lifted his arm.

'And some of us hasn't got a mind above beer,' Philby said.

'Give over, lads.'

'We make pretty potent stuff.' Todd smiled more easily now, Claire thought, now that they were on their way. 'Sorts out the men from the boys.'

'That means you can wait for us outside, Philby.' Ainsworth took Dawn's arm as they once more set off to cross the yard. A steady, fine, wetting rain was falling. Little puddles were forming in the tyre tracks across the stained sand.

'Watch where you're leading me, Ainsworth. I've only got one spare pair of tights.'

'Well, I'm going to get a move on, lads and lasses. Them as gets in first might get a second squeeze of t'pot.' Mrs Crowther nipped smartly to the head of the group, following Mr Todd into a small office at the end of the building nearest the main gate.

It was furnished with a large desk, some folding chairs, a couple of green metal filing cabinets, and a safe. Behind the desk, covering one wall, was an enormous map of the North Atlantic, with Ardnabegh as the centre. There were numerous small holes all over it, as if flags or labels had once been pinned there.

'Interested in cartography?' Todd asked Claire, taking out a stone jar from behind the desk and beginning to fill the glasses.

'Quite interested.' She took the glass he handed her.

'That's an old one, I'm afraid. Last war. Ops map. Someone found it at the airfield.'

Claire raised her brows. 'I thought no one liked to go up there?'

'That maniac Menzies again? Oh, they go up there when they want to, believe me.'

'Pilfering?' Philby called over.

'And other things.'

Claire took a step nearer the map. 'The airfield's marked.' She screwed up her eyes, spelling out the letters. 'Crann Tara.'

'Aye. Gaelic, Menzies would tell you, for Fiery Cross.'

'Eeh, lass, I don't know what the folks at chapel'd say.' Mr Crowther smiled fondly as they all sat around with large glasses of the colourless liquor clasped in their hands. 'You supping neat spirits.'

'Folks at chapel reckon I *am* a spirit, sitting on a cloud luiking down on them.'

'Well, bottoms up!' Ainsworth raised his glass.

'The good health and fortune of the assembled company.' Signor Borghese sniffed his glass for bouquet, took a sip, rolled it round his tongue, and then let it trickle down his throat.

'Well?' Mr Crowther asked.

Signor Borghese kissed his fingertips. *'Bellissima! Dulcissima!'*

'D'you have to say that, lad? That's what you said before about yon wine in your story, think on.'

'Slainte.' Mr Todd drained his glass at a swallow, immediately refilled it and took another gulp. His previous tension seemed to smooth away. In a friendly tone he said to Mrs Crowther, 'It must be a very strange experience for you all.' He lounged back in his chair, nursing his glass, his eyes half closed like a cat's in the sunlight. 'To be alive. And yet back there they all think you're dead.'

'Better'n being dead and thinking you're still alive, lad.' The liquor had gone to Mrs Crowther's face. Her cheeks wore a bright purply-pink flush. Her eyes snapped merrily behind the round spectacles. 'I could name you half a dozen folk 'at's dead 'an they don't know it.' She laughed with disproportionate glee at her own joke. 'I wonder, lad – ' she took off her glasses and wiped her eyes – 'if t'Oddfellows will have a two minutes' silence for thee?'

'Tonight? At lodge meeting? Happen they will.'

'My brother freemasons,' Herr Hagedorn said with sudden wry humour, 'will not know where the acacia spray to send.'

'Just so long as no one's collecting our insurance.' Ainsworth grinned, holding out his glass for a refill.

'It's not really funny when you look at it.' Philby stroked his beard thoughtfully. 'In fact, it's a nasty situation. If we're already dead, anyone could bump the lot of us off, and it wouldn't matter at all, would it?'

'Would to us, lad.'

Mellow with the raw spirits, they all laughed uproariously.

'Besides, who would want to?' Todd asked softly.

'Quite.' Ainsworth drained his glass. 'Of course I can think of individual members whom someone might just want to . . .' He glanced meaningfully at Philby.

Mr Todd looked at his wrist-watch and frowned.

Immediately Claire stood up and Mr Todd followed suit. 'I hate to break up the party,' she said, 'but we really must go. Captain Lampeter will wonder what's happened to us.'

'Well, if you must, you must.' Mr Todd made no attempt to detain them. He brushed aside Claire's thanks with a shrug, and opened the office door. He cursed the blustery wind under his breath.

'The tide is rising rapidly too,' Hagedorn said, as thick curds of spume smacked wetly on the sand of the yard.

'Does at this time of year.' Todd stepped lightly ahead of them over the grease and puddles of the yard. Somewhere the engine still chugged and the plume of steam curled upwards wavering in the wind. But the yard was deserted and not another soul moved.

Mr Todd unlocked the gate and pulled it back.

'Well –' he shook Hagedorn's outstretched hand – 'a safe trip home.'

Still holding back the gate, waiting for the last two people, Signor Borghese and Mrs Ewart, he looked up at the grey mesh of the rain. 'Begh's disappeared. D'you still reckon you'll get off tonight?'

'We're keeping our fingers crossed.'

Todd gave Claire a thin mocking smile, and then turned to frown at Mrs Ewart.

'These wretched shoes. Now it's the heel,' she wailed, finally limping up. 'Thank you so much, Mr Todd, for a very memorable visit. When I get back to Montreal, I shall tell just everyone. They're to drink nothing but the real Ardnabegh whisky.'

'Do that.' Mr Todd bowed and smiled. The big gates shut smartly behind them. On the other side, a lock turned.

Despite Ainsworth's groan of irritation, Mrs Ewart leaned against the gates, sighing.

'I really did have something caught on my shoe. I trod on something back there. A nail, or a bit of wire. That yard's just awfully messy.' She slipped her right foot out of its shoe and bent down and picked it up. 'There. What did I tell you? No one believed me.'

'I believed you, signora.'

Mrs Ewart held out her shoe. Caught fast round the slim heel was a small but heavy steel cap, with a strong chain attached which was embedded into the soggy sole.

'Land's sakes, where did that come from?'

'That's what Todd would call pilfering,' Philby said. 'No wonder he keeps everything locked. You've probably just walked away with the most valuable piece of machinery in the whole distillery. The place'll break down without it.'

'You don't really think so, do you? Should we knock on the gate and hand it back?'

'Let me see, please, one moment.' Signor Borghese leaned forward authoritatively and took it from her. He examined it carefully, turning it over in his hands, running his nail over the unfamiliar hieroglyphic – a large capital S but facing the wrong way – stamped into the outside and then, as if it were wine, smelling it. He shook his head.

'That, dear signora, has nothing whatever to do with whisky distillation. Take no notice of them. They tease you, these young men. It is simply a very small fuel cap. Of no importance or significance whatsoever.'

'Keep it for luck,' Mrs Crowther said, beginning to stump off up the hill towards the churchyard. 'Put it in thee pocket and keep it for luck.'

'Bill!'

They left the aircraft and began exploring the maintenance room and offices. Clearly this was where Barrett had got his extra tools and bits and pieces in addition to those in his own extensive tool kit. A table greasy with oil, a lathe, lockers, a desk with a wooden chair beside it, a pile of gear wheels, half a Merlin engine, plugs, screws, a box of nails. On a green baize notice-board was pinned a ragged sheet of yellowing paper headed *Maintenance Order, 299 Squadron.*

They went from room to room, but there was no sign of Barrett. But clearly he *had* been here. Peering through a broken pane of glass, Lampeter saw other buildings through the mist, a Stores perhaps, and what looked like another hangar.

'I wonder where he's put the bicycle, sir.'

'Perhaps he's gone off on it to look for some more stuff.' Lampeter led the way outside, walking slowly, his eyes never still. Looking up at the sky, down at the state of the perimeter track, over his shoulder at the rusted, derelict buildings, his eyes narrowed, assessing the visibility.

It was increasing with the rising wind. Drifts of torn-off cloud trailed away towards the north-east. Now they could see almost a mile right into the centre of the airfield where the two main runways crossed each other. Lampeter glanced at the intersection, then stared a little longer, then stopped altogether. Beside him Spence stopped obediently and gazed intelligently at this core of the airfield which so held his Captain's eyes.

'See anything odd, Mr Spence?'

'Odd, sir? What about, sir? Very derelict this field of course, sir.'

'About the runway intersection?'

'No, sir.' And a little more worried, 'Nothing there, sir.'

'Can only remember seeing that once before. That intersection looks exactly at right angles, wouldn't you say?'

'Yes, sir. Exactly, sir.'

'The runway we landed on was east-west true. So the short runway is exactly north-south true.'

'Oh . . . oh, yes.'

'Interesting!'

'*Very*, sir,' Peter Spence said, thinking airline operating really did throw some strange bods up on the beach. Barrett and his bloody engines. Lampeter and his fascination with flying. Here they were with an unserviceable aircraft, cut off from the outside world, on an island of half-wits, with visibility as uncertain as a politician's promises, and Lampeter was fascinated by an unusual heading of some wartime runways. And, lest his thoughts had leaked like a balloon above his cap, he said earnestly, 'Very interesting indeed. What d'you make of it, sir?'

'Oh, nothing. Just one of those things.' Lampeter's voice sounded impatient. 'That's a bit of a store or something over there. Come on, let's see if it's there Bill's gone on the scrounge.'

A hundred yards down a broken concrete path, an old Nissen hut still stood like some decrepit dead centipede. The door had gone. A notice still hanging by a single rivet said *B Flight Electricians,* and in smaller letters *No issue without 658.*

Further on were the underground fuel tanks, their cocks and pumps poking up surprisingly preserved like periscopes.

'Might be some fuel in those, sir?'

Lampeter shook his head. 'Dundas has promised all the kerosene we need from the distillery.' He turned, 'Well, there's no sign of him here. We'd better get back to the hangar.'

As they walked away there was the sound of an engine, and a Land-Rover materialized, slowed down and slid to a slippery stop.

'Well, there you are!' Dundas was clearly trying to keep the irritation out of his voice. 'Found you at last! Why did you move the aircraft?'

'That's it, we didn't. Surely your chaps moved her?'

Dundas parked the vehicle just outside the hangar doors and climbed down from the driving seat.

'*My* chaps? Why should they?'

'Who else?'

'Your engineer!' Dundas looked around. 'Where is he, by the way?'

'He's not here.' Lampeter pointed to the neat patches on the port wing. 'But he *has* been here.'

Dundas grunted. 'Made good progress, too. You'll be able to get off soon, eh?'

'Bill's got to mend the starboard wing.'

'Well, the sooner the better. He can't be far away from here.' He went to the back of the Land-Rover and, helped by the pilots, unloaded tools, copper pipes, duralumin strips, and ten-gallon cans of kerosene. 'We've got everything you need here, anyway.' His voice was now unmistakably impatient. 'Where *is* the man?'

'We've looked all round here and there's no sign of him.'

'What about the bicycle?'

'No sign of that either.'

Dundas looked at his watch. 'Does he believe in fasting?'

Lampeter smiled. 'No, he likes his grub.'

'Well, it's half past twelve. After working through the night, he'll be ravenous. Come on, jump into the Land-Rover. I'll bet he's back at the inn with his legs under the table, knocking back Maiyrat's potato soup!'

Coming up from the harbour, the wet wind pushed in their backs and the steep cobbled street had been turned into a shallow fast-moving stream. By the time they reached the

Oak, they were all soaked through, and the effects of the 140 proof whisky had worn off. Inside the bar, they huddled round the fire trying to get warm. Above them on the wall, the pendulum of the big round clock ticked to and fro. Rain sluiced down the windows. A silence hung round all of them till Mrs Ewart said suddenly, 'I kinda got the impression Mr Todd wasn't too pleased to see us.'

'Oh, but he was a dish.' Dawn clasped her hands against her bosom. 'Those dark blue eyes.'

'And those dark blue bags under them,' Ainsworth scowled. 'Looked as if he had been up all night.'

'Doing what?' Philby asked.

'Not making whisky. The cold, you understand, so inimical to the esters.' Signor Borghese shook his head.

'D'you think he could be up to something?' Ainsworth asked hopefully.

'But what,' Philby said slowly, 'could there possibly be to get up to in Ardnabegh?'

'The islanders,' Dawn said, 'are well known for their . . .'

'And Mr Todd gave you all a fine time showing you the distillery, that iss so?'

As if he had been lurking behind the half-open kitchen door, Menzies suddenly appeared with the speed of a jack-in-the-box. Clearly he was in a calmer temper than earlier. Wiping over the wood, he gave them all what was intended to be a friendly smile. In return, from their circle round the fire, they regarded him warily. There were self-conscious nods and murmurs. Each of them remembered what Todd had told them about the landlord; they noticed afresh his muscular strength, and they were assailed with doubts and fears about the meaning of his improved temper.

'He iss a fine man, Mr Todd. And he knows many, many things.' The remark was received in silence. The only sounds, the rattle of the rain, the hiss of moisture on the glowing peat, and the howl of the wind in the chimney blowing smoke in their eyes.

Menzies tried again. 'Mr Todd could show you many other things. Very wonderful things that you will not ever have seen before, that iss so. I could ask him for you, maybe . . .'

'That's very kind of you,' Claire said, 'but we shall be leaving tonight.'

The landlord's friendly smile froze. 'But the aeroplane. It iss not ready!'

'It soon will be. All the crew are working on it now.'

'But the weather.' The innkeeper nodded several times at the streaming window-panes. 'It will not let you.'

'They think it will clear.'

'How so?' The heavy frown returned. He nodded towards the radio set. 'Who says it will clear? Have you heard something, then?'

'No,' Claire admitted reluctantly. 'But the storm's got to blow itself out some time.'

'We shall see.' Menzies looked at the clock. Then, ponderously, all trace of his smile gone now, he lifted the flap of the counter, walked over, switched on the radio. Then he retreated back to the bar.

There was a crackling of static in which a disc-jockey and his music were drowning. No one spoke. Arms folded over his massive chest, the landlord continued to regard them solemnly and silently. Then the time signal cut through the static. 'Here is the weather forecast and news at one . . .' The BBC announcer's voice surged and faded on the waves of interference. The landlord suddenly turned his back on them all, and ostensibly busied himself with the bottles behind the bar.

'. . . disturbances associated with a deep stationary low-pressure area extending over the north-western approaches, Faroes and Rockall will continue . . . heavy rain, low cloud. Thunder at times, poor visibility . . . winds moderate easterly, backing to . . . further outlook in the north remaining unchanged.'

The group by the fire let out a collective groan.

'I'd say that means there was a good chance of it being fine,' Claire said. 'Weather forecast is always fifty per cent wrong.'

'Hundred per cent,' Philby said, coming to her assistance for once. 'Medical fact.'

'It iss not so.' Unable quite to conceal his triumphant smile, the landlord turned. 'That –' he jerked his head towards the set – 'iss always right when she says it will be after raining.'

'There's a place like that in England,' Mr Crowther called across to the landlord. 'Name of Manchester in Lancashire.' But his wife dug her elbow into his side for silence.

The announcer's voice was struggling again with the first news item.

'. . . agency report that fierce fighting is now going on in the Ah Fezim area . . .'

' 'sall right, lad, it's not us!'

But everyone now remained quiet.

'. . . an Arab group led by Sheik Ben Yussef is attacking an Israeli armoured division, using the most modern weapons. Tanks and field guns are in action. Captured mortars and bazookas have been declared by observers to be of a modern, until recently restricted, American type. The United States has categorically denied supplying such weapons to either side, and at the same time submitted a report on Russian flame-throwers found abandoned after a similar attack on a desert Israeli patrol . . . an Army tank was ambushed in Belfast last night by a group of youths with home-made . . . in Vietnam a helicopter carrying wounded . . .'

'Same dreary stuff.' Ainsworth scowled. 'God what a world.'

'Even if it is,' Dawn sighed, 'I still want to get back on . . .'

But none of them, Claire suddenly noticed, was really listening. They were all counting. It was like being back at school. Marks being read out. First, second, third item of news had gone by. Their importance, their reality was dwindling away. Then . . .

'The massive search for the survivors of the missing aircraft of Celtic Airways, which continued all last night, has now been called off. Ships and aircraft in the search area report heavy rain, thunderstorms, and mountainous seas, in which no raft could survive. Celtic Airways say there can now be no more hope for the thirteen people on board, and next of kin have been informed . . .'

'Well, they'll get a surprise when us all turns up,' Mrs Crowther said. But nobody answered. Menzies fished out the same faded cloth from a shelf under the bar. He rattled some plates and knives. The triumphant smile had deepened. From time to time Claire saw him glance at them all with a weird possessive look, as if, Gulliver-like, he itched to lean over and clutch them all in his great ugly hands. Beside her Philby punched a discord on his guitar.

It was into this atmosphere five minutes later that Lampeter strode, closely followed by Dundas and Spence. He took one look round the group by the fire, and then said sharply, 'Barrett's missing. Have any of you seen him?'

It was in fact – quite rightly so in the circumstances – the laird who took over. After all, he knew the island and the islanders. He had the transport and the equipment. He had the ghillies and he knew their capabilities. Maiyrat, who was the most noisily fearful – not so much for Barrett as for her bicycle – was firmly silenced. Dundas produced a map, and started delineating areas, organizing search-parties and making plans.

'Everything I have, Captain – ' he turned to Lampeter – 'cars, men, ropes . . . is yours. I know I can say the same for my distillery manager. We'll do everything we can.' He spoke very quietly. 'Of course we may be jumping the gun. Barrett will probably walk in this door before very long. But I agree . . . you've seen for yourself the terrain, and we can't minimize the dangers.'

Watching him, Claire was struck by the efficiency and good sense of his arrangements. Barrett's known movements were marked in ink on the map, then his possible movements pencilled in. After that, Dundas coloured in red the areas where Barrett was most likely now to be.

'Now we'll divide everyone into parties,' Lampeter said, eyeing his charges thoughtfully. 'We'll put someone who knows the terrain in charge of each group.'

'Excellent idea.' Dundas nodded. 'And if I also might suggest, this area and this are the most tricky ones . . .'

Between them they decided on Spence, Hagedorn and Menzies to search the short cut to the aerodrome along which they had come last night. Ainsworth, Todd and Borghese would take the segment between the short cut and the coast road. Lampeter and Mr Crowther would search the coastal sector of the airfield.

'Most likely spot,' Lampeter said. 'Hangar and dispersals. That's where he'll have gone nosing around.'

'The most tricky too,' Dundas said. 'Cliff erosion . . . sure you wouldn't like me too? Well then, take my head ghillie . . . he'll see they come to no harm.' He smiled across at Mrs Crowther.

Mr Dundas for his part was to take Dawn and Claire in his car; they would drive slowly along the perimeter track and search the small roads along the inland sector of the airfield.

'And, Claire . . . bring the rest of the food and blankets back with you.' Lampeter gave her a quick direct glance that singled her out as the confidante of his unexpressed and carefully concealed anxiety. 'We may not get away from here for quite a while.'

'What about the old shepherd?' Claire asked, colouring slightly and giving Lampeter a faint, acknowledging little smile. 'He might have seen something.'

'Oh, him,' Dundas interposed swiftly. 'He's bound to have seen something.' He shrugged and gave a sad, dismissing smile.

'He was after being round here this morning,' Menzies suddenly broke in. He addressed himself to Dundas. 'Old Duncan McDermott, the same. Enquiring about the strangers, whilst they were away at the distillery. Likely he only wanted a free drink.'

'Very likely,' Dundas said drily, 'and now if you'll excuse me, I'll go and get hold of Todd and any equipment, ropes, torches, what have you, that we can lay our hands on.' He buttoned up his jacket. 'Meanwhile I expect our friend Menzies here can find you a bite to eat. Put on whatever warm clothing you've got.' He paused and smiled mischievously. 'And this time, don't anyone move till I get back. There's good chaps. I won't be more than an hour at the most.'

In fact he was back in fifty minutes, but thickening cloud or the early northern twilight was already making the afternoon dim. The laird had Todd and one of his ghillies with him. The other ghillies would meet him at the hangar.

'I take it your friend hasn't turned up yet?'

'No.'

'Well then –' he checked the old black-painted clock on the wall with his wrist-watch – 'three-fifty. Shouldn't we have a time to report back here? Collate our findings?'

'A thorough search'll take hours in this terrain. Say we'll all come back here round about nine.'

'Eeeh,' Mrs Crowther said as spokeswoman for the older ladies, 'us'll all be sitting on pins till you all get back.'

'Right then,' Dundas said, 'don't any of you do more than you've been given. And do what the local chap says.' He smiled faintly. 'They may look thick but they know the place best.'

'Watch it, Peter,' Lampeter said.

'Yes, sir.'

'Don't take any risks.'

'No, sir.'

Before he departed Signor Borghese kissed Mrs Ewart's hand, and in a sudden excess of emotion she stood on tiptoe, cupped the sad salesman's face in her hands and planted a delicate little kiss on his furrowed forehead.

'You'll follow us then, will you, in the Land-Rover, Captain?' Dundas bustled Claire and Dawn out of the bar.

'Think on, lad, don't get thee feet wet,' Mrs Crowther called after them.

It was drizzling again outside. A little more light had drained from the sky, Claire thought, like grey sand from an hourglass. It was shadowy inside the back of the car. The ghillie was already sitting in the driver's seat with the engine running. Dundas climbed in beside him, and checking first that Lampeter was ready to follow him, nodded to the ghillie and said something to him in Gaelic.

Mr Dundas glanced anxiously at his watch and at the sky again. The car pulled smoothly away into the myriad puddles between the cobblestones. The tyres hissed, the springing carrying them comfortably over the uneven surface.

As the car came out from the shelter of the line of cottages it was buffeted by a strengthening sea wind. Rain rattled on the windscreen. Below, they could glimpse the sea – huge elephant-grey rollers swelling and swinging in under the cliff.

'Whirlpools,' the laird said, pointing to the only place in

the bay where the grey waters churned.

At the headland, they got their first real view of the island. The jagged, inhospitable coastline, the little village clustered round the harbour, a hint of muzzy purple where the wild moorland began, and to their right, the cloud-beheaded shoulders of Begh.

'Once a sacred sacrificial mountain to the Druids,' the laird said. 'I believe they used to throw their victims off the summit. The islanders still treat him with great respect.'

'I would too.' Dawn shivered.

Down below a few gulls swooped and glided on to the oily surface of the sea. The cloud on Begh altered its shape.

At about five miles an hour, the ghillie eased the big car round the headland. 'You get cross winds, little sneaky draughts and funnels, just here.' Dundas seemed to sense Claire's impatience. 'They can topple you over just like that.'

A vision of Bill unwittingly cycling along this road in the darkness came into Claire's mind. She bit her lip.

'At one time there were a lot of accidents here. The islanders said Begh was angry.' He smiled. 'Till I got around to explaining about upcurrents, down-draughts and what have you.'

All four of them in the car had their eyes travelling the roadside, the rocky crevices, every gorse bush. Now light was draining out of the murky sky. At a sharp bend further on, the ghillie switched on the headlamps, throwing strong cones of light on to the glistening road. Claire's heart-beat quickened. The world outside seemed more baffling and desolate still.

'I'm afraid Fergus only speaks a few words of English, and those most likely swear-words.' Mr Dundas smiled. At the sound of his own name the ghillie shrugged and coloured slightly, but he kept his eyes fixed ahead.

Dawn said, 'He's a good driver.'

'And he needs to be. You can't see it now, but there's a three-hundred-foot drop your side, Miss Playfair.'

Dawn wailed and moved a little closer to Claire.

On the laird's other side, by pressing her face hard against the window, Claire could still see the landscape beyond the white wash of the headlamps. Ahead and to the right, the plateau that was the airfield glowed through the darkness with a curious luminous green.

'Sure sign of bogs, that colour,' the laird said, watching her.

'Why did they build the airfield there in the first place?'

'Good anti-U-boat field. And a first-class refuelling post for aircraft from Labrador and America.'

Claire kept her nose pressed hard against the glass, her eyes straining for a sight or a movement or a clue of any kind. Cutting through the glimmer of green, she could just distinguish the black cross of the runways, the gaunt skeletons of old hangars, the concrete black of the control tower. For a fraction of a second, as they rounded a curve, light seemed to glow from it. But when she looked again it was gone.

'I thought I saw something from the control tower.' She leaned forward and spoke to the laird.

He peered out. 'As we turned?'

'Yes.'

'Just reflection. There's still glass in some of the windows.'

They drove round another bend, heading now parallel with the perimeter track. They were momentarily out of the wind. Shapes of resting sheep tucked in the shelter of overhanging rock and clumps of whin bushes lay at the roadside like city snow after a thaw. Twin green lights bobbing in the radiance of the headlamps raised a quick false hope, before the dazzled sheep dragged itself away and on to the airfield.

The car glided past the wreck of the guard-room, turned right for a few seconds, and then left, gathering speed up towards the hangar. Rainwater spurted from the tyres. On either side of them now was total darkness, without light or visible landmark, giving a curious eerie dimensionless quality. And ahead, a faint wet pink stain marked where minutes before the sun had set.

The headlights swung round the perimeter track, flickered over the hangar, and then caught the silver skin of Tango Foxtrot in a bright yellow spotlight. They came to a halt. Behind them, the Land-Rover had stopped, and Lampeter and Crowther were already walking towards three more ghillies gathered in the illumination of the car headlamps. They wore long rubber boots, windcheaters, and tweed shooting caps with the ear-flaps tight down, and all held torches and hurricane lamps.

As they stood stolidly side by side in the curious mixture of shadow and glare, Claire kept looking at them. Was that all she saw last night? A ghillie scared out of his wits by an invasion of strangers? A cap wet with rain could look like a helmet, a windcheater was not so different from a flying jacket.

She sighed, wishing now that Bill's disappearance could be as easily explained away.

Lampeter and Crowther had rolled back the huge hangar door, and the headlamps now focused on Tango Foxtrot's long white tail. The laird gathered his men around him and said, 'Now, which of you had the Land-Rover last night?' They shrugged and stared.

Dundas spoke again, this time in Gaelic, very slowly, as if he had learned the language with difficulty.

One of the ghillies nodded and pointed at himself. Dundas asked another question. The man's face melted into absolute astonishment. He shook his head, shrugged, let out a spiel of Gaelic.

'The Captain here –' again Dundas spoke in English – 'said that he left this aeroplane at the end of the runway, and now suddenly it's here.' He searched their faces, and again went into Gaelic.

There followed an incomprehensible exchange. Then Dundas said, 'William here had the Land-Rover, and he didn't move the aircraft. Neither did any of the others.'

The information had a curious chilling effect on Claire. It all seemed so much in line, this mystery moving of an aircraft, with the shepherd's story and the ghostliness of this island.

But Lampeter didn't press the point as to how the aircraft had been moved. He had formed his own opinions. He began walking forward, shining his torch around the hangar. As he walked under the tail of Tango Foxtrot, Dundas caught up with him.

The cone of light reflected on the skin of the aircraft, flitted over the dirty concrete floor, sparkled for a split second on something lying under the wing.

'What was that, Captain?' Dundas pointed. 'I thought for a moment I saw something . . .'

Lampeter swung the torch round.

'Was that there before, Captain?'

'The soldering iron? No. It was on the wing.' Lampeter bent quickly and picked it up. 'Still warm. Feel.'

A relieved smile began to dawn on the laird's face. 'That means, surely, Captain, that your friend's been back . . .?'

But Lampeter had walked away from him again. He was under the wing, shining the torch along the leading edge. Over his shoulder, he called, 'And all this soldering wasn't done this morning either.'

Immediately everyone began to press forward.

'So he has been back.' Dundas spread his hands, the expression on his face a mixture of relief and exasperation.

'Apparently.' Lampeter narrowed his eyes. 'Only the port wing tank was repaired when we left. Now he's begun on the starboard.' He turned the soldering iron in his hand. 'This is warm and the solder still soft. Which means he's been back here and working in the last hour. But where in hell is he now?'

'Barrett. Bill Barrett.' On the wet tarmac just outside the open door they stood shouting out into the mist. Lampeter blew a succession of three short alarms on the flight deck whistle, pausing to listen after each. Eerily, mockingly from the direction of Begh, came a thin attenuated echo back. It mingled with the disturbed cry of guillemots in the cliffs, the turning of the sea and the threshing of the rain.

Silently, and grim-faced, Lampeter loaded the survival kit pistol in the light of the headlamps. Thoughtfully Claire watched him.

He fired the first cartridge towards the centre of the field. The explosion triggered off the same mocking echoes from the mountain, and made some heavy birds rise flapping and squawking from the grass between the runways. The star burst in a brilliant pink incandescence, showing up the billowing inside of a dense nimbus cloud, struck a quick glitter of fire from the granite of Begh, then, sinking in a dying arc, glowed on the iron roof of a hangar, and abruptly went out. It left behind a pungent smell of fireworks and the illusion that the night was darker than before.

Without saying a word, Lampeter fired again. This time,

westward. The red star spread itself on a whiter sea mist, expanded for a second, hung and slowly descended. A vicious rocky promontory rose in brief silhouette, and vanished with the light.

'That should bring t'lad running back if owt could.'

'Enough to wake the dead.' Dundas smiled ruefully. 'Of course, fog blankets sounds. And if he's searching around in a hangar he likely wouldn't notice . . .'

'One more,' Lampeter said as if speaking to himself, 'then we'll start looking.'

'You're still searching as planned, are you, Captain?' Their faces were all upturned to the blossoming chrysanthemum of light. In the faint sifted glow Lampeter's expression was unreadable. He said nothing till the light had vanished. Then simply, 'Yes.'

Dundas hesitated, then he said slowly, 'I think perhaps you're right, Captain.'

'Happen the lad has knocked off work and is on his way back home by now?' Mr Crowther wiped the rain off his face. Dundas looked sideways at Lampeter and when the Captain didn't reply, again said slowly, 'I think perhaps Captain Lampeter prefers to search while we're up here?'

'I do.' Lampeter stowed away the pistol in its case. 'See that's put back where it belongs, Claire.' He gave her a brief abstracted smile. 'And don't you take any risks either.'

'You'll take Jamie, won't you, Captain?' He nodded towards the chief ghillie, standing in the middle of the silent group. 'He's got more sense in his little finger than the rest put together.'

Over his shoulder, he spoke to the man slowly in Gaelic. 'And he's got the most English. I've told him where you're to search. Take his advice, mind. It's a tricky part, but he knows it well.'

Lampeter nodded. 'We'll be off, then.'

'Well, lass,' Crowther said to Claire, 'I must love you and leave you.'

'Mind how you go.' She included Lampeter in her glance.

He nodded, smiled faintly and walked out into the darkness beyond the headlights of the car. He stood for a moment with his hands in his pockets, staring about him, getting the feel of the night, and letting his eyes adjust their focus. The cloud ceiling was higher, and the wind had dropped. A light breeze fanning his cheek was wet, not so much with rain as with sea fog rolling in.

'Mr Crowther?'

'Here, Captain.'

'Keep close all the time!'

'You don't have to tell me, lad. I'll be hanging on to t'tails of yor shirt.'

'Jamie?'

'Aye.' The man had a high pitched sing-song voice.

'You lead the way, you understand? We need to search over there. The man we're looking for, did Mr Dundas tell you, is about your height, reddish hair. In this uniform.'

'Aye.' The man nodded as if he understood.

'Now we've each got a torch and a whistle. If by any chance we get separated, remember fog distorts sound, so flash your torch three times, and shout and whistle like hell. Understand?'

'Aye.'

Along the wide apron, the ghillie walked silently beside them. He had fastened the earpieces of his cap under his chin with tape. The collar of his jacket was turned up, so that all Lampeter could see of his face was the point of his nose and the shadows of his eye-sockets.

'How long have you worked for Mr Dundas?' Lampeter asked him pleasantly.

The ghillie seemed at first as if he wasn't going to understand. After several seconds he answered surlily, 'Long enough.' And making the apparent excuse that the perimeter track had narrowed, placed himself in front of the other two, presenting a stiff uncompromising back that inhibited conversation.

Somewhere to the right, the light sea wind rattled a loose piece of corrugated iron on an old concrete hut.

Lampeter shone his torch on the derelict building. 'We'll look in there.'

It lay about twenty yards off the tarmac. A pathway thick

with weeds led up to the door. One hinge had rusted away so that the door blocked the entrance. Impatiently Lampeter kicked it in.

Immediately faint sounds came from inside the hut. Bits of wood and old iron rattled on the walls. Something moved in the far corner.

'Bill?' Lampeter stepped over the threshold, kicked the rubble aside, sending the torch beam flickering into that corner. Beady eyes glittered frantically. A huge brown rat scuttled desperately across the floor.

'Lad would never have come here any road, else t'door wouldn't have bin stood up like that.' Mr Crowther shook his head reprovingly. 'An' he'd have shouted back to us an all.'

'You never know.' In Lampeter's mind were turning all sorts of possibilities. He might be hurt, stunned, unconscious –

He pulled himself up sharply, not allowing that train of thought to continue. They left the hut and walked up the perimeter track. Now it was pitted with potholes and scarred with cracks.

'Careful!' Lampeter said. 'You can break your ankle in some of these potholes.'

'Looks as if it's had a bit of wear round here.'

'Gets the prevailing wind.'

'Aye, an' a dose of salt.'

Somewhere beyond the now ill-defined rim of the perimeter track, water tinkled through marshy ground. From away over the headland the sea thudded dully, but there was no other sound. The wind had dropped. The fog now rolling in thick over the cliff blanketed their footsteps like a snowfall.

'We'll stop and shout. Ready? On the count of three. One . . . two . . . three . . . *Barrett!*' Lampeter's voice, Mr Crowther's a shade deeper, then the ghillie's in a high-pitched hallooing warble.

Nothing came back except the faint echo of their voices from the wall of sea fog.

'Sounds queer somehow,' Mr Crowther said, mopping his brow. 'Name like Barrett in a place like this.'

Far away, disturbed by their shouts, a sheep bleated. The

cry was taken up by others from the centre of the field and from up in the moors.

'There's another building over there,' Mr Crowther said as they resumed their walk. 'That be more workshops?'

But it was a lavatory block, with the roof still on but the doors all gone. The pans were broken off at their stained roots on the concrete floor. A dozen green eyes gave back the light of the torches. The whole place was full of sheltering sheep.

'By heck, it fair puts you off mutton,' Mr Crowther sighed.

'Bill . . . Bill Barrett!'

This time an owl hooted in answer.

'*Barrett!*'

The ghillie stepped forward and put his finger to his lips urgently. Lampeter waited and listened. The sea seemed to boom louder. But maybe it was only his own heart-beat in his ears. After a second the ghillie simply turned and walked on. Lampeter caught his arm. 'Did you think you heard something?'

'Nay, nay. But – ' the man hesitated for his words – 'it is ill luck to cry a living man's name while yon bird cries.'

Lampeter scowled. Mr Crowther raised his brows, but not with complete derision.

Out of the mist on the right-hand side a grey circular shape emerged.

'Air raid water-tank,' Lampeter said, walking round it slowly.

'Ground aye soft, sir.'

'You're right! Stay where you are, Mr Crowther.' He negotiated the wet ground carefully. The tank was standing on a thick concrete base. It was full to the brim of sour-smelling water. Lampeter shone his torch down on twigs and lumps of wood littering its oily surface.

'Was this where you were this morning? Where the old planes were?'

'No, that's the other side of the hangar. Dundas is looking there. Looks as though that was a dispersal hut, though.' He pointed ahead. 'And something beyond it.'

They moved on. Now the fog was lifting a little with the

onset of night. The indefinite shapes of twilight had disappeared, and the powerful torchbeams were illuminating sharper and further.

The ghillie had stopped. 'We will call again?'

Together and in unison, they shouted, 'Barrett.'

The mist smelled strongly of the sea and caught at their throats. The tarmac under their feet was crumbly and soft.

'No further,' the ghillie said firmly, as Lampeter began to move on.

'He'd never come round here, would he, lad?'

'We can't be sure. Anyway we've got to look everywhere.'

'Bet you he's back at t'pub now getting my missus to get him some nice hot grub.'

'If he is,' Lampeter said gently, 'I promise you I'll kill him.'

'Barrett!' Lampeter broke off his shout to say, 'That looked like a hangar over there. Blast! Can't see it now. The bloody mist swirls so damned much! No, there it is. It's a dispersal hut. And there's another hangar beyond. See it, Jamie?'

Even in the shadows Lampeter saw the man start.

For some reason that he couldn't explain to himself, Lampeter shone the torch on the ghillie's face. It looked deathly pale, and the thin lips were set and closed.

'There is marsh and cliffs,' he said at last. 'Not safe.'

'You show us the way.' Lampeter began walking to the hut. It had once been a row of offices, but the partitions had all fallen down, though even in the torchlight he could see where the corridor had been. There was still linoleum on the floor, but the rats or dry rot had been at the boards and it was full of great jagged holes.

'Stay outside,' Lampeter called to Mr Crowther. 'I'll have a look through. See you at the other end.'

He edged his way carefully, supporting himself on here an upright, there a pile of rubble, a broken chair. A tall green metal cupboard still stood in one corner of the middle office. 'Bill?' he called softly, making his way over, chiding himself for letting his imagination run away with him. He reached a firm piece of floor and pulled the cupboard door open. A mass of old chewed-up papers slid to the floor.

Outside he heard Crowther's voice shouting to him.

'OK, just coming,' he called back.

He flickered his torch over the walls. An old cork notice-board, bleached with the weather, still stuck to one inner wall. A red fire-bucket, half full of sand. There was a nasty hole just before the exit doorway. As he negotiated it, Crowther's figure appeared, his torchlight flickering.

'Sorry. Were you getting worried?'

'I am that, lad. Have ye got Jamie with you?'

'No. I left him with you.'

'Well, he walked on. Mist's come down again, thick as sauce. He said summat, but I couldna mek head na tail on it.'

'Which way did he go?'

'Towards the hangar.'

'Come on then, let's go. *Jamie!*' Lampeter yelled. Nothing. He yelled again. The hangar had disappeared from view in the mist. So had the huts. There was no landmark. They yelled again and whistled.

Then in the darkness came three bright flashes.

Suddenly, Mr Crowther yelled, 'There he is, lad!' He walked forward, calling, 'Good lad, Jamie, are you all right?'

The three flashes came again, and this time there was a strange sobbing shout that was abruptly broken off.

Crowther dashed forward, away from the direction they were walking in towards where the light had been.

'Stop!' Lampeter yelled urgently. 'Wait!'

Again the three lights flicked on and off. Mr Crowther ignored Lampeter's shout. His thick-set figure lurched forward, began to merge with the mist, and then suddenly, too suddenly, disappeared.

This time the shout was unmistakably Crowther's.

'Lad! Lad! Watch it, lad!'

'Where are you?'

Shining his torch, moving forward with as much speed as he could, Lampeter picked his way forward. The ground here was stony. The bushes stunted and salt-bitten. There was no sign of bogs. But the mist tasted of salt and the sea sounded near. Then abruptly his torch picked out something white. Lampeter froze in his tracks.

A hand. A hand clenched round a whippy shrub bending

perilously towards what Lampeter saw was the lip of a crevasse. Lampeter bounded forward, throwing himself on the ground, and clutched Mr Crowther's wrist. Mr Crowther's head was visible a foot or so below the rim of the fissure. A shower of pebbles screed and bounced down as Crowther kicked to try to find a foothold. Lampeter listened to their long fall.

'Hang on.' Inwardly he cursed that he hadn't kept a more watchful eye on their direction. The whole of this westerly coastline was indented with these narrow granite faults.

'Can't for much longer, lad. Me feet aren't on anything.'

Lampeter felt himself break out in a sweat. 'Try and dig your toes in. Or brace your knees.' He leaned right over and grasped Crowther by the elbow, taking as much of his weight as he could. He screwed up his eyes but he couldn't see the bottom of the crevasse. He could just glimpse the other side, masked like this with small bushes.

'Steady on, lad. I'm heavier than you. I'll go an' pull pair on us over. An' it's a helluva way down.'

Then Lampeter remembered Jamie. He shone his torch desperately three times and yelled.

But no light answered him. Only the sound of the sea funnelling and moaning below.

The fifth time Lampeter yelled for Jamie, the echo was less pronounced. The thick wall of mist was breaking up. But the temperature was dropping too. Crowther's hand felt as cold as a lump of lead.

'Listen, lad, give over trying to get me up! You need a rope or happen a winch.' He gave a snort of attempted laughter. 'Go on back an' get t'others to help. I'll hang on. I'll be all reet.'

God, Lampeter thought desperately, the old boy's going to do a Captain Oates on me. Get me safely away, and when his hand gets too numb, just disappear.

'Quiet,' he said, 'save your breath. You're going to need it. I'll sort something out.' And raising his voice again, 'Jamie!'

He shouted more to quench the eerie, sea-filled silence and give himself time to form some rescue plan than with hope now of a reply. Lying flat on his stomach, his eyes and mind were frantically busy. Though the terrain and circumstances were alien, all his old habit and training asserted themselves. He observed, he assessed, he deducted. He weighed risk against risk.

'Jamie!'

'Hope *he* hasn't gone and took a tumble. How far's t'bottom?'

'Can't see.'

Still gripping Crowther's wrist, Lampeter went on shining his torch down the side and along the lip of the fissure. The bottom disappeared behind misty darkness. The depth limit of the torch's focus was the skeleton of a salt-burned shrub silhouetted against the dark grey of the foam of the incoming sea. Lampeter gritted his teeth.

Crowther had chosen a singularly bare and precipitous part to drop over. The lip of the crevasse had a shaley top soil. Ferns and stunted shrubs grew intermittently all along. Here and there were a few precarious handholds, unable to support weight, but possible to permit of a moment's purchase.

Lampeter leaned further forward. Trails of mist no longer smoked across the beam of his torch. Black pebbles glistened out of the scree. Some of the paler rocks sparked with crystal. He tilted the beam further. Four feet or so below Crowther's dangling feet, he spotted what looked like a narrow ledge. He lay on his side, and twisted the beam. The ledge, if ledge it was, could only be about eight or nine inches deep, but it ran for a yard or more. Lampeter thought for a moment, then he asked suddenly, 'Can you hang on a while, without me holding you?'

'Aye, lad. 'Course I can. Are you going for help, then?'

'No.' Lampeter stood up. 'Just you hang on. *I'm* coming down.'

Three and a half miles away in the darkness, Peter Spence looked at his watch. For nearly two hours now he and his party had been meticulously searching the south-westerly side of the short cut to the airfield, flashing their torches, whistling and calling.

There had been no answer. No sound except the movement

of the wind through the whin bushes, the tinkle of marshy water, and the flap and squawk of a frightened bird. Apart from Menzies's dire prophecies, sometimes in English, mostly in Gaelic, they had hardly spoken.

'He shouldnae have gone to the airfield, yon wee red man,' he kept saying, 'all alone and at night. It is . . . *sgteat aidh*.'

'Forbidden, he means,' Herr Hagedorn said.

'*Cunnartach*.'

'Dangerous.'

But unlike Dundas, he was not talking about physical dangers, windswept cliffs, bogs, treacherous inlets. He was obviously talking about the peril of flouting the taboo on the airfield ground itself. As the shepherd had done, he muttered about the earth shaking, strange lights and figures, not of this world, but '*Sith*'.

'Fiery or ghostly. I think that would be a fair translation,' Hagedorn said, dashing a waterfall of rain from the brim of his Homburg hat.

'Folk have been lost, that iss so, spirited away when the ground shook and the thunder came.'

'Thor-rr.' Herr Hagedorn nodded to Spence as together they shone their torches down a dark cave in a shallow hillside. 'Interesting . . . yes?'

'I wish he'd shut up,' Spence said heatedly. The cave smelled musty and sour but it was empty even of sheep.

'I postulate,' Hagedorn said, looking as if at any moment he might bring out his notebook, 'that mine host believes that Thor-rr, thunder, brought Bill Barrett here, and now has taken him away again. The Lord giveth and the Lord taketh away.'

'Different Lord.' Spence dusted the wet bracken off his knees.

'The old gods remain with all of us. Very much more so here. Remember the inn is called the Oak. There was mistletoe hanging.'

Droplets of rain winked in the light. Mist hung between the gorse-bushes like wet cloths.

'Barrett! Bill Barrett!'

Peter Spence kicked a lump of peat off the path. 'You get pubs called the Oak all over.'

'Precisely.'

'And mistletoe at Christmas, at least you do in England.'

'Precisely. And we in our masonic craft venerate the acacia. Little golden suns, like the mistletoe. You see our gods do not really change.'

'Well, if you ask me,' Spence said, shining his torch in an arc from side to side, 'Menzies is round the twist, as Mr Todd said.'

'Twist? What twist?'

Hagedorn's English did not run to the colloquial, and Spence thrashing along through the rain-soaked heather was in no mood to translate, only to add under his breath, 'And you too if it comes to that.'

A few yards ahead, Menzies was still muttering away to himself. Once he broke into a strange nasal incantation. Far away beyond the mist they heard another search-party call, 'Barrett! Bill Barrett!' After another half-hour, they looped back to the path of the short cut itself.

'I want to look at this carefully,' Spence called to Menzies. 'See if there's any sign of tyre tracks.'

'Aye.' Menzies paused, shook his head and didn't bother to look. He stood very still, with his face lifted to the rain, his head cocked on one side, listening.

'Not a sign,' Spence said to Hagedorn. 'Look, there's some of our prints from last night. And nothing overlaying them.'

'Not there, perhaps,' Hagedorn said. 'But here, surely, feet have come?'

'Could be.' And to Menzies, 'Isn't that a track to the left?'

' 'Tis only a sheep track, you understand.'

'Still he might have mistaken it for the proper path. Anything's worth trying.'

'If you say so.' Menzies led them, shoulders hunched, mumbling to himself.

The path was narrow and thick with sheep droppings. It was strewn on either side with boulders. 'Going seawards,' Peter said, feeling the salt mist on his face, wishing to hell he'd got a compass.

Suddenly Menzies stopped. Ahead in the mist someone or something stirred. There was a sound like a cough, and a long-drawn-in sigh. Spence pushed forward and shone his torch. A man sat in the shelter of some overhanging rock. He was crouched over, head resting on folded arms. The posture was one of utter exhaustion.

'Bill . . . thank God . . . we've all been looking . . .'

The head raised itself. Spence's torch shone on a nimbus of grey hair, and a flowing beard. The shepherd raised one arm slowly, shaded his eyes against the light and then imperiously waved Spence to lower the beam. He didn't rise as they came hurrying up, but shuffled over in his shelter so that they could stand beside him in the dry.

A great spiel of Gaelic broke from the innkeeper. The shepherd listened to him courteously, from time to time inclining his hand, inserting a word here and there, not watching any of them, his strange light eyes fixed on the rain slanting down beyond the overhang of the rock.

Suddenly the shepherd turned to Menzies. Though the voice remained quiet, the tone was caustic and accusative. Menzies heard him out. Then he seemed to try an indignant bluster. Gradually his voice faded to a whine. The shepherd flung him a contemptuous glance, turned to Spence and speaking slowly he said, 'No. There hass been no one passing here.'

'Have you been here long?' Spence asked, the beam of his torch sparkling on the recent puddle of water dripping from the old man's boots. There were bracken fronds clinging to his trousers, and a jagged tear in the sleeve of his jacket.

'Aye. It seems so.'

'Where are your sheep?'

'I have driven them tae the ither side. The wind will change, the night. They will get more shelter there.'

'Didn't you hear us call?'

'Perhaps. Perhaps not. Then, too –' the old man seemed to be making his excuses as he went along – 'I would not be after confusing you by calling back tae ye.'

'Did you know that one of our crew is missing?'

'I know that now.'

'Have you been up at the airfield today?'

'Aye. And last night.'

'Did you see anyone?'

'Aye.'

'The man we're looking for is short with reddish . . .'

'I mind fine what he looks like.'

'You saw him then?'

'Nae. Not yon wee fellow. He wasnae there.'

'Who did you see then?'

The shepherd closed his eyes in a gesture of great resignation and despair. Then, moistening his lips, he said sorrowfully, 'I saw *them*.' He paused, 'I felt the ground shaking, I heard strange noises. I saw many lights. I saw *them*.'

Menzies held up his crossed fingers and muttered to himself.

'Oh lord,' Spence said, 'can't we get any sense out of anyone?'

Far away, the other search-party was still calling, 'Barrett. Bill Barrett.' Behind them a night-jar answered. The wind was rising, driving the rain in front of it. It moaned round the piles of rocks, and the shallow hillocks. It stirred the gorse-bushes, rasping their harsh branches.

'So he is gone,' the shepherd said, shaking his head, 'your wee red man.' He sighed. 'Likely he saw *them* too.'

'Likely,' Menzies said heavily in English.

'Ye will nae find him now,' the shepherd said. 'Ye best go home.'

There came a few more words in Gaelic from the shepherd. Menzies listened attentively and nodded. Then he said to Spence. 'There iss nae more paths round here to follow. Duncan McDermott will be here. He will listen for your friend.'

Spence looked at his watch. Nearly ten to nine. 'I suppose we ought to be getting back,' he said to Hagedorn. He forced a smile. 'Maybe Bill's back at the inn by now. I don't like giving up, though. Maybe leaving him stuck somewhere on his own . . .'

'He will not be on his own.' The shepherd shook his head. 'He has gone. He has been changed. There will be others.'

'Come.' Menzies began to move along the path towards the way they had come. He lifted his hand to the shepherd, '*Moch-eirioh 'luain a ni'n t-suain 'mhairt.*'

'Amen,' said the shepherd.

'What does that mean?' Spence asked.

The shepherd and Menzies exchanged glances. 'It means,' the shepherd began, and then paused for several seconds, 'early rising in Monday gives a sound sleep on Tuesday.'

'Interesting, yes?' Hagedorn said, as they were once more thrashing their way through the sodden heather. 'In one northern dialect the meanings of the word for sound sleep and death are interchangeable.'

In the centre of the island, struggling against dripping bracken and thick mud, Todd was leading Ainsworth and Borghese slowly forward, searching sheep tracks and calling out, 'Barrett.'

Here the land was higher, and low cloud alternated with driving rain. At times the range of their torch was only a few yards before the light hit a wall of mist.

For the past half-hour they had hardly spoken. Borghese had given up his hopeful allusions to Todd as the good shepherd and was now conserving his strength. He was gasping as he scrambled, pausing every hundred or so yards to catch his breath and mop the wet off his face, seeming utterly disorientated by this sodden, alien landscape. Ahead of him, inadequately dressed and shod and soaked to the skin, Ainsworth was muttering repeatedly, 'Hell to this.'

Rough drystone walls, fragments of rusty barbed wire fuzzy with sheep's wool, formidable rocks carved into weird shapes by the weather, loomed out of the rain. Birds flapped up from under their feet, squawking. There was a distant high-pitched clamour which Todd said was from roosting gulls.

'Hell to this.'

Now they were going down a steep incline, skidding along the wet wiry turf till suddenly Ainsworth sank to his knees in ice-cold water.

'Careful,' Todd's voice floated through the mist, 'hill loch ahead.'

'Now he tells us,' Ainsworth muttered, and, raising his voice, 'Bit late in the day!'

The distillery manager materialized from just behind him. 'I'm up to me . . . in icicles. Hell to this.'

'Don't press on so fast. We've got to go left here.'

'Soaked to the bloody skin.' Ainsworth took out a packet of cigarettes, put one in his mouth, struck a match and then dropped it.

'Let me.' Todd flicked a flare out of a silver lighter and lit the cigarette.

Ainsworth inhaled gratefully. In a more reasonable tone he said, 'We're not doing a damn of good here.'

'No.'

'The chances of finding friend Barrett like this are just about bloody zero.'

Todd shrugged. 'You can see for yourself how dangerous it is.'

'Hell, I didn't need this tour to realize that.'

'People often just disappear.'

'You don't surprise me, mate.' Ainsworth puffed quickly at his cigarette.

'*Local* people.'

'Not much hope for a stranger, then, on a night like this.'

'Frankly, no. Still, we must try, mustn't we?' He began to move forward, 'We'd best get on.'

Ainsworth finished his cigarette and stamped it out on the wet ground. 'Where's that Eye-tie?'

'Wasn't he on your side?'

'No. He was way behind. No stamina, these chaps.'

'But he was just beside you a moment ago. I saw him.'

'Wasn't.'

Todd hissed something under his breath and went splashing through the marshy ground, shining his torch from side to side.

'Borghese,' Ainsworth yelled, 'Borghese, where in hell are you?' And then, 'Hell to this. Oh, Christ Almighty.'

'When did you last see him?' Todd came up, shining his torch on Ainsworth's face.

'I didn't. Least not actually see him. Not for the last twenty minutes. I heard him though, moaning and groaning. Heh, put that thing down. It's not my fault. I'm not his wet-nurse. Though wet is the bloody word.'

'Borghese!'

'We'll call again,' Todd said irritably.

Over the loch, the mist hung in a continuous shroud,

muffling their voices.

'Hell to this, don't say the little sod's gone and drowned himself.'

They began retracing their steps up the turfy slope. 'Climb one foot, fall back two,' Ainsworth groaned, his thin shoes sliding on the grass. 'Come out and look for one. Lose another. Borghese! Barrett! Anyone, answer! Hell to this. Talk about the ten little nigger boys.'

Over the top of the slope a shadowy head and shoulders appeared, and then, materializing out of the rain, a wet mackintoshed figure sliding down to join them. Todd shone his torch on the anxious features of Signor Borghese, the brim of his battered sodden hat pulled down for protection over his ears. Borghese mopped his streaming face, struggled for breath, 'I thought someone called me.'

'Wonder you heard anything with your ears full of wet hat. It was us calling you, nit.'

'No, no. This was close at hand.'

'Trick of the fog,' Ainsworth felt for another cigarette, at the same time moving forward. He stepped once more in the marshy margin of the hill loch.

'Hell to this,' he said, hurling the unlit cigarette into the mud. 'For Chrissake, before we all drown let's go home.'

Left alone in the inn, the three older women sat by the fire, making a determined effort to keep up their spirits. Frau Hagedorn had her knitting, and every now and again nodded her head and said '*Ja*,' though it was unlikely she was following what they were talking about.

'Pour a nice brown gravy over the chitterlings, and then if you offer a bit of sweet cake and make a pot of tea to follow, you've got a meal the Queen herself . . .'

It was doubtful if Mrs Ewart and Mrs Crowther were listening to each other. Every few sentences, their eyes would turn away towards the window. They had left the shutters open. Grey fog pressed against the panes, reflecting themselves and the lamplight, turning them into figures on a stage set in ectoplasm. Figures back in time, long dead, mistily remembered.

Then their eyes would go back to the clock.

They had been told it was important they should stay at the inn lest the engineer turned up, or one of the search-parties came back with a clue to his whereabouts. They had, however, not been deceived into believing that it was for any other reason than that they would be liabilities rather than assets, searching rugged and unknown territory in this sort of weather.

For two hours they had sat in the bar while Mrs Crowther handed out tricks for making Yorkshire pudding rise, for baking bread and creaming tripe. Mrs Ewart capped her dishes with Graham cracker pie, maple flapjacks and sea-food stews, until Mrs Crowther suddenly observed that it was opening time, and yet no one had come in for a drink.

'Funny sort o' pub, if you ask me.'

'Mind, there's not many folk on the island,' Mrs Ewart said.

'All the more reason to come to t'pub of an evening. Be sociable, like.'

'Do you figure what men there are could be helping our boys?'

Mrs Crowther grunted doubtfully and got to her feet. 'An' where's our Maiyrat gone off to?'

They had from time to time heard the girl's heavy foot-steps round the place, the rattle of pans, the sound of water running, but Maiyrat herself had not put in an appearance.

'Eeh, but she's a rum lass, that. Just like her dad.'

Mrs Crowther walked over to the bar counter, stood on tiptoe, and peered over as though to see if the girl were crouched down with the barrels and the empties.

'Would you like a drink of something, honey?' Mrs Ewart asked.

'A drop o' whisky would warm us up.' Mrs Crowther spoke very loudly and slowly as if hoping thereby that the German woman would understand. On the other side of the fireplace Frau Hagedorn's face remained set in its perennial sweet smile. She nodded several times and said, '*Ja.*'

'I figure it'd do us all good.'

Mrs Crowther nodded and smacked the little push-button bell on the counter several times. The noise pinged round the room. But no one answered. She gave up the bell and knocked vigorously and for several seconds on the bar counter, calling sharply, 'Anyone at home?'

Nobody answered.

Mrs Crowther rapped again. 'Eeeh, but that lass is a right wilk. If she was mine I'd warm her jacket.'

'Maybe she's out.'

'Where, pray?'

'Out for a walk?'

'Not in this!'

'Then where d'you figure she is?'

'That, love, I intend to find out.' Mrs Crowther marched out. 'I'll get her off her backside . . .' She stepped into the corridor, with Mrs Ewart close behind, shouting, 'Service. Service, please.'

With only a perfunctory knock, she pushed open the kitchen door. There was a smell of onions and fat, kerosene and washing. In the far corner by the stove, her elbows on the table, sat Maiyrat in a battered wicker armchair. She was facing them. But she didn't look up as they burst in. A magazine was spread out on the table in front of her. She was apparently lost in rapt concentration, her heavily painted lips moving as she read.

Mrs Crowther threw a triumphant glance over her shoulder at Mrs Ewart, as if to say, 'I told you so,' and, advancing into the kitchen, stood over the girl with her hands on her hips. 'Are you deaf, then?' she asked crushingly. 'Or have you got cloth ears, then?'

She looked scornfully down at the magazine which the girl was hastily closing, the glossy cover showing a slip of a girl in the clutch of a Mr Universe-type bronzed man, under the title, *Real Life Romances*.

'American trash.'

Maiyrat stared back at her impudently.

'I was never let read trash like that when I was a lass.'

'That was a long time ago, that iss so,' Maiyrat said saucily, and then getting up, towering above Mrs Crowther, 'Was it something you were wanting, then?'

'It is that.'

'Will ye be after ringing, then, instead of walking right into my kitchen?'

'We've had us fingers on the button for the last ten minutes. Now, three double whiskies, you cheeky lass, and look sharp about it.'

Maiyrat stared down at Mrs Crowther's puggy little face for a second, her lower lip thrust out pugnaciously. Then suddenly she slipped the magazine into the table drawer, and flounced through into the bar. Taking her time about it, she produced three glasses, set them on the counter and unscrewed a bottle of whisky.

Standing a little away from the other side of the counter, Mrs Ewart whispered, 'Did you get a good look at that magazine she was reading?'

'That I did. If she was my lass I'd give her Real Life Romances.'

'But the date, didn't you see the date?'

'Nay, I saw t'price. One dollar!' She clicked her teeth. 'But not the date, no.'

'It was Saturday, 26th October. Two days ago.'

'Couldn't 've bin.'

'It was.'

'Nay, lass, you've bin seeing things. Us eyes isn't getting any younger.'

'It was, I promise.'

'Then how the heck did *she* get it?' Mrs Crowther reached over and took two glasses from Maiyrat. Then she walked over and presented one to Frau Hagedorn, miming that she should knock it back at a gulp. The other she handed to Mrs Ewart. 'Mebbe it was on board *us* aeroplane. They do have papers, magazines, suchlike,' she whispered at the same time.

'But who gave it to Maiyrat?'

'I'll bet her bad old dad's bin up there!' Mrs Crowther lifted the glass to her lips. 'Whatever it is, I don't like it.' She drained her drink and shuddered. 'An' I wish them daft lads'd come back. I got a nasty feeling in me bones that summat's up.'

He took one last look by the light of his torch, printing the footholds on his mind like a map. Grasping handfuls of fern, he slithered over the lip of the crevasse. Gravel and pebbles and sand screed down. He lowered himself carefully, face to the rock, till his left foot found the first hold, a jutting lump of shaley rock. It held just long enough for him to thrust his right foot into a shallow hole, before it went crashing down. He heard it bounce twice, then splinter into a hail of little pieces.

'Hey, lad! Careful!'

'I'm OK.' He steadied himself with his chest and hand pressed against the cliff, one foot resting on another shaley niche. That too crumbled. He grabbed wildly for a clump of woody fern.

It held. Now he swung by one hand for a perilous moment like a monkey. He dug his fingers into the shalcy surfaces, then grabbed at something growing out of a narrow vertical niche and winced as the gorse spines dug into his skin. But the fissure itself gave him a grasp. He reached down with the toe of his right shoe, and found the ledge he was aiming for.

He paused for an agonizing moment, disciplining his muscles lest he drop too quickly and bounce backwards. Then slowly he put more pressure on his foot and let himself painfully down, using his body as a brake pressing against the cliff face, till his feet reached the ledge. It felt smooth like granite, slippery and perilously narrow.

'Not long now.' His voice echoed weirdly against the funnel of the crevasse.

He could just make out Crowther's shape, dangling like a hanged man a few yards to his right. Lampeter glanced down below. Something blacker and shinier than the darkness with a white toss-back of curdling foam raced in below. The incoming tide rushing up the vortex fifty feet or so beneath.

He inched along the ledge, right foot first, with weight on his left foot, and his hands grasping tufts of fern or pressed against the rock face. Ten sideways paces on, the rock was smoother. His fingers encountered only soft pads of the kind of moss that grows on granite. Crowther's feet became clearly distinguishable within a couple of arm's lengths. But his right foot found nothing.

Cursing softly to himself, he brought his foot back, and

felt in his pocket for his torch. He snapped it on. The ledge began again, about half a yard this side of Mr Crowther's feet. There was a long circular fault in the rock like a chimney about four feet across. He felt the hairs on the nape of his neck prickle. His leg muscles ached. He shuffled to the extremity of the ledge. The chimney effect meant there was no support above. He took a long sideways stride. His toe waved wildly at nothing. He brought his foot back and waited till his heart-beat slowed a little. Tried again. Nothing. The sickening knowledge came to him that there was no way across except to pass his point of no return. To leap sideways, and hope to land.

He gritted his teeth and leapt sideways. He landed on the ledge, wobbled, pushed himself forward, pressing his face to the cold rock. Mr Crowther's limp foot dangled against his shoulder.

'Lad, are you there, then? By heck, that's a marvel!'

'Don't let go yet, for Chrissake!' He drew a deep slow breath. 'Let me get it exactly right. We can't afford to make a mistake.'

The urge to hurry, before Mr Crowther's arm went numb or his hand relaxed its hold, was overpoweringly strong. Not unlike, he told himself in grim warning, the urge to get under the cloud, or hurry down to the runway on a blind dark night. And just as dangerous.

Slowly, as his breathing steadied, he began to move sideways again, keeping his chest flat against the side of the rock. Very clearly beneath him he could feel the boom and break of the tide. Every few seconds a large wave broke, sending reverberations up the side of the crevasse. Sea mist breathed coldly on his cheeks. As he shuffled sideways, his fingers scrabbled for every hold, digging with his nails into the scree, fastening on anything that grew, but not giving it enough weight to unbalance him if it broke away. He held for a moment some tough-stemmed plant, its feathery leaves scraped his face. He gripped them between his teeth, moving them aside. He carefully edged his head under Mr Crowther's left foot. 'I'll take your weight in a moment, sir.'

'Me foot's going to sleep. Don't know if I can feel it, lad.'

'Oh, Christ,' Lampeter said to himself. 'If he can't brace

himself enough to leap, that's it!'

Two more sideways shuffles, and he was between Mr Crowther's dangling feet.

'Got pins and needles in me arm, lad.'

Lampeter's fingers encountered a hard smooth ledge, further to the right than he'd have liked, but at a good height.

'OK, sir. Ready for you now. Listen, carefully! And do exactly what I say.'

'Heck, Captain, you've got no mutiny on the *Bounty* here . . .' A laugh that turned into a sob.

'Ssh! Now keep hold of that bush. I'm going to guide your feet on to my shoulders.' He grasped Mr Crowther's left ankle and eased the left shoe on to his shoulder. 'Feel it?'

'Aye, lad. It feels grand.'

'Still a bit numb?'

'Aye.'

'Wriggle your toes. Now I'm putting the other on. How's that?'

'A treat.'

'Not numb at all?'

'No, lad.'

'So when it comes to it, put your weight on your right foot. Don't let go of that bush,' Lampeter said sharply, as it seemed as if his shoulders were bearing a heavier weight than he'd bargained for. Gently he flexed his feet on the shelf of rock, feeling cautiously for any sign of giving, gripping the handholds, *just in case . . .*

'I don't want your full weight yet. But relax your hand a bit at a time. Let the blood get back in it. How much d'you weigh, Mr Crowther?'

'Fourteen and a half stone, lad.'

Lampeter groaned inwardly. Aloud he said, 'Feel along the rock, with your left hand. Is there any handhold above shoulder level?'

Little fragments of shaley rock spattered down as Mr Crowther did as Lampeter told him. 'Nay, lad, nowt.'

'Brace the palm of your hand against the rock if there isn't.'

The little shower of pebbles and grit went on cascading. 'Hey! Just a minute! Got something, lad. Bit of rock jutting out.'

'Firm?'

'Far as I can tell. Bit high, though.'

'Better still. Right. Get ready to grab it! Now when I say *Go*, I'll give you a shove. Lever up at exactly the same time. Pull with your left hand, grab that ledge. Try to lever your chest over the top. If you can't make it, try to get your left foot on that ledge.'

'An' if I can't?'

'I'll take your weight.'

'Happen –' There was a second's pause. 'Happen I got ter make it,' Mr Crowther said quietly.

'Now remember, kick off with your *left* foot!'

'Sounds like Come Dancing.' And when Lampeter didn't say anything, 'Well, lad, might as well die laughing.'

'Start getting ready. Now give me more weight while you tense yourself.' Lampeter held on to the handholds at either side of him.

'Ready. Take a deep breath.' He transferred his hands quickly to the calves of Mr Crowther's legs. '*Go!*'

With all his strength he shoved Mr Crowther's fourteen and a half stone up the side of the crevasse. Bits of rock and pebbles and sand and dirt rained on to his upturned face. He kept his own feet straddled wide on the ledge, his body leaning against the face, his arms ready to bear Mr Crowther's weight, though God knew, if he did fall back, that would be it!

About eight feet above his head, the older man's feet kicked wildly. Hopelessly. There was a heavy grunting sound.

More scree rained down.

It looked as if Mr Crowther was going to follow it.

Then the left foot made a hold. The right disappeared. Then the left. Finally, grunting and shouting and panting, Mr Crowther disappeared. Two seconds later his head and shoulders reappeared at the lip of the crevasse, dark and solid against the paler darkness of the overcast sky.

'Made it, lad! Eeh, I never thought.' He wiped his face with the torn sleeve of his jacket. 'Now *you*, lad. How're we gonna do you?'

'That's easier. There's a firm footing here, and some holds further along. I'm not bad at climbing, and you'll be a damned good anchor man.'

Five minutes later, Mr Crowther lying flat on his stomach, had succeeding in pulling Lampeter over the lip of the crevasse about twenty yards to the right of where he had fallen down.

They sat for a moment on the mossy grass, panting. The mist was clearing a little. Like a man slightly drunk, Mr Crowther walked unsteadily to the lip of the crevasse. He shuddered. 'Nasty old place, that . . . You don't reckon, lad, that Jamie . . .?'

'Fell over? No. We'd have heard him. Besides he knows the area. Besides, the hangar's away behind me.' He stretched his legs luxuriously on the wet grass. Mr Crowther had turned his back now on the crevasse and was just about to walk back to where Lampeter was sitting when suddenly he stopped. He opened his mouth wide, swallowed, then whispered to Lampeter 'By hummer, lad . . . Look behind you.'

About thirty yards behind, moving quickly along the perimeter, was a white cone of torchlight. Behind it, just distinguishable in the trailing mist, a dark shape ran forward.

Lampeter jumped to his feet.

'Jamie!'

The figure froze in its tracks. The torchlight turned, hesitated, came bobbing towards them.

'Sir . . .' a spiel of Gaelic . . . 'sir . . .' the torchlight travelled over first Mr Crowther, then Lampeter. Behind it they could see only the pale shadowed moon of Jamie's face. More Gaelic.

Lampeter leaned forward, and caught the ghillie's wrist, gently taking the torch from him, and lowered the beam. In the muffled light the man's face loomed clearly, blanched and set in an expression of terror.

'Where did you go to?' Lampeter asked.

'Over there . . . where you wished it . . . the . . . the big . . .'

'Hangar?'

'Aye.' His hands clenched.

'Why didn't you wait?'

'Someone, something was following. I saw the light. Heard steps. Your own, that iss so, I thought, coming wi' me. I went to the hangar. There was not a soul there . . . no red-faced wee fellow. Nothing at all.'

'Nor us.'

'That iss so. Then – ' the man looked wildly behind him – 'something shut the door. I couldnae git oot.'

'And there was no sign of Mr Barrett?'

'None, sir.'

'You weren't over there at all?' Lampeter shone the torch in the direction of the crevasse.

The man shook his head violently. 'No, that is away off the field.' Urgently he thrust his face towards them, ' 'Tis an evil place, this! Evil things happen here.'

Lampeter glanced from the ghillie's face to Crowther's. The last half-hour had been too much for the older man. He was swaying on his feet.

'You're sure no one was in that hangar?' he asked the ghillie sharply.

'Aye, sir. I had plenty of time to look around.'

'Come on, then. Let's get to hell out of here.'

He led the way back to the tarmac. The mist was rolling away. He could see almost as far as the beginning of the coast road. A sheep bleated. And not very far away, he heard a sound like that of the shepherd whistling to his dog.

At approximately the same time, Claire got out of Mr Dundas's car at the hangar and called hopefully, 'Bill!'

The slow drive, punctuated by frequent lengthy stops down the south-easterly sector of the field, had revealed nothing but the green eyes of sheep bobbing in the full cones of the headlamps, dripping derelict buildings, and deserted overgrown tarmac. Twice an apparent answering flicker of light had raised their hopes. But both times it had turned out to be only their own reflection sparked from an old unbroken window-pane.

'You won't find him here now.' Dundas came up and stood between Dawn and her. 'He'll have knocked off and gone back to the inn. And who's to blame him?' Dundas smiled. 'Only wish I could find workmen like him.'

'Bill! Are you there?'

Something, a rat or a mouse, scraped in the far corner of the hangar. But no one answered.

'Well, he's not in our sector.' The laird brought out his map. 'That's for sure. We couldn't have searched more thoroughly. I suggest I bring the car forward with the headlights on, and we collect the stuff your skipper wanted.'

'*And* have a good look round the aircraft.'

In the full light of the lamps, the hangar remained exactly as they had left it. There were still the wet footprints just inside the door where they had all stood before setting out. There was even a faint smell of cordite from the pistol cartridges, and the whole hangar was cupped in a curious unscratched quietness that convinced Claire no one had returned.

The silence echoed their feet as they walked over the concrete. The old metal doors rattled. She paused beside the aircraft at the crew entrance.

'Mind if I come up as well?' Dundas asked. 'I don't think I've ever been inside a jet.'

'No, of course not.' She shivered. 'I'd like you to.' She began to climb the ladder, and edged herself up on to the flight deck. Dawn, after a moment's indecision as to whether she would wait for them both down below in the hangar, decided to follow.

'Didn't want to be on my own,' she whispered. 'The hangar gives me the creeps.'

'My goodness – ' Mr Dundas swung himself up – 'it's all very plushy.'

'Nice, isn't it? More roomy than they used to be. That's the captain's seat on the left, first officer's on the right. Behind here is the engineer's console and panel.'

'Mr Barrett's?'

'Yes.'

'Well, he's certainly not sitting in it.' Dundas gave a relaxed smile.

'He always used to keep the chair screwed down because his legs were so short.' Claire felt a sudden sick feeling. Why am I talking about Bill in the past tense? We're all fairly sure he's all right. The search is just Lampeter being extra conscientious.

'What's this little place through here?' Dundas called.

'Rest compartment and mail locker. Beyond is the passenger cabin.'

'Very comfortable indeed. One of these days I shall tear myself away from Ardnabegh and jet off to the sun.' The smile faded from his face, as Claire came and stood beside him, her eyes slowly travelling over the cabin. 'You're still worried about your friend?'

'A little.'

The twin cones of light came in through the portholes making a geometric pattern of light and shade. Momentarily it seemed a dark figure might be huddling in the corner, or the shadow of a seat looked like the shape of a small man.

'Did you think he might have had a nap?'

'Yes. I rather hoped to find him asleep somewhere.'

'Goldilocks –' Dawn smiled – 'with red face and ginger hair . . .'

'He will have a red face after all this.' Mr Dundas surreptitiously looked at his wrist-watch.

'Is it time we should be getting back? I don't think you've eaten all day.'

'We're all right. Take your time. It's just after eight. I'm in no hurry.'

He sat down in one of the rear seats, while the girls walked up and down the aisle. 'No clues?'

'Not a thing.'

'I tell you, the bird's flown.'

'You're not worried, then, Mr Dundas?'

'I was at first. But now I know he's been back, no.' He got up and stretched. 'Are these the blankets Captain Lampeter wanted?'

'Yes.'

'Shall I start loading them up?'

'If you would.'

Claire walked to the end of the cabin and opened the doors of the gentlemen's lavatory and the ladies' powder room. No light leaked in here from the headlights. She switched on her torch. They still smelled of Imperial Leather shaving cream and Arden talc and soap. There was some powder spilled on the floor of the ladies' room, and a crumpled tissue with the imprint of Dawn's luminous pink lipstick. She shone her torch round. Nothing was changed. Not a footprint in the powder, the bowl dry. In the gentlemen's, it was the same. She touched the cake of soap. It was dry and hard. So Bill hadn't washed his hands all day. But then he had been too busy, surely.

She walked back into the cabin. It still held that same rather sweet, stuffy smell of mingled aerosol freshener, upholstery and burned kerosene. Dundas was waiting.

'Everything all right, my dear?'

'Exactly the same.'

'Well then . . .?'

'I'll just collect the bits of food from the galley. Dawn, could you give Mr Dundas a hand with the blankets?'

Claire walked into the galley. There was still the stack of empty glasses from the drinks she had served after landing. They, like some faulty drain, gave the galley a stale, mouldy smell. She opened a drawer and took out some plastic bags and set about filling them with coffee, tea, wrapped cheeses, crispbread and biscuits. She began picking out the fruit that was still sound. Suddenly she paused with an orange in her hand.

Everything was exactly the same. She had been looking for something different. But surely everything was too much the same. Bill working all day in this cold would get terribly hungry. No one knew better than he that the galley was full of quick snacks. Yet not a biscuit packet was opened, not a piece of cheese cut. Even the remains of the apple pie were untouched.

Dawn put her head round the galley stanchion. 'Are you ready? His lairdship is making noises as if he'd like to be awa'.'

'Yes. Quite ready.'

'Mind if I bring my make-up box? I'm low on eye-liner.'

'No. Of course not.' She walked down the cabin behind Dawn. 'If I'd thought, we could have asked the others if they wanted anything.'

'No one was in the mood then to think.' Dawn slid gracefully through the exit, while Mr Dundas held up his hand to steady her. 'Anyway we'll be on our way tomorrow.'

'I shall be happy for your sakes.' He waved his hand in a resigned, gallant gesture, 'But very sorry for my own. It's rare we get such unexpected and delightful company.' He walked between them towards the car, 'So everything was normal?'

'Exactly as we left it.' Claire toyed with the idea of telling Mr Dundas about the untouched food, the unused soap, but it would take so long to explain and really it all seemed very slight. Besides, it seemed they were likely to find Bill back at the inn, or that Lampeter would have made contact with him.

'It is getting colder, isn't it?' Mr Dundas asked as the two girls climbed in the back of the car. 'But a drop in temperature sometimes clears the fog.'

There was no sign yet that it was doing so. Faint swirls of it smoked in the headlights of the car. Further away at the far end of the apron they could just distinguish the Land-Rover. So Lampeter and the other two had not yet finished their search. Beyond there was no sky and no horizon. Just a wall of solid darkness.

'They won't be long,' Dundas said gently as if reading her mind.

'No.' The two girls huddled gratefully in the warmth of the car. Fergus drove at some speed down the runway, and apologetically Mr Dundas smiled. 'I let him have his head here, because he's got to watch it once we're on that damned road.'

Obediently Fergus slowed down once they were past the guard-room. The fog was still rolling in from the sea in eerie billowing shapes. Occasionally they hit a clear part. The headlamps glittered on wet black macadam, and the darkened granite of the low sea wall, fronds of bracken and gorse bushes sparkling with iridescent droplets. Then a wall of fog would bend back the beam, showing them nothing but their own blurred and muzzy radiance.

'Mind if I wind the window down?' the laird said. 'Help him to steer.'

'No. Please do.'

He said something in Gaelic to Fergus. And then to the girls, 'Just telling him not to brake suddenly even if one of these damned sheep come out. Can't risk a skid. Surface is slippery.'

Sitting close together in the back, they could smell the salt in the mist mixing with the scent of bracken and heather and the deathly smell of sodden leafy earth. The boom of the waves sounded above the smooth hum of the engine.

'We're too damned close to the sea to take any chances,' Mr Dundas said. 'Ah, that's better. Thinning a little here. Once round the headland and we should see the lights of home.'

The right-hand turn came up, and was neatly negotiated. Then the left-hand. The fog was indeed less dense. Their spirits rose. They sat back in their comfortable seats and relaxed.

'I do believe,' Mr Dundas said as they rounded the headland, 'that I caught a glimpse of a light . . .' Then his voice trailed to a horrified stop.

Claire sat forward. A light. No, not a light. The headlamps had reflected on something metallic. Something at the side of the road. The seaward side, against the low wall. Mr Dundas's hand, resting on the back of the seat, gripped the upholstery. The knuckles were white. Fergus stared ahead, his eyes wide.

Just in front of them, in the full radiance of the headlights, lay a bicycle on its side. A wrecked, buckled bicycle. Its front wheel crumpled, its handlebars twisted to one side. There was no sign of a rider. Only the roar of the waves at the bottom of the sheer drop far below.

A splintered refraction from the bike glittered in the head-lamps of the Land-Rover as Lampeter returned to the inn nearly an hour later.

'Barrett's back!' he shouted to Crowther as he pulled on the handbrake and switched off the ignition. Then, about to douse the headlamps, he paused and leaned forward. The bike was spotlit in the full radiance and something of the truth began to dawn on Lampeter. The scene suddenly became one to be printed on the eye, and afterwards meticulously remembered.

The bike was propped on the far side of the inn. The front was at right-angles to the rest, like a broken neck. The handlebars were buckled and the headlamps flung their distorted shaky shadows on the cement wall. On the near side of the door, the bar-room window was unshuttered. The room was full but no sounds leaked out. In the smoky wavering lamplight people stood in groups, every gesture, every glimpsed profile, bearing an invisible caption, 'Bad News'.

Only one figure was detached from the rest. Mrs Crowther had commandeered the bar counter lamp and was holding it above her head at the window, peering out into the wet night, waving it like some forlorn signal to guide them in. The blob of yellow light clearly delineated her tired puckered face. Had he not seen the bike, Lampeter thought, her face alone would have told him.

He stood for a moment with Crowther beside him. A sixth sense told him there was something in that scene that he ought to remember. But he could see nothing except a melancholy ordinariness.

He shrugged his shoulders, exchanged a meaningful look with Mr Crowther. Then he gritted his teeth, opened the door of the inn and went inside. The bar smelled of coffee, kerosene, wet clothes and defeat.

For a moment no one spoke. Mrs Crowther set down the lamp, hurried towards them. She stopped half way across the room, her boot-button eyes suddenly misty and tender, travelling over her husband. She looked for a moment as if she was going to act completely out of character and throw herself into his arms. Then she tightened her lips, blinked her eyes, and, chuntering angrily, began searching in her handbag.

Lampeter glanced quickly round the room. A solitary local inhabitant – an old man in a fisherman's sweater – was sitting in the corner, trying to follow the whispered conversations.

All the search-parties were back, which was a relief. Claire, Peter, Borghese, Ainsworth, Hagedorn, he mentally ticked off his charges. Claire, Mrs Ewart and Maiyrat were handing round sandwiches. They all looked pale and Maiyrat had been crying.

'Mrs Crowther,' Lampeter said softly, pushing her husband gently forward, 'he needs a bit of looking after.'

'He allus does.'

Then, raising his voice without any preamble, Lampeter asked crisply, 'Who found it?'

'We did,' Claire and Dawn answered. Dawn was sitting close to Ainsworth, holding his hand tightly.

'When and where?'

'On the way back. At the headland.' Claire walked over to him. She had herself well under control, but her eyes looked unnaturally wide and bright.

'How long ago?'

'About thirty minutes.'

He glanced at the clock above the bar. 'Shortly before nine, then?'

'Yes. We got back here about five minutes ago.'

"Tell me about it.'

Someone, Ainsworth or Philby, thrust a large glass of whisky into Lampeter's hand.

'Drink it first,' Claire said softly. 'Then I will.' She leaned her elbow on the bar counter, cupping her chin to steady it. But when she spoke her voice was as calm and clear as if she were reporting up front after take-off on a routine flight.

'And where is Dundas now?' Lampeter asked when she had finished.

'He went straight off to organize a boat. He took Todd with him.'

'Is there any chance Bill could have fallen on a ledge part way down?'

'Not a hope. It's a sheer drop. Slightly concave. We shone our torches over the edge. And Fergus swung the car round to get the light.' She shook her head. 'But there was nothing. Absolutely nothing.'

'You shouted?'

'Yes. There was no answer. But the sea was loud.'

'And well up?'

'Just after high tide, the laird said.'

'So the worst time to fall. He'd be carried out on the ebb tide.'

She nodded. 'That's why Dundas wanted to get the boat. There was just a remote chance . . .'

'Did he tell you where we could meet up?'

'He said you were to get some rest. Leave all this to him.'

Lampeter's jaw tightened but he said nothing for a moment. He watched Mrs Crowther busily selecting dressings out of a red Elastoplast tin. 'Crowther had a bad time. I'll tell you about it later. But how about the rest?' He raised his voice questioningly.

Spence drained his drink. 'The interior's a bit grotty, sir. But you and I should be able to manage the cliff by ourselves.'

'There is a saying in my country – ' Borghese buttoned up his sodden jacket – 'that many muscles make light loads.'

'I a word of the Celtic language have,' Hagedorn said and, gently patting his wife's arm, walked over to join Lampeter.

'You stay with the women, Ainsworth,' Philby suggested. 'You're not built for cliff climbing.'

'What, and be torn apart in the rush? Hell to that.' Ainsworth finished fastening on the sole of his shoe with a strip of Mrs Crowther's Elastoplast.

'Well, *this* old lad's staying in, any road,' Mrs Crowther said firmly, and turning to Claire added, 'but see *your* lad gets summat to eat afore he goes.'

Claire, smiling for the first time, proffered the plate of sandwiches. Lampeter took a couple absent-mindedly and swallowed them ravenously.

A sudden memory of Bill Barrett's voracious appetite and the untouched food in the galley disturbed her, but was quickly crowded out by other more pressing anxieties.

'Don't do anything foolish.'

'You know me.'

'Yes, I know you.'

He looked at her gently and whispered with apparent irrelevance, 'What a time and place to pick.'

She didn't ask him what he meant. She followed the men out to the front door. Steely pencils of rain slanted down. They stood in a huddle looking down at the wrecked bicycle.

As if not to miss whatever excitement was going, the old man in the fisherman's sweater came pushing past her.

'*I dairt – Crann-tara*,' he said, passing the group by the bicycle. He held up his crossed fingers.

'*I dairt – Crann-tara*,' Hagedorn said. '*I dairt* means victim and *Crann-tara*, fiery cross.'

29th October   TIWESDÆG

The Day of Tiw, god of battle, related to Woden

Half past nine, ten, ten-fifteen . . . the pendulum of the clock on the bar-room wall ticked down Bill's chances as dispassionately as a totalizer.

At half past ten Menzies appeared with some thick white ointment in an old fish-paste jar and a glass full of purple syrup, which he handed to Mr Crowther as a cure for his bruises.

'This will calm the swelling in the *bruthadh*, you understand. And this you will drink, please, all at one gulping, so she will make you sleep the night through without any pain, that iss so.'

At eleven, he came through from the kitchen to bar the shutters and announce, 'Well, I'm awa' to my bed,' though he had the kindness not to close the bar. Instead he produced from under the counter a wooden box with a coin slot cut in the top.

'The honesty box,' he said earnestly, handing it to Claire. 'Maiyrat's written doon the prices on this wee slate. I dinna have the reading mysel' . . .' Then, turning to Mr Crowther, 'Mind ye drink that now. Ye'll have a bonnie sleep . . .'

He walked through into the kitchen. Claire listened for his footsteps on the stairs. Instead she heard the back door softly open and as carefully shut.

'Well, I don't reckon much to the luik of that for a start.' Mrs Crowther rested her sharp nose on the rim of the glass

126

and sniffed. 'Can't say I like the sound of the bonnie sleep overmuch either.'

Dawn huddled herself inside her coat. 'How *long* a sleep one asks oneself?'

Mrs Crowther raised the purple glass to the lamplight.

'Pretty colour,' Mrs Ewart said. 'Kinda like blueberry juice.'

'*Ja.*' Frau Hagedorn's face had lost its seraphic smile. From time to time she paused in her knitting to listen. But she still nodded enthusiastically.

'Perhaps it's home-made elderberry wine,' Claire suggested, her eyes on the hands of the clock as if by watching them she could stop them moving.

'Home-made deadly nightshade more likely,' Mrs Crowther said roundly. 'We're not having any of his pegmeg. A bismuth tablet's all you're taking tonight, think on, lad.' She got to her feet. 'Luik. We're not doing anyone no good laking around like this. Bed.'

'I'll wait for a while in case the men want anything,' Claire said, looking at the clock again. In the time it had taken the rest of them to gather their things together and say goodnight, it had leapt forward again.

Eleven-thirty, eleven-forty-five. Midnight. She shivered in the empty room. She thought that somewhere an outer door opened. A draught of cold air fanned the dying peat fire. The shutter rattled.

Twelve-thirty, one o'clock. There was the sound of a car engine swelling, then slowing and stopping. She heard the squeak of the Land-Rover's brake. Then the slamming of the doors, people getting out. She listened for the tone of the men's voices. No one seemed to be speaking.

The front door opened. She walked to the bar-room door, counting the figures in the beam of light. Lampeter, Spence, and the three other men. All there. But without Bill.

'Not a sign.' Lampeter ran his hand through his wet hair. 'We've seen Dundas. No joy from the boat either. Peter and I will drive round the coast road just once more. The rest are going to turn in now.'

Claire lifted the flap of the bar counter, walked round and reached down a bottle of whisky, and poured them each a good measure. She pushed the plate of sandwiches over to the silent, dispirited group. No one seemed hungry.

'Where's Menzies?' Lampeter asked.

'He said he was going off to his bed.'

'It's where you should go,' Lampeter said gently.

'I will presently.' She frowned. 'He gave something to Mr Crowther before he went to bed. For his bruises.'

'Ah, yes, Crowther.' Lampeter stared at Claire as if he wasn't really seeing her. He swirled the whisky round in his glass. Then after a moment, as if he had been weighing something in his mind and had now come to a decision, he announced suddenly, 'I'm going to work on the aircraft tomorrow. First light.' And turning to the First Officer, 'Pete.'

'Sir.'

'You organize tomorrow's search.'

Spence drained his glass. 'Don't you want me to . . .?'

'No. You stay down here.' Lampeter put his glass on the counter. He smiled thinly. 'Very generous of Menzies.' He jerked his head to indicate the open bar.

'Don't worry. It's not on the house. He left what he calls the honesty box.'

'He would.' Lampeter glanced at the clock and straightened. 'Don't forget to put the money in.'

'I'll sort something out in a moment. Anyone want any more?'

'I think everyone should go to bed,' Lampeter said.

Ainsworth opened his mouth to make some pithy comment, but instead yawned wearily and rested his head on his hands, his eyes shut.

'Come on. You can't go to sleep here.' Philby took his arm. 'Time to climb the wooden hill, laddie.' There was no answering crack from Ainsworth. 'Take his other arm, Hagedorn. There's a good chap.'

Slowly the passengers creaked up the stairs. There was the sound of Frau Hagedorn's voice talking rapidly in German, and her husband's reassuring reply.

'We'll be on our way.' Lampeter jerked his head at Spence. And to Claire, 'Don't wait up. Menzies might charge us extra for the oil.'

'I won't.' She watched the two of them walk to the door. She didn't ask them how long they would be. She knew they would not this time return until Lampeter was satisfied that there was no more hope of finding Bill alive.

She stood for a moment listening to the fading sound of the Land-Rover. Then she walked back into the bar-room. Silence. A cold silence had shrunk down over the inn again. Not even a creak or a footfall came from upstairs. The fire had died to a white ash. She trimmed down the hanging oil lamp to a blue-white skimmed milk glimmer. She stacked the empty glasses. She tried to carry them through into the kitchen. But the door was locked. About to dim the light on the bar counter, she remembered the honesty box. She reached for her handbag and sorted out some change. Then she picked up the slate.

She frowned at the slate in concentration. Written in sprawly schoolgirlish printing was:

BEAR – 5p
Whisky – 12$\frac{1}{2}$p
Lemonaid – 5p

And then, between the Lemonaid and Brandi 15p, an item where Maiyrat's spelling appeared to have got completely out of hand. Idly, Claire wondered if the girl had been trying to write Gin. She blinked at the words sleepily. Then they seemed suddenly to leap out at her. 'Go. Killed else.' And lest her father had some glimmerings of reading, 15p.

Dawn had gone to sleep with the lamp still on. She woke when Claire put it out and asked if they had found Bill Barrett yet, but she had dozed off again before Claire had time to say no.

It was icy cold and uncomfortable on the floor. Her back seemed to find every rough patch in the planks, and when she did manage to twist herself into a slightly more comfortable position, her mind wouldn't let her sleep. She lay awake listening to the turning of the sea, the moan of the wind, the creaking of the sign, the rattle of the rain. Cold air through the tiles blew intermittently as breath on her face. Her ears imagined alien sounds. She thought she heard a voice, a footstep, an engine, the shutting of a door. All the time her mind asked the one question: if Bill was alive, why didn't he return? And always there was the half reply. He had been alive that afternoon, but had not returned. Why?

She seemed to lie for hours staring at the oblong of sky-light above her head. It was grey-black, the texture of baize. She must have drifted off into a light sleep, for when she woke the skylight was clear and a single star shone. She had the curious certainty that some definite sound had alerted and wakened her. She lay still, all her muscles tensed and listened. Nothing. Then faintly, but getting louder, an engine. She got up and walked to the little window. Two headlamps cut through the darkness and slowed down the cobbled street. The Land-Rover's brakes squeaked as it stopped. The lights were switched off. Peter Spence and Lampeter got out. No one else. They walked slowly, heads bowed, into the inn.

Claire dozed intermittently. The next time she woke the skylight was still dark, but the faintest glimmer from the small window told her that it was almost first light. There were sounds of someone moving down below, and the clatter of a bucket in the yard outside. She got up, dressed quickly and went downstairs.

Everything was dark except for a light glowing in the kitchen. The door was open. Maiyrat was standing with her back to Claire, engrossed in pumping up the flame of the oil stove. Then suddenly, before Claire had time to speak, she turned quickly. The lineaments of her face looked pouched and ugly in the yellow incandescence. She nodded curtly in answer to Claire's good morning, and turned her back again, apparently intent on her task.

'That smell of paraffin – ' Claire took a step into the kitchen – 'reminds me of the aeroplane.'

The girl didn't turn, but her body tensed like some stout gun dog pointing. Claire looked behind her to make sure there was no one else around. Then she pulled back the half-open door from the kitchen to the bar. It was still very dark in there with the shutters tightly closed, but in the beam of light from the kitchen she found the slate still lying on the bar counter.

'Maiyrat,' she whispered urgently, stepping back into the kitchen, 'why did you write that?' She came round and thrust the slate in front of the girl's face. 'What did you mean?'

Maiyrat frowned, sighed resignedly, wiped her oily hands on the sides of her apron, and took the slate from Claire. She peered at it short-sightedly, her eyes travelling with nerve-shattering slowness over each line, her lips soundlessly forming every syllable like a child, her head nodding at each item. Outside, Claire heard a heavy tread in the yard. Something that sounded like a milk pail rattled.

'Why,' Maiyrat repeated, 'why did I write it?' The puffy blue eyes were innocent as a fox's. 'So you would know what it iss to pay, that iss why.'

'Not the prices,' Claire said urgently. Now she could hear people outside in the street.

'Tell me, please, Maiyrat, before anyone comes. Please.' She took the slate from Maiyrat's hand, and pointed to the line between the lemonade and the brandy. 'Why did you write this?' She turned it so that she could read it aloud. Then she looked again. She took the slate over to the lamp. There was nothing there now except the faint chalky blur where a finger had erased the few words written there.

Maiyrat gave her a secret little smile. The blue eyes seemed now wholly guileless. 'The prices are very reasonable. For what you get. Everybody says that iss so.'

This time, the women insisted on coming. The beach was flat. It was low tide. There was no danger to watch, except, presently, the queer looping ways of the incoming tide. Besides, anything was better, as Mrs Crowther said, than being left at the inn with that Job's comforter the landlord. Spence divided the beach into strips, and for safety's sake, they searched in pairs.

Claire had Herr Hagedorn with her. They were to search the area beneath the cliff where the wrecked bike was found, walking right down to the flats at the water's edge, and back up among the rocks and pools at the foot of the cliff.

It was a cold morning, and by half past ten the cloud had lifted and a blustery wind was blowing. It raised white caps on the distant sea, flurried the shallow tide pools into cat's-paws, and flapped the ends of Herr Hagedorn's scarf as, neatly dressed in Homburg and Crombie overcoat, he negotiated the slimy rocks and spongy sand.

There was no one else in sight. Their neighbouring two searchers, Philby and Spence, were far beyond an outcrop of rock. She and Hagedorn might have been the only people left in the world. Far behind towards the harbour, not a plume of smoke rose from the huddle of cottages. High above, heavy rain clouds trundled in from the sea. But nothing seemed alive. Herr Hagedorn kicked at lumps of sodden driftwood, overturned an empty packing case, stirred mounds of seaweed lying like dead dogs, peered into little tarnished pools.

Then as they reached the shallow waves at the water's edge, the altitude wind parted the heavy nimbus heads. A stray finger of sunlight cast a silver disc on the gunmetal sea.

'Zo –' Herr Hagedorn pointed – 'an omen perhaps? The first time since we arrive the sun has come!'

'And gone,' Claire said turning away, wondering by what strange primitive awareness in her, by what mysterious infection of this place, she should know as certainly as if his body lay at her feet that Bill was dead.

'The clouds always darker seem when the sun has gone.' Hagedorn held up his face to the blackening sky. Then eyes down again to the sand, scanning sideways, bending to pick up every likely object like beachcombers. Glancing behind, watching their own footprints fill with water. Then off the flats on to the coarser sand, the shingle, the pebbles, pulling a scarf of weed from a cleft in the rocks, picking up a coin glittering among the stones.

Now with the sea half a mile behind them they could just distinguish Spence and Philby, dwarfed by the beach to minute figures in a landscape, walking heads down twenty yards or so apart. A single gull hung very white against the darkening cloud, hardly moving.

There were more rocks here, weed-covered and slippery green. The pools gave back the heavy colour of the sky. Rubbery red lumps of anemones clung to the sides. Herr Hagedorn bent and picked up an old plimsoll ribboned with weed. He held it up.

'His?'

Claire shook her head. She prodded a thick mush of weed with her toe. A tiny pink translucent crab ran out of it, slid in sideways to a pool. Nothing else.

Then she became aware that Herr Hagedorn was hurrying forward. Picking his way with careful speed over the slippery rocks to the round elephant-grey boulders that footed the cliff. He said something aloud in German but to himself, not her.

Half wanting to hang back, Claire forced herself to follow him. Here, immediately under the overhang, huge flat granite rocks formed themselves into a rough platform to the headland. They were pitted with shallow pools that reflected the face of the cliff, but otherwise smooth. Hagedorn was standing with his back to her, staring down at what looked like a cairn of small boulders.

'Stay away, please!'

Hearing her close behind, he turned fiercely waving her back. She hesitated for a moment, and then as he turned back again, came slowly on.

As if he had forgotten all about her, Hagedorn was bending over the cairn. He appeared to hesitate for a moment. Then slowly, and with reluctance, removed the top stone.

In a sudden moment of prescience, Claire thought; I shall always remember Herr Hagedorn thus. Hand outstretched, in that moment of mournful hesitation.

When she came and stood beside him, he had removed half the stones. They were roughly graded, most of the heavier ones towards the base, and Hagedorn was panting now with his efforts.

'It is not good, to do this.' The apology was not just to her. 'But I must.'

'What does it mean?' She asked softly, crouching beside

him, glancing over her shoulder at the bare clean boulders, wishing she could dismiss the cairn as the haphazard workings of the tide.

'This is the same as the primitive cairns. Erected to house the human spirit. They should not be disturbed. For they are to stop it wandering.'

'You mean . . . you think . . .?'

'Yes.'

He did not now attempt to stop her as, gritting her teeth, dreading what each would uncover, she began to pull the stones and pieces of rock away.

But there appeared to be nothing. Herr Hagedorn pulled at one large stone at the base and the rest tumbled away. She watched them bounce over the granite and rattle into a rock pool just below. She saw the surface distort into small splashes, and then re-form into its mirror-like surface again. But now there was more in it than trails of weed and a reflection of the sea wall.

There was a distant tiny face in it. Someone was standing at the top of the cliff staring down over the sea wall. Claire raised her eyes. She could see a head and shoulders outlined against the sky. The figure of the shepherd loomed unnaturally large. What light there was made an eerie lambent aura of the grey fuzzy hair. She thought he looked as daunting as some Old Testament prophet with his right hand outstretched and pointing.

Then she saw that the shepherd wasn't pointing at them. She turned her head. Far away to the south above the sand flats was a flurry of what looked like snowflakes. Above the sound of the sea came the sad scream of gulls. They were coming out of the dark sky, circling lower and lower, calling.

And below them, a little huddled shape, very still on a stretch of sand.

'Poor chap . . .'

Spence turned his head away. 'I suppose you've seen a good many dead bodies, Philby.'

'None like this.'

The little engineer lay on his back in a shallow sea-water pool, his head twisted grotesquely half under his right

134

shoulder. His uniform jacket was unbuttoned. Two of the buttons were missing and there were brown threads of weed round the two that remained. His shirt was grey and sodden, stained down the front a dreadful washed-out pink. There was a round bruise on the side of his head, but it was his face that was terrifying – leech-coloured, both eyes wide open and the whites a brilliant red.

Philby closed his eyes tight and opened them again. It was the small personal things that were so pathetic, he thought, trying to summon up what two and a half years at medical school had taught him; the gold ring on the lifeless hand, the bright Austrian braces holding up the uniform issue trousers, one button off on the left-hand side.

One by one he raised the arms and, letting them drop, saw by the strange way they fell how broken and mangled the bones must be. The ribs were crushed in the front, and there were multiple fractures in the legs. So great were the injuries that it seemed that only Barrett's clothing was holding parts of his body together.

Philby raised his head and saw Claire and Hagedorn approaching from across the sand. He called out, gesturing them to keep away.

Spence shouted, 'It's no good. It's too late,' and then helped Philby pull the body on to the dry sand, do up the clothes and close those luminous scarlet eyes.

'Must have hit hard,' Spence said.

'Terribly hard.'

'Rock or water?'

'Don't know.' Philby shrugged his shoulders. 'But he's been in the sea a while, judging by his skin.'

'Tide washed him out, you think?'

Philby nodded. 'And brought him back.'

They knelt there on the beach, straightening up Barrett's uniform, pulling his tie to the front – uselessly and ironically, Spence thought, but somehow trying to keep the full horror away from other eyes who would see, adding a kind of dignity to the body, covering the worst of the wounds. High overhead the gulls were still screaming, and the noise was so loud that they did not hear the soft pad of rubber soles in the sand, and were startled by the voice behind them that suddenly said very quietly, 'So the search is over.'

Looking round, they saw Dundas standing above them.

'And it must've been quick, which is a mercy.'

The two younger men said nothing.

'I mean . . . he would have felt nothing.'

Spence and Philby stood up, and still neither of them spoke.

'McDermott told me it'd been found. I've got the car on the top of the cliff, if you could give me a hand.'

Together and carefully they picked up the body.

'He's light,' Philby observed.

'He was always small and thin,' Spence said, 'in spite of the amount he ate. But he was tough and a tower of strength in trouble.'

They were walking over the edge of the rocks.

'Pity he didn't wait till morning . . . as I said.'

'He was always a press-on type . . .'

'Sad,' said the laird. 'It's all very sad. For him . . . for Ardnabegh.'

At the south end of the bay the cliff flattened out and there was a rough track upwards. Dundas had driven the car over the grass as close to the edge as possible. Without much difficulty they managed to get the body in the back seat, and with the three of them in the front they drove off towards the village.

'Is there a doctor?' Philby asked.

'Of sorts. Most of the islanders go to Menzies for what little troubles they've got. But there's old MacPhee. Retired really. He lives in a cottage on the northern headland. I'm taking you there now.'

'And a constable?'

'Well, I'm the special constable here ، ، ، not that I've ever much to do.'

'Burial?'

'You seem to be used to this sort of thing.' The laird smiled wryly.

Spence said, 'Philby used to be a medical student.'

'Did you now?' Dundas looked at the boy with new respect. 'But you didn't finish?'

'Preferred to see life with my guitar,' Philby said lightly, and as if to stop further questions, 'About the funeral?'

136

'Well, as soon as the doctor's seen him and signed the certificate and the grave's dug, we'll bury him.'

'When?'

'Tomorrow.'

'Isn't that rather soon?' Spence asked.

'The dead are always buried quickly here,' Dundas said softly. 'The islanders lead a hard life. They are a superstitious lot. They won't rest easy till your friend is buried...'

They were climbing now, and over on the left the clouds were breaking. The shroud of mist that had covered the cliffs and hills momentarily melted, and there high above them in all its steep and rocky majesty towered the mountain of Begh, dwarfing everything in sight – its shape sharp and black looming in the drifting shreds of cloud, everything around it desolate and deserted.

There was a silence while Spence and Philby watched awestruck as the mist again wove itself around the summit, gradually covering the mountain till again there was nothing but a wet grey veil.

'Perhaps you see now why the islanders fear Begh,' Dundas said.

It was the last thing any of them said till they reached a croft, rather better built than the ones in the village. A white-haired man was already at the door when they drove up, alerted by the sound of the engines. Dundas introduced him as Dr MacPhee.

'You have heard about the aeroplane, Doctor?'

'Aye.'

'And about the man who was missing?'

'Aye . . . Fergus was over here yesterday and I was after looking a wee while with him.' The old man peered into the back of the car. 'He has been found, then. And as I feared.' He opened the door and stiffly got inside the car. Perfunctorily he began to examine the body. 'He fell from the Head, I hear.'

'Yes.'

Sighing, the doctor unbuttoned the uniform, felt the ribs under the pink-stained shirt, opened for a few seconds the bright-red eyes.

'Death would be immediate, Doctor?' Philby asked. 'As soon as he hit?'

'Oh, aye. He wouldna feel a thing.'

'You're sure?'

'Oh, *air chinnte,* man. The Head's five hundred feet, and the puir wee *leanabh gille* has scarce a bone of his body unbroken.'

The doctor climbed slowly out of the car and closed the door. 'Well then, Mr Dundas, in your capacity as constable I suppose you'll want a death certificate signed.'

'If you please, Doctor.'

Indoors, the old man rooted around short-sightedly in an untidy desk, found a death certificate and in old-fashioned handwriting wrote it out and signed it, giving the cause of death as 'fractured skull and multiple injuries from an accidental fall'. He handed it over to the laird.

'And the funeral?' Dundas asked him.

'Ah, *gru grad*! Immediately.' The old doctor seemed shocked at the question. 'You must surely know the islanders now? Shall we say the noon hour tomorrow? You will tell Todd?'

'Noon.' Dundas turned to the two young men and explained, 'The Ardnabegh minister never comes out these days. It is the good doctor here who reads the services.'

With only a pilot's brief education in maintenance and engineering, like many of his breed, Lampeter was surprisingly unacquainted with things mechanical. Of course he had to do his Air Registration Board technical on the Astroliner – the hydraulic and electro system, the engines, instruments, fuel system, emergencies. But these he had learned for the purpose of the examination – on a theoretical basis – and after passing it had promptly put to the back of his mind all those details which would not immediately concern him in the air, since he had so much else which he had to have on the immediate fingertips of his memory. He had never done any practical repairing of aircraft. His intention was to use the work Barrett had done on the port wing as a blueprint to carry out the plugging of the similar holes in the starboard wing.

Alone he took the Land-Rover down to the hangar, and then climbed up on to the wings of the jet.

The neatness of Barrett's repairing on the port pipe was immediately apparent. He had used thinner and stripper to clean the surfaces, then cut the pipe, tinned it, and soldered on the sleeve.

He climbed over the top of the fuselage to the other side, and took a look at the holes in the starboard wing, two of which had been plugged, and the other fractured pipe.

He frowned, bent down and ran his fingers over the top of the repairs. It was rough and badly done. There had been little effort to clean and tin the fractured pipe surface and where it had been done, the cone had become too hot and the metal had bullied. He straightened up and glanced back at the work on the port wing.

The difference was most marked. There is a sort of signature about all work, like handwriting. And here were two different imprints – one careful, meticulous, professional, the other quick, careless, slapdash.

Of course, he thought to himself, Bill would be dead tired by the time he started work on the other wing. That would affect his work. All the same, it was odd. Yet another odd happening that would not be satisfactorily explained.

The work on the starboard wing looked as though someone other than Barrett had done it. Suppose someone had? Perhaps Barrett never had come back to continue the work, perhaps someone else, very anxious to get them off and away, had hurriedly done these repairs.

Thoughtfully he began cleaning the skin surface round the break, heating the solder, meticulously starting the starboard mending operation all over again.

It was dark when he returned to the inn. Spence was waiting to break the news of the finding of the body before Lampeter went in to the others.

Immediately he walked down to the distillery. Already it was dark, and the little cobbled street, slippery with rain, glittered in the beam of his torch. Todd met him at the door, and silently led the way to a small shed at the far end of the courtyard.

In Lampeter's mind, there was some strange hope that all this hadn't happened. It couldn't be Bill Barrett, it was somebody else. Giddy with tiredness, after working all day on

Tango Foxtrot in the hangar, his mind had fixed on the idea that there would possibly be so much disfigurement that there had been a mistake in the identification.

But there was none.

They had tidied up his uniform, buttoned his jacket, brushed his hair, washed his face, almost as though he was reporting for some service. The grotesqueness of it made Lampeter close his eyes and turn away.

'You will want these.'

Todd's voice, handing over a pitiful collection of what was left of Barrett's belongings: the ring, a salt-stained wallet with three pound notes in it, three ten-penny pieces and two half pence, a handkerchief, a photograph, a car key, two pencils and a pen. He took them mechanically, heard the hollowness of his voice as he thanked the man.

'I shall see you tomorrow,' Todd said. 'It is at the noon hour.'

30th October   WODENSDÆG

The Day of Woden, father of Thor, god of the
dead, to whom human sacrifices were made,
and whose palace was Valhalla

It was at the noon hour exactly that the coffin arrived at the lych-gate.

Lampeter, Spence, Hagedorn and Borghese carried it down the flagged path between the rounded headstones into the bare damp-smelling nave. The rest of the male passengers, Dundas and the innkeeper in a high white collar and Sunday black came after them, and bringing up the rear, Claire and Mrs Crowther, the only woman passenger who had insisted on attending.

'I'm not bothered if it's customary or it isn't! If my old lad's going, I'm going! I don't want him slipping in after t'coffin!'

'It would be best,' Mr Dundas had warned them, 'if you

140

do not go to the graveside. In Ardnabegh, it is only for the men.'

When the coffin-bearers were half-way down the aisle, the old doctor came hobbling forward to meet them.

Mrs Crowther dabbed her face with a fancy lace handkerchief. 'He's got more'n one foot in t'grave hissen by luik of 'im, think on.'

Claire nodded, but said nothing. All the time she was trying to keep her eyes from the coffin, crowned not with flowers because the island didn't have any, but with a rough wreath of rowan berries made by Maiyrat. Though she tried to look away to the plain glass windows barren of any decoration except a soft green mould that edged their frames and the mottled imprint outside of years of rain, the coffin drew her eyes back. The grey of the wood against Lampeter's dark head, the brightness of the berries like the colour of Bill Barrett's blood. She caught her breath and closed her eyes.

She twisted her hands in her lap. Already the scene had imprinted itself too vividly on her mind. This weird, godforsaken island with its queer folk had taken an uncanny hold on her. That was why she had lain awake all night, listening to the wind and the rain and the creaking of the old building, thinking she heard other people talking. There had been talk all right in the men's room. She remembered hearing Peter Spence's voice and Philby's, and the slow deep rumble of Mr Crowther.

When she did doze off to sleep, she dreamed violently. Always the same dream, that they were all running along the beach, Captain Lampeter, Peter Spence and the passengers and her, but though they forced and forced themselves, they couldn't make any progress. And whatever was pursuing them was coming closer and closer, but she was too afraid to turn her head. Then suddenly a shadow was cast over them, the shadow of their pursuer, and the shadow was Begh, and there in the apex of the shadow was Bill Barrett's body. Whenever she woke, she was always bending to pick up his body, and wherever she touched him her hands were clotted with blood.

The coffin now was resting on a plain wooden table. The men had shuffled into a pew. The doctor stood with old, trembling hands tucked into the sleeves of his black suit his head bent. There was no sound but the slight squeak of a chair, and the rattle and moan of the rain outside, and the interminable, unquenchable ringing of the bell. Then abruptly and it seemed simultaneously, the bell stopped, the door opened. A sharp gust of sea wind dispersed the smell of death and mould, as the shepherd came in.

The funeral service began.

Claire couldn't hear if it was in English, Gaelic or Latin. It seemed to be a jumble of all of them. There was no address and the service was brief. The dreadful bell began clanging again above the rafters. The shepherd had opened the doors, and they were carrying the coffin out into the slanting rain.

'Do you want to go back, or do you want to wait?' Claire asked Mrs Crowther as the men filed out and there was nobody else left in the mouldering little church.

'Wait,' Mrs Crowther said firmly. 'I'm not letting that lad out of me sight.' She dabbed her little boot-button eyes with her handkerchief and set her mouth grimly.

Outside, the knot of village men had melted away. There was no one in the churchyard except the little group of mourners, led now for some reason by the shepherd. He was striding in front, head high, the wind blowing his long prophet's hair, then the coffin and the pall-bearers, and the rest of the men. They made their way down an old moss-covered path and turned left.

'Aye, there he is, the old lad, safely at the back.' Mrs Crowther pulled her hat firmly down on her head and narrowed her eyes. Little feathers of spume were blowing in with the wind from the sea. Thick as snowflakes, white as birds. It reminded Claire of the awful birds wheeling over Bill Barrett's body. The little procession was turning left, far left, to the little sandy dune of a freshly dug grave. Then the men stood quite still as the coffin was lowered and the shepherd threw down a handful of earth.

Watching, Lampeter felt at that moment more alone than he had ever done in his life. He had recently taken a number of decisions, upon some of which the lives of the people in his care depended. Decisions which he had discussed with no one. Now as he watched the last of the raw elm of Bill's

offin disappear under its cover of stony soil, he was not sure
that he had decided well. A cold wet wind blowing straight
up the harbour slope ruffled his hair like icy fingers. From
where he stood at the head of the grave, Lampeter could see
on the one hand the wild race of the wind-whipped water,
and on the other, the heavy cloud fingering its way down the
banks of Begh. Given weather like this, in a hastily repaired
aircraft on a cracked and pitted runway, *dare* he take off? Yet
dare they stay longer?

Go they must. Somehow of that decision he was certain.
Something as nebulous as the mist and just as dangerous
menaced them on this island. The island was out of true –
like an aircraft he had once tried to fly which years before
had broken its back.

Slowly Lampeter's eyes travelled round the faces of those
assembled at the graveside. Peter Spence was standing immediately opposite. He still looked pale from the shock of
finding Barrett's body. Next to him stood Dundas, head
bent, eyes lowered again as the old doctor began to chant
another prayer. Dundas must wonder, Lampeter thought
wryly, when he was going to be shot of them all. He at least
had been unfailingly helpful. But now, despite his helpful-
ness, it was obvious he had had enough. He wanted them on
their way. Did he in fact know more about the island than it
was politic to say? Or more than he dared say?

Next to Dundas was Philby, and then Jerry Ainsworth,
and beyond him Crowther, visibly moved, remembering perhaps his own brush with death – the accident that to Lampeter's thinking was no accident. Lampeter tightened his
lips. Just behind Crowther, the landlord stood with his eyes
closed and his lips moving, watched curiously by Herr
Hagedorn, still with his grey scarf neatly folded and carrying
his Homburg hat.

Now it was all over. The old doctor had turned away from
the grave, and was hobbling with what haste he could back
down the overgrown path to the gate. Eyes still lowered, the
mourners fell into step behind him. A few of them knew
a little more than they would admit, Lampeter thought
grimly. If each would contribute his piece, would the jigsaw puzzle fall into place?

At the gateway, Lampeter shook hands with the docto
thanked him for conducting the service, and watched hi
being escorted into Dundas's car. The landlord walked brisk
down the street back to the inn, followed more slowly b
Crowther and the other men. Lampeter waited for a mome
by the gateway, with the wind and the rain blowing full on hi
face. Then he retraced his steps.

The grave was shallow and the shepherd had stayed be
hind to fill it in. He was standing staring down at his hand
work. He had placed the rowan wreath in the middle of th
freshly turned soil.

Without looking up he said in his sweet, lilting voice, 'Yo
will all be going away now, that iss so?'

'In a couple of days.'

'You must go even before that, sir.' He raised his eye
suddenly and stared at Lampeter. The irises were so pal
that Lampeter seemed to see nothing but the glistening whit
eyeballs. 'You must go now. Without more talk, you under
stand, that iss so. You walk a narrow path between life an
death. What has happened to your friend will surely happe
to all of you.'

'Tell me what you know,' Lampeter said urgently.

'I see death all around.' The shepherd covered his eye
with the tips of his fingers. 'I see the bird will rise and th
bird will fall.'

'Is that all you can tell me?' Lampeter asked. Despite hi
scepticism he heard his own voice rise a tone.

'Aye.' The old man didn't look at him again. His eyes wer
still fixed on the bright orange berries of the rowan wreath
And then with a sudden chill, Lampeter saw it wasn't th
wreath that he was staring at, but an object just below it.

Speared on a stick, with its outstretched wings nailed on a
crude cross, was a tiny brown wren.

Nobody felt like lunch, though Maiyrat – perhaps this too
was an Ardnabegh custom – had put on a spread of oatcakes,
cheese, boiled eggs and sliced tinned ham from Tango Foxtrot. Lampeter had gone upstairs to lie down for half an hour
before going back to the airfield to continue work on the
starboard wing. The Land-Rover had again been put at his

144

disposal by the laird and was parked just outside the inn under the swinging sign of the Daroch.

He lay on his back with his eyes closed, an aching, twitching tiredness in all his limbs. The events of the last three days had made their impact on him. Practical and realistic, used to judging the environment around him on needles and gauges, he had no such definite guidelines to steer him through the weird other-worldliness of Ardnabegh.

Not given to flights of fancy, he was now certain that there was something going on beneath the surface of events – as if there were two planes of existence continuing at the same time. The people were not as they seemed. They turned different faces to them, the strangers, than to each other. It was as though Hagedorn's Thor had hurled his bolt, and after that tremendous thunderclap they had slipped through some crack in time, beyond science and aerodynamics and logic to ancient mysteries, and old ways.

In spite of being almost dead on his feet, he couldn't sleep. One after another the events on the island since they managed to land chased each other through his mind. There appeared to be no pattern and no meaning. The footsteps that went away, Claire hearing the night sound of engines, the moving of the aircraft, the fact that somebody other than Barrett had been working on the aircraft, Crowther's close shave in the crevasse, and finally Barrett's disappearance and death.

Did the islanders resent their presence? Were they hiding some secret, and therefore wanted them away? Had something happened for which they were all collectively guilty?

The only person who had gone out of his way to help them was Dundas. He had done everything he could and Lampeter was grateful.

But he was not an islander, and behind his obvious loyalty to them were hints of strange unnatural doings. Dundas's attitude was more one of a benevolent father towards backward children than that of the conventional laird. On an island as isolated as this, inevitably there would be intermarriage, and as Dundas had said, worse. Abnormal streaks would be accentuated, not only by inbreeding but by the environment itself. Strange ideas obviously flourished – the fear of the airfield called after the fiery cross, the mistletoe hanging all the year round on the oak beam, the crucified wren thrown down into the grave.

Were these just local legends and customs? Cold northerly versions of Christmas kissing and maypoles? Or did they hold some hidden warning? Was Barrett's fate to be the fate of them all?

Not only had Lampeter the difficult problem of patching up the aircraft and taking off on that execrable runway, but also the safety of his passengers and crew on this mysterious island against forces that he could neither see nor identify. Lampeter knew he was all right when he could recognize who or what was his enemy; the weather gave the right warnings before becoming dangerous, mechanical failures showed up on instruments. Red lights flickered and fire bells clanged in an emergency on an aircraft. But in Ardnabegh there were just shadows moving in the mist.

He lay listening to the whistling of the wind, the turning of the sea, and people moving about below in the inn. Somebody was coming upstairs – two people in fact. He heard the door of the bedroom open. Spence's voice saying softly, 'He's asleep.'

Footsteps coming cautiously inside.

'Don't wake him, Philby.'

'I wasn't going to.' The squeak of bedsprings. 'Might as well kip down too.'

Whispering voices. 'Probably nothing to it anyway.'

'Maybe not.'

'You can't really call yourself a medical man.'

'Thus spake my masters at Tommy's.'

A silence. Then Spence's voice a little louder. 'Mind you, Barrett's eyes . . . those red eyes . . . they were terrible!'

Another silence, longer this time.

'You reckon that if he'd been killed instantaneously by the fall, the whites of his eyes wouldn't have been bloody.'

'Medical fact.'

'It would only be if he had died a number of minutes after the blow on the head that the blood would have time to flow into his eyes.'

'So the remnants of my medical knowledge tell me.'

'And what you're really saying, Philby, is that he was dead *before* the fall off the cliff.'

'Am I? Yes, I suppose I am.'

'And that pink stuff on his shirt couldn't have been blood?'

'No.'

'Then what was it?'

'Ah, there you have me.'

A third silence even longer this time. Then Spence's voice, irritable now. 'I don't believe you. I don't think you know what in hell you're talking about! You're going round the twist like the rest of them here.'

'What is sanity, one asks oneself?'

'Well, we're not going to worry the skipper with *your* theories. He's got enough on his plate.'

Philby sighed, picked up his guitar and began strumming very softly.

'I said not to wake him.' Spence turned round and saw Lampeter's eyes wide open, watching them.

'It's OK, Peter. I was awake.' With a new energy Lampeter raised himself and swung his legs on to the floor. 'I heard what you said, Philby.'

'If you ask me sir, it's a load of . . .'

'I'm not so sure.' Lampeter stood up and looked down at the ex-medical student assessingly. His fingers still plucking at the strings of his guitar, Philby's shrewd red-rimmed eyes stared back up at him.

'It would be in keeping with the island,' Lampeter said grimly.

Softly, crooningly Philby began singing 'Thunder on Sunday . . .'

'You reckon his dead body was flung over the cliff, and the bike arranged to look as if he'd crashed and fallen.'

'. . . dead on Monday . . .'

'That he was murdered.'

'. . . Which is it going to be? The butcher, the baker, the candlestick-maker. Or why not say all three?'

'Murdered.'

Like an immediate echo of the last word Lampeter had spoken, the three syllables came out of Dundas's mouth to reverberate round the steel vaults of the hangar above them. 'Good God, man!' Dundas walked forward in considerable agitation. 'Are you saying it just on *that*?'

Still working on top of the wing, Lampeter glanced keenly down at the laird's upturned face. Something lay beneath the surface expression of shocked surprise. Something pained, regretful, deeper than that, something terrified that confirmed his own suspicions. The shadows in the fog, he thought grimly, touching a rim of solder with the tips of his fingers, were beginning to solidify.

'Not just that, no.' Lampeter frowned. His decision to confide his suspicions to Dundas had been almost automatic. The laird was the only inhabitant who could possibly understand or conceivably help them. Yet Dundas had his Achilles heel, his blind spot, his wall eye. He would protect his islanders and whatever strange secret he held about them. For that reason, Lampeter had confined himself to Philby's so-called medical facts, and the queer stain on the body.

Now he drew a deep breath and said, 'I had a look at the bicycle.' Satisfied with the leading edge solder, Lampeter jumped down from the wing and stood in front of Dundas.

'Pretty badly smashed up.' Dundas shook his head.

'Very. But if it had smashed into the wall and he'd braked at the last minute, the front tyre should have been in a helluva mess.' Thoughtfully Lampeter kicked the front wheel of Tango Foxtrot.

'And wasn't it?'

'No. The handlebars were buckled and scratched as if they'd had *sideways* blows.'

Dundas said nothing.

'Furthermore, the saddle was too high.'

'What could that possibly mean, Captain? He'd just borrowed the girl's bike. He probably didn't bother to alter it.'

'That wasn't like Bill. Everything had to be just so.'

'Well, you knew him, Captain, I didn't.'

'Then, as I told you, the work didn't look like his. See this place here? Notice how smooth. Now look at the far end. Just here! The cone of the flame was too hot, the metal bullied.'

'Maybe he had an off moment, we all do.' Dundas raised his hands and let them fall to his sides. In the cold grey light his rosy face looked for the first time haggard.

'Then, sir, though he was working here all day, he didn't eat.'

Dundas smiled faintly, 'You've worked all day without eating to *my* certain knowledge.'

'It was out of character. Besides, Claire tells me he didn't wash either.'

'And that was out of character too?'

'Yes.'

'Maybe he was acting out of character all day?'

'Yes. But if he hadn't washed –' Lampeter opened his own hands, and held them palm uppermost; they were covered in grease, and grains of solder – 'there'd have been marks all over the handlebars. Now wouldn't there?'

Dundas stroked his chin and said nothing. He began walking slowly up and down the hangar. Over his shoulder he said, 'The rain might have washed them clean?'

'Unlikely.' Lampeter began wiping his hands on a rag. He paused deliberately for a few seconds, giving the laird time to digest what he had already told him. Then softly, 'Oh, another thing . . .' and he began to tell him about the crucified wren dropped into Bill Barrett's grave.

The effect on the laird was instantaneous. He had his back to Lampeter, but he paused in his tracks as if Lampeter had struck him. Then he slowly turned.

'Now tell me,' Lampeter said sternly, 'what is really going on.'

Dundas upended the last of the ten-gallon kerosene cans and sat down. In the last ten minutes he had aged twenty years. 'I wish I knew for certain, Captain.' He spoke slowly. 'As you know, I've always wanted you to get away quickly. I *sense* you're in danger. I've tried . . .'

'You've been most helpful, sir.'

The laird smiled wanly. 'For their sakes as well as yours.'

'You think the islanders might do something?'

'Yes.'

'Does this mean that you think, *now*, that Bill was murdered?'

'Perhaps.'

'Did what I told you have some meaning?'

'Some of it. The crucified wren, yes.' Dundas sighed. He spoke slowly as if his lips were swollen. 'The broken bones, yes. But the pink on your friend's shirt . . . no. Haven't *you* any ideas?'

Lampeter shrugged. 'All I can think of is hydraulic fluid.'

Dundas looked startled. 'But surely your first officer would recognize that?'

'Doubt it. You see, everything's electric on the jetliner.'

'No hydraulic oil?'

'None.'

'Then how . . .?'

'Exactly. It couldn't have been. Bill wouldn't have been soaked in the stuff unless he'd got inside another aircaft. A bomber for instance. Bomb doors are opened hydraulically. When I was in the RAF, if there were any hydraulic leaks it was always in the bomb bay.'

'But the old bombers on the airfield, he wouldn't have gone in those, would he?'

'I shouldn't think so. And anyway, they'd have no fluid left in them now.'

Dundas shuddered. 'I hesitate to use the word magic, but it might have some magic significance.'

'Such as?'

'I don't know.' A spasm crossed Dundas's face. He paused for a moment to regain his composure. 'When I came here four years ago at first there appeared to be nothing but an odd legend about an airfield called the fiery cross. Only gradually did I find out other things.'

'Why didn't you leave?'

'I nearly did. But I'd sunk a lot of money in the place. And I'd got fond of the islanders by then. It was mine. It all seemed harmless enough. I even understood their fears. The island is ageing, dying. Like a human being. They needed youth and the sun again. Very rarely does the sun shine here. The old folk remember the old days. We all remember the sunny summers of our youth.. So Ardnabegh sought to bring the sun back. It has gone back to its old Celtic ways.'

'What d'you mean?'

'The worship of the sun, the secret tradition, druidism, I suppose you'd call it.'

'But surely in this day and age . . .?'

'Have we changed so much?' Dundas gave Lampeter a quick wry smile.

Lampeter shrugged. 'All this apart. Why Barrett?'

'That I don't know. I think they hold their ceremonies here on the airfield. That's why it's taboo. All this is guesswork, of course. But it's something to do with it being sacred ground. Then the readymade circle, and the intersection of the runways. That I think is why –' he jerked his head at Tango Foxtrot – 'they had to move your aircraft.'

'*They* did it?'

Dundas nodded. 'And maybe your friend surprised them. Perhaps some secret ceremony.'

'And who are *they*?' Lampeter asked grimly.

'That I don't know. They have a high priest, I understand, but his name is secret.'

'But surely they don't really believe this nonsense?'

'All legends, Christian and pagan, run into one another . . . mistletoe means the seeds of life to them. They have the cup, the chalice, a litany, to them all this is sacred.'

'So sacred that they would murder?' Lampeter asked sharply.

In a low voice, Dundas said, 'What I'm afraid of, Captain, is something worse than murder.'

'*Could* anything be worse than murder?'

Then again very softly, 'Yes, Captain, sacrifice. Human sacrifice.' And in the horrified silence. 'Your friend's bones were all broken, you say. The Druids used to drop their victims in wicker baskets from some high place. A cliff or mountain top.'

'And you think Bill . . .?' Lampeter clenched his fists. 'They wouldn't dare . . .'

'Why not, Captain? To the outside world he's dead already.' Dundas stood up. 'Don't you see, that's what I fear. You've all been given up. Officially you don't exist any more. They might even think in their mad way that you were sent. By lightning, don't forget! Sacred lightning. For sacrifice.' Dundas wiped the sweat off his face. 'That crucified wren in the grave. *That* meant sacrifice. The wren is the god of the winter solstice. He needs to be propitiated. And tonight, the thirty-first of October, the old year ends.'

'Hallowe'en?'

'It survives with *us* as that. It's *their* night of the Hallow Fires.'

'The fires. The fiery cross. You don't think . . .'

'I think, after that,' Dundas said, trembling, 'that they might try to kill you all.' His face crumpled. He seemed suddenly an old, old man, as old as the shepherd, as old as the island. Then with a tremendous effort he seemed to pull himself together. 'So you see the urgency. *You must get away.*'

'What about you, sir?'

'Oh, they wouldn't harm me.' Now he was once more the practical man, the laird. 'Your repairs, are they nearly done, Captain?'

'Pretty well, yes.'

'All that remains, then, is the refuelling?'

'Checking and refuelling, yes. Then there are some holes could do with filling in. There are masses of weeds, of course. But Spence reckons it'll do.'

'I don't think there's much time to lose.'

Lampeter looked at him thoughtfully but said nothing.

'We can give you a hand, Captain, refuelling this afternoon. And I can get two or three of them filling up the worst parts of the runway. So what time shall you fix to get away?'

'Before dawn. At first light. That'll be seven-fifteen.'

'Don't let it be any later, Captain.'

'I won't. Seven-fifteen. On the dot. You can rely on that.'

'Maiyrat must know something,' Claire whispered to Dawn as they lay that night in their loft room, with the rest of the inn apparently asleep.

It had been a sad day, with the rain and the grey skies adding to the melancholy. With the exception of the Crowthers, whom Lampeter had told to stay behind so that the old man could rest up and give his hand a chance to heal, everyone else had spent the afternoon and early evening, helped by Dundas and Todd, either moving ten-gallon cans of kerosene down by Land-Rover to the hangar or filling in the worst holes on the pitted overgrown runway on which they hoped to take off, while Lampeter and Spence went on repairing the holes in the starboard wing.

Conversation had centred on the weirdness of the island. Everyone seemed to remember the small odd things they had noticed about the place – Signor Borghese had reaffirmed that he didn't think much whisky production was going on at the distillery, and Mrs Ewart had produced the little metal cap and chain for Lampeter's inspection, though he too had declared it to be of no importance.

Now, in spite of feeling dog tired, Claire could not get to sleep. Maiyrat's babyish handwriting giving that chalked warning on the slate that next morning had been rubbed out and denied kept coming vividly in front of her eyes. Everything on Ardnabegh seemed to appear and then disappear, like the man in the flying jacket, the sounds of those aircraft, even poor Bill Barrett before he died.

'They're all kinky, that's my opinion.'

'There's something more behind it than that.' Claire huddled the blanket into a tight cocoon around herself. 'That cairn of stones . . . I . . .' She shuddered.

'You think someone had already found the body and said nothing?'

'Perhaps.'

'Who do you think it would be?'

'The shepherd or maybe old Menzies.'

'He's the worst of the lot. That stuff he gave Crowther for his hand –' she tried to mimic Mrs Crowther's voice – 'fair brought it up like a pumpkin.'

'But it's better today.'

'Then don't forget Menzies gave Mrs Crowther a draught for him which she, bless her, poured out of the window.'

'That doesn't prove anything.'

'No . . . but Mrs Crowther isn't the kind to frighten easily.'

'Nor am I, sweetie, but I'm frightened now.'

Above their heads, the skylight showed the rain-speckled blackness of the night outside.

'Did you tell Captain Lampeter about Maiyrat's message?'

'I've told no one else but you. Didn't really take it seriously at first. And now so much else has happened.'

'That's exactly why we've got to find out what there is behind it.'

'How?'

'There are ways,' Dawn said cryptically. 'I'll tell you this . . . I'm not going to be kept in suspense any longer. Something's bloody odd about this island, and there's already been a death. If there is danger, and Maiyrat knows about it, she's going to tell us.'

'We could try bribery,' Claire suggested. 'Perfume, lipstick. She's keen on make-up.'

'She needs to be.'

'Or we could offer clothes.'

'As long as my skin's left intact.' Dawn reached for her handbag and lit a cigarette. 'She can have the rest.'

'And if she still won't talk?'

Dawn inhaled deeply and blew the smoke out in a long puff towards the ceiling. 'She'll talk.'

'She's scared stiff of her father.'

'She'll be scared stiff of me before I've finished with her.'

'Dawn . . . what are you going to do?'

'You're in this too, sweetie, and we'll make her talk.'

'Make?'

'Christ, sweetie – you've led a sheltered life! You don't get anywhere by saying "fasten your seat-belts", "hope you enjoyed being sick on the trip". Me . . . I haven't been in the modelling business for nothing. Red of bloody nail and claw. And if their eyes weren't scratched out, darling, it'd be yours.'

There was a silence between them. Then more gently Dawn said, 'It's the jungle, sweetie . . . surely you know that now?'

31st October   THURSDÆG

The Day of Thor

Next morning, immediately after breakfast, all the men left
to continue work on the airfield. Dundas and Todd arrived
with the Bentley and Lampeter continued to drive the Land-
Rover. Crowther insisted on being enrolled in the party
which was going on with filling in the holes on the east-
west runway, in spite of his wife's forebodings. The women
were to be left at the inn to pack everything up for departure
as soon as possible.

'Keeping us out of harm's way,' said Mrs Ewart.

'Gettin' rid o'us more like. All men are fools. My man's
no different to t'others.' Mrs Crowther glowered at Menzies
as he came in from the kitchen dressed in black mackintosh
and gumboots to join Todd in the Bentley. 'Though there's
worse things than being a fool, and that's for sure.'

After the Land-Rover and Bentley had gone, organized by
Mrs Crowther, the women cleared away and washed up.
Upstairs, Maiyrat could be heard cleaning and tidying.

'That lass'd turn milk sour,' said Mrs Crowther, taking
the chair nearest the smouldering peat fire beside Frau
Hagedorn, who had taken out her vast knitting of orange
sweater and sat in the rocking-chair as inscrutable as ever,
clacking her big white needles, 'Is it her bicycle she's still
frettin' over?'

'No,' Dawn said. 'She's got more on her mind than that.'

And without any further ado, while Frau Hagedorn rocked
and smiled and clacked her needles, Dawn told them about
the warning on the slate.

'I allus knew there was something up,' said Mrs Crowther.

'She is a very strange girl,' said Mrs Ewart.

Mrs Crowther agreed. 'She's her father's daughter an' no
mistake.'

'But she knows something,' Dawn persisted. 'And we've

got to find out what it is.'

Around the inn could still be heard Maiyrat's heavy footsteps. They sat over the fire, talking over the mysteries and dangers of the last few days, trying to work out what was behind the chalked words on the slate. In spite of Claire's reluctance, it always came back to the need for a direct confrontation.

'But if she won't tell us?' Claire said.

Dawn said very slowly, 'Well, in that case . . .'

'It's a bit much if she's trying to warn us,' Claire said.

'But *is* she trying to warn us? She may just be trying to frighten us. We've *got* to find out.'

She stopped. The five of them stared into the smouldering fire in silence.

'That's the ticket, lass,' Mrs Crowther said at last. 'Nowt else t'do.'

They sat there, quite still, listening to Maiyrat's footsteps along the landing. Now she was coming downstairs. The sound of the kitchen door opening, then the footsteps faded.

'Come on, Claire.' Dawn got up and moved to the door. 'Let's get it over with.'

Left on their own by the fire, the three other women appeared to be galvanized into garrulity. Even Frau Hagedorn was moved to speak a guttural waterfall of German.

From the other side of the wall could be heard the soft coaxing voice of Dawn.

'. . . what they call a Fair Isle sweater, that's what my old lad's always wanted.'

The disembodied voices grew louder and more insistent.

'. . . in Canada, of course, there's a lot of skiing, and he had to wrap up warm . . .'

Actual words – isolated from sentences, came in from outside. Foreign sounding names like Schiaparelli and Dior that mixed strongly with the scent of whisky and peat smoke in the bar.

'Dior,' said Frau Hagedorn, nodding her head vigorously in approval. 'Schiaparelli.'

'. . . lavender water, when I was a girl. Them fancy perfumes . . .'

'. . . a dab of eau-de-Cologne behind the ears before going

156

to a sorority hop . . .'

'Eau-de-Cologne,' put in Frau Hagedorn patriotically.

The sound of voices from outside reached a crescendo, then died down completely into an ominous silence.

'. . . a little parsley sauce . . .'

'. . . maple syrup . . .'

'. . . not a pricey dish and one you could serve in Buckingham Palace and no disgrace . . .'

A door slammed. There was the sound of a chair falling over. Frau Hagedorn smiled and nodded.

'. . . the money these young girls earn these days . . .'

'. . . a good day's work . . .'

'. . . some of them don't even know the meaning of the word . . .'

Now the voices had started up again, low and insistent rising to high and shrill. There was a crisp sound of a hard slap.

'. . . and every penny goes on their backs . . .'

Pans began rattling, a ripping sound of material.

'. . . and such shoddy stuff . . .'

'. . . never wears . . .'

'. . . and tears so easy . . .'

A tremendous banging noise from outside. Hanging from hooks above the bar, glass tankards tinkled. A thud, followed by the smack of an open hand on bare flesh.

'. . . cheese scallops done to a treat,' said Mrs Crowther raising her voice.

Equally loudly, Mrs Ewart began chanting the preparation rites for a Thanksgiving turkey.

Pandemonium now was coming from the kitchen. The crack of crockery breaking, bumps and bangs. Then sounds of sniffing and weeping.

'. . . in a hot oven for five hours,' yelled Mrs Ewart.

'And careful with the gravy,' Mrs Crowther shouted back at her.

Suddenly on the other side of the wall there was complete silence. Then Dawn came in, followed by Claire with a long scratch all the way down her left cheek.

'Well.' Dawn brushed the hair away from her eyes. 'We found out – the hard way.'

'Eeh, lass, but these things have got to be done,' said Mrs Crowther, now very quietly. 'And what's to happen?'

'There's to be a ceremony down at Crann-Tara. They're going to light the Hallow Fires, she said the Druids would make sacrifices.'

'Druids,' said Frau Hagedorn happily, a beam on her placid pink face. 'Thor-rr. Thor-rr-sday.'

'. . . and then there was that business of the disappearing footsteps,' Spence said.

'And our lad's fall.'

'And the moving of the aircraft,' said Ainsworth.

'And the repairs to the starboard wing that Bill didn't do,' said Claire.

'And this.' Mrs Ewart rather shyly produced from her handbag the metal screw cap with the tiny chain attached. 'Wouldn't you say this was kinda mysterious?'

After Lampeter and the other men had returned that evening from working at the airfield and been told what the women had extracted from Maiyrat, they had all sat round in the bar-room, producing any odd bits of information, trying to work out the pattern of this sinister jigsaw.

Lampeter picked up the screw cap, turned it over in his hand and examined the mark inside it. The thing looked as if it might have been the top of some very large brandy flask. 'Interesting,' he said, giving it her back, 'but I don't see any connection.'

Mrs Ewart slipped it into her bag. 'I'm going to keep it as a souvenir.'

'Of this place?' Ainsworth exclaimed. 'Hell to that. You must be joking.'

'Then there was the cairn of stones,' Philby contributed.

'And the mistletoe. Over my bed too!' Dawn shuddered.

'An t'date on that daft lass's magazine,' said Mrs Crowther.

While the pieces did not fall into any discernible pattern of what was likely to happen, everyone recognized that the most careful plans must be laid for their departure tomorrow. They recognized too that Lampeter as their commander should lay down the drill that was to be followed.

'As far as the islanders are concerned,' he said, 'we'll all be here at the inn till first light tomorrow. But I shall slip out later tonight to make sure no one tampers with the aircraft. Peter, you arrange some sort of guard rota – one person awake – through the night. At seven in the morning, bring everyone down in the Land-Rover . . . it's outside now. I'll be in the hangar waiting for you.'

He smiled cheerfully at them. 'Then we'll take off at eight-fifteen on the dot.'

There were a number of demurs that he was running the most risks and offers from all the men to accompany him. But there were good sound reasons for going alone and he brushed their protests aside. After settling everything and making sure they all understood, he told them he would go up to his room.

Menzies had returned, and could be heard shuffling around in the kitchen. As Lampeter opened the bar-room door the landlord appeared.

'Are ye awa' to your bed then, Captain?'

'Yes. It's been a tiring day.'

'Will ye no have a wee bite of supper?'

'No, thanks.'

'A guid night to ye then, Captain.'

'Good night, Mr Menzies.' Lampeter yawned.

At the bottom of the stairs, he waited for Claire. He stooped down to whisper in her ear, 'Watch yourself with that maniac.'

'I will, don't worry.'

'I do worry.'

'Watch *your*self,' she whispered, standing on tiptoe. 'I worry too. There are plenty of us here.' Her voice faltered. 'But you've got no one.'

He put his hand on her shoulder and gave it a little shake. She flushed at the expression on his face.

'Here,' she said, 'you'd better have this.' She thrust something into his hand.

He opened his palm and looked down in the shadowy lamplight at the little silver brooch of the squat Icelandic figure.

'I don't think,' she said in a shaky voice that teetered

between laughter and tears, 'that there's anything in company regulations about captains wearing jewellery.'

'You're wrong,' he said, pinning it on above the left-hand pocket of his jacket. 'The regulation is quite specific.' He tilted her chin. 'Wedding or engagement ring.' He bent down and brushed her lips with his. 'Or tokens.' He patted the little brooch, smiling, but his eyes questioning. 'Or tokens,' he whispered, 'of similar significance.'

Lampeter slipped out of the inn, just before ten. No one saw him go, not even the other inhabitants of Tango Foxtrot who were making themselves noisily conspicuous in the barroom. Menzies had gone off again, and the plan, hastily made after Maiyrat's disclosures, had been put into operation.

Anxious to keep away from the road, Lampeter chose the short cut to the airfield. At least it had stopped raining, though the perennial mist was rolling in from the sea. He half walked, half ran, jumping streams, sliding over the wet turf, his mind busy with possibilities and conjectures of what was to take place at midnight.

Tango Foxtrot, at any rate, when he reached the hangar, appeared to have been untouched. He went over her carefully, shielding the beam of the torch with his hand so that it cast a pink glow on the duralumin skin. Pink, the colour of the stain on Barrett's shirt. He shivered, slowly continuing his inspection inside the aircraft. All was exactly as he had left it.

Next he walked round the hangar searching for any piles of inflammable material. Nothing had been moved, nothing had been brought in. Softly he closed the hangar door, paused for a moment to accustom his eyes to the misty night light and inspected the outside of the building, his eyes searching the tarmac apron, then the heathery grass on the other three sides. Nothing. His own feet made the only tracks in the wet, bending the coarse grass, snapping the heather. Everything was, as Claire had said before, extraordinarily ordinary.

He looked at his watch. Eleven-twenty-five. Just over half an hour of the old Celtic year left. Practical man though he prided himself on being, he felt the hairs on the back of his neck prickle. The airfield seemed cupped in a silence more empty and profound than anything he had ever experienced. Not a sheep bleated, not a night-jar called.

He stepped back on to the perimeter track. Walking quickly, head down, shoulders hunched, eyes darting on either side of him, he reached the end of the east-west runway by eleven-forty. The mist had lifted slightly. It hung head high, luminous and pearly with diffused moonlight. Here on his right an old command post loomed clear but beheaded in fog. Close to, water tinkled through the marshy ground. And distantly, the waves boomed.

He turned down the runway. The weeds thrusting up through the tarmac muffled his feet. But he had the curious feeling that somehow through the emptiness he was being watched. Twice he stopped in his tracks and turned. He could have sworn that a footfall, not an echo, had followed his own. Once he risked shining his torch, shading his eyes to see if the petrified shadow at the edge of the mist was a figure or a shrub. Gorse bushes littered the heathery grass between the runways. The air smelled of them, more sweet and pervasive than he had ever remembered.

The wind seemed to have changed direction and to be blowing off Begh. It was parting the mist, rolling it this way and that, bringing down the bleat of sheep from the mountainside, heightening the musky scent of autumn flowers. By the time he reached the intersection, the mist had parted sufficiently to show all four arms in a black macadamed cross. There was no sign of anyone or anything else.

He hadn't known what he had expected to find, but his first reaction was one of relief, followed quickly by an irrational certainty that something was *going* to happen. The feeling of emptiness subtly changed. It was a vacuum, a held breath surrounded, pressed upon, threatened by imminent activity. An emptiness cupped in awareness, as if, just by standing there, he was the target of alert, assessing eyes.

He found himself hurrying away from the intersection, looking for somewhere to hide himself. Still with head down, shoulders hunched, he ran off the tarmac. He was half way up to his knees in mud before he remembered all the warnings about the marshes. He dragged his feet clear, cursing. Wet ooze squelched. He turned right, picking his way carefully towards where he had seen the gorse bushes growing. After casting around for a minute or so, he found a thick wind-burned clump about thirty yards south of the runway cross. The ground was fairly dry, and the branches fanned by the prevailing wind so that they formed a neat shelter, through which he could peer. He dropped to his knees, wriggled through, grateful for the feeling of safety. He had half expected there to be a sheep sheltering in the dry, but there was none. He had seen none on the airfield come to that, as if someone had already driven them away. There were strands of their grey wool clinging to the spines of the bush. And their stale smell mingled with the crushed heather and the sweetish smell drifting down with the wind.

Every few minutes Lampeter looked at his watch. Eleven-forty-five and still nothing had happened except that the visibilty had improved..

Low cloud arched above his head. It glimmered with a muffled incandescence, giving the feeling of being inside some domed amphitheatre. The sound of the sea had turned into a soft continuous murmur. The fog hung in curiously patterned patches.

As far as his eye could see on all four quadrants his vision ended in white walls. Then suddenly he saw the white walls move.

From the north, from the south, from the east, along the arms of the runways were coming figures, draped from head to foot in white robes like Ku Klux Klansmen. Three from each direction, carrying something stretched across between them.

Lampeter felt the palms of his hands sweat, and at the same time the cold seemed to numb his bones. The figures glided forward making no sound at all. And then he realized that the murmuring was not from the sea, but was high-pitched humming, broken by a simultaneous chant like the breaking of a wave.

The nine figures advanced slowly. Lampeter strained round anxiously to see if others were coming from the west.

But though the fog there was white and solid as if it contained someone, no one came.

He raised himself just a little on his elbows, peering above the thorny brush as the figures came closer. He could distinguish what the ones nearest him were carrying: a long wooden plinth. He still couldn't see their faces. The white hoods were pulled down so that they had no profiles. Their robes brushed the ground. Now, below the chanting of voices, he could hear the swish of garments and the smack of bare feet.

Simultaneously the three groups reached the intersection. Two placed down heavy stones. The group nearest laid the heavy wooden plinth over them, to form a simple altar. Then they slowly backed away, formed themselves into an incomplete circle, heads bowed, arms folded within the sleeves of their white garments, all facing west. Waiting now in absolute silence. Clearly whatever was to come was to come from behind him. The hairs on Lampeter's neck prickled. He tried to swivel himself round. A gorse spike caught on his sleeve. The branch shook, the spines rasped. The noise seemed to scratch the silence. But no one stirred. It was as if their ears were pitched to one sound only.

Then suddenly the chanting started up, swelled to a crescendo. A sound soft at first but regular as a heart-beat came from behind. Lampeter shifted round.

Three figures had materialized out of the mist. Lampeter wriggled back a few inches and peered round a branch. Hardened, practical man though he was, he felt a quick shiver of fear. A collective shiver of fear trembled the broken circle of acolytes, harshening their chant to a bird-like scream.

The central figure was somebody Lampeter had never glimpsed before. He was an enormous hunchback, tall as Lampeter but huge in his deformity. Was this, Lampeter wondered, the taboo, the secret they had, as the hunchback advanced, head thrust forward. He wore shoes and he trod ponderously, making a heavy sound doomful as some feverish nightmare. A sound that at first masked the other noise. A quick tip-tapping.

Lampeter craned his neck. Half hidden by the bulk of the

other two men, the third led forward a small shorn sheep. Lampeter felt a sudden quick relief. If sacrifice there was to be, it would not be them. But relief gave way quickly to disgust, and disgust to fear again.

Every rhythmic step forward of those heavy feet released something as certainly as if they were hammer blows. Something best left covered. In the night. In them.

Twenty paces and the hunchback was level with him. Lampeter strained his eyes. He could distinguish nothing. The voluminous robe was held tight over the misshapen figure. He could smell something, though. The figure on the hunchback's left and nearest to Lampeter had a metal bowl. From it came that musky flower scent mixed with something harsh and pungent, distantly familiar.

Then, abruptly, the sheep bleated. It was a signal for the chanting to fall to a soft urgent murmur. The shivering animal pulled at its leash. Its hooves scraped against the tarmac as the man dragged it forward.

In through the broken circle, the three advanced to the altar, the hunchback first, the other two respectfully behind. The circle closed softly behind them. The whiteclad figures bowed to the hunchback, clearly the Chief Druid. The chanting stopped.

The thick-set man placed the metal bowl on the altar, and prostrated himself. The circle broke, formed a line. One by one, the figures advanced and tossed something, Lampeter couldn't see what, into the bowl, retreated, and like ballet dancers formed the circle soundlessly again.

Seconds ticked away in silence. The prostrate man raised himself, lifted the bowl and brought it over to the hunchback and knelt. With a quick gesture, a hand appeared from under the hunchback's robes. He scattered a few drops of liquid from the bowl towards Begh.

Everyone waited. Lampeter was conscious of a collective expectancy. Nothing happened.

Then for the first time, the hunchback spoke. The stout man sprang to his feet. Some sixth sense must have warned the sheep. It kicked, bucked, tossed its head, screeched. Its eyes glittered in the half moonlight.

The large man took the bowl and placed it on the ground.

He threw back his shoulders. He raised his right arm. There was a flashing arc of metal. A strangled broken-off cry from the animal, and the large man was kneeling, catching its blood to mingle with the fragrance in the bowl.

A terrible moan of pleasure stirred the prostrate figures. And then there was silence, broken only by the scrape of the metal bowl on the tarmac, a sigh as the big man got to his feet, walked over and presented the bowl to the hunchback.

Lampeter was almost afraid to breathe lest their heightened excited senses catch the sounds of his presence. Slowly, like figures under water, the hunchback received the bowl. The other two prostrated themselves again.

The hunchback turned his back on them. He chanted softly. He raised the bowl high. His shoulders straightened though the hump remained. He seemed to grow in size. The others lay still as snow on the cold tarmac.

Then he stopped chanting and in dead silence emptied and cast aside the bowl.

Now Lampeter was no longer conscious of the spines scraping his face. He waited as they all waited. He could feel his own quickened heart-beat. His mouth was dry. The mist was clearing, opening up the airfield before his eyes as if he were travelling down the runway. Now he could distinguish the outline of Begh coming, it seemed, out of cloud towards them.

Everything was black and white and soft muted greys. Even the stain of blood was black. Then the hunchback let out a high-pitched scream as if something were being wrenched from him. The scream gave way to a rushing, whooshing sound. And the black sky came alive.

Between the sky and the figure curled a whip of golden flame. It twisted like lightning and out of the cloud drew a strange pewter glow from the flanks of Begh, flared to glowing orange and plangent red. It billowed over the ground, making the moss and the heather glow an evil green. It soared upwards, illuminating the grey turbulence of the cloud, and thinned to a blood-red wriggling rope, joining it like an umbilical cord to the white figure below. It glowed fitfully across the white robes of the prostrate worshippers. Then shrivelled away.

Lampeter's first thought was of absolute astonishment. Somehow, unbelievably, the Druid had made fire. Fragments of legends flitted through his mind. Greek fire, Celtic fire, lightning itself tamed. The secret . . . was *this* their secret handed down through thousands of years?

Very slightly, he raised his head to get a better view. And then something pressed in the small of his back. A hand bore down on his shoulder, so that he sank forward, scraping his forehead on the spines and the dried heather.

'Keep your head doon, if ye dinnae hae a mind to be torn limb frae limb.'

A few inches away from his face the strange light eyes of Duncan McDermott stared sternly at Lampeter. His right hand still bore down, though more gently now on Lampeter's shoulder, forcing him under cover of the sheltering bush. 'Those folk are not in their proper minds, the night.' The shepherd touched his own head and sighed softly. 'Inside now they are savage as foxes. But they do well to wear the white, for they are silly as sheep, that iss so.'

The white hunchback figure still stood with his back to them. The rest of them lay in the wet and the cold, chanting in ecstasy.

'See,' the shepherd whispered, 'he has them now. Whatso he says they will do. He could turn them on ye like a pack of hungry wolves.'

'And would they harm *you*?'

'Ach! Folk dinnae mind me. They ken that I see tae the sheep. When these strange times come, I herd the loons awa'. But always there is the foolish one.' The old man's eyes went to the stained body of the sheep. 'Ye saw what they did tae yon wee *uan*? They wouldnae tak what wasnae their ain, nor kill like savages, except *this* night.'

'Hallowe'en?'

'Aye. They are burning the old year. Sometimes they burn other things. What they call evil. To cleanse themselves, and bring the sun and life.'

Out at the intersection, the Chief Druid had begun a nasal gabbled chant. The tone was interrogative, hectoring, and weirdly frightening. The tuneless voice seemed to echo in the mist. From the ground a humble chorus answered.

'How long's this sort of thing been going on?' One of Lampeter's feet had gone numb. He shifted himself into a more comfortable position. A dead root cracked. The shepherd held his fingers to his lips. But no one stirred. The litany continued.

'For ever. That iss certain. For thousands of years. The secret order was aye strong in the isles. My mother came here from the Hebrides. There they burn a big ship and a good one, aye.'

'But this is different. When did this start up?'

'Not so long. Not this manner. Mind, this ground itself is strange. Yon mountain too. He has power. Even I can feel it.' He pressed his hands to his chest. 'Can ye not?'

'In a way, yes. But then mountains usually frighten pilots.'

'Aye. They say that the Druids worshipped that same mountain from just about here. When they builded yon airfield, folk said she would be without luck. So she was. Then Begh began to claim some aeroplanes for himself. And when the war was over, times got worse.'

'And then this worship started?'

'Perhaps. No, I mind not so soon as that.'

The Druid put his hands under his robe. The chanting stopped. Silence swished down like a curtain. A couple of seconds ticked by. A faint wind stirred the Druid's garment. The strange whooshing noise came again. There was a sudden gush of flame.

The hood had fallen back a little. The flames reflected on the hunchback's profile.

'Todd!' Lampeter said the name out loud in astonishment.

'Wheesht.'

'Did you know?'

'I didnae *know*. I had it in my mind, *maybe*.'

'Do you know how he does it?'

The shepherd shook his head. 'Divine fire, *he*'ll be telling them.'

'That big man who killed the sheep . . . isn't it Menzies?'

'Aye. Poor fool.'

'He's more than that.'

'No, no . . . no indeed. A fool. They all think it is I that am the fool.' He touched his own grey head respectfully. 'That iss not so. Menzies is a big soft bairn for all his fierce face. A great bladder of lard. Nae more. Always hankering after being the seer, the *faidh*. He wants the secret of yon fire. Be content, I tell him. Ye have the gift of healing. But he seeks this. The fire. So one day he can be chief.'

He turned for a moment to watch the flame. The golden light reflected in the pale eyes, the gaunt face looked like something beaten out of bronze.

'He began this, I mind, in a silly foolish way. But others took hold from him.'

'Is there always sacrifice?'

'That I do not know. Maybe if the fire doesnae come without.'

'Would they kill a man?'

'When they are like this, aye.'

The flame was dying down. A plume of smoke hung like a black gull over where it had been.

'Do you know what trick produces that fire?'

' 'Tis an age of marvels, that iss so. Aeroplanes. We know they are there. But few of us know how they stay in the sky. And them that come here to this place . . . where do they come from and where do they go?'

He was off again, Lampeter thought, into the realms of his own fantasies.

'But that's just a tale surely. Ghostly aircraft.'

The shepherd shook his head as if trying to clear his mind.

'Perhaps.' He fixed his light gaze on Lampeter's face. 'Perhaps I only see them with the other eye. 'Tis hard for me to separate the one from the other.'

Lampeter put his hand gently on the shepherd's shoulder. 'But you really think you saw them?'

'Aye. The whistlers frae the west and north. With the fire itself glowing behind them.'

Lampeter drew in his breath sharply. 'Jet engines. Could be jets. That could be the cause of *their* fire.' Excitement made him raise his voice and then he quickly dropped it to a whisper again. 'And for how long have you seen them?'

'For three summers. Maybe four. I cannae be sure.'

There was another high nasal call from the Druid. A muttered, humble reply from the rest.

'About the same time as yon *crochaire* has been here,' the shepherd jerked his head towards Todd, now beginning to send another jet of flame towards Begh. In the glowing backwash of light, Menzies cautiously raised his head, and furtively began to watch. 'But the ither fools are being led. Like yon silly peeper.'

'And the chief ghillie?'

'He came with Todd. The other ghillies, local men, are fools, nae more.' The shepherd put his hand lightly on Lampeter's arm. 'This *boilich* will soon be done. 'Tis time we were awa'. See, the moon has gone and the cloud has come doon. Go with care. 'Tis evil they deal in. I have it here.' He pressed his fingers on his closed eyes. 'There is fires not yet lit that will be lit. I see it. Go, all of you from this place. While ye can.'

Lampeter reached forward and gripped the other man's arms. 'What about you?'

In the glow, the shepherd's eyes shone with a curious prideful light. 'I shall not leave. Ever.' He squared his shoulders, held his head high. Lampeter saw a fleeting illusion of magnificence. 'It is mine, it iss *me*, this place.'

Then he glanced again at the soaring flame, and the illusion died. Crouching now, he eased himself backwards, turned, and, hands hanging loose in front of him, like some old hunted hare, he darted away to the shelter of a more distant bush. In that last sight of the shepherd, Lampeter thought, he did indeed seem the embodiment of the island, ageing, decayed, oppressed with poverty. He listened to the faint brush of the shepherd's feet over the turf dying away. Perhaps Todd's alert ears heard something too. He suddenly turned. The flame reached like an orange searchlight over the sodden heather. The white garment swished back. The light glittered on a nozzle of steel in Todd's hand, the buckle of a harness, the outline of what made the humped back.

A fuel cylinder.

'God!' Lampeter muffled his own exclamation against the heather. Portable fuel cylinders. Flames. Flame-throwers. Why hadn't his mechanical mind thought of it before? Why had even he been so bemused by all this weird magic? His mind seemed to work in short bursts like the hideous weapon in Todd's hands. He had a sudden memory of little Mrs Ewart showing him the carefully made tiny steel cap and chain she'd found at the distillery. And of himself, as Borghese had done, not recognizing the Russian C, dismissing it as of *no importance*. God! Weapons. War. The old role of the island as an aircraft staging-post. The island at the joining of the world.

Apparently satisfied that there was nothing, Todd turned the flames to their rightful direction again. He screamed in what seemed a final incantation. No, too sharp and authoritative. An instruction more like. Were there really, then, other fires to be lit? Whatever it was, an obedient sheep-like response came back. The whiteclad figures rose to their feet. The flame swelled, rushed towards Begh, showed the huge brooding shadow of its shape.

They all raised their hands, then down they sank to the ground again. The last was Menzies. He was still watching Todd. Lampeter glimpsed his astonished face. Then, abruptly, the flames died. The night became as black as a burned-out match.

The cloud was lower now, and it had begun to rain. One by one, the acolytes stood up, bowed deeply to Begh, and resumed their former roles. The man who had led in the sheep now flung its body into the heather. In threes the others dismantled the rough altar, and carried their former burdens away with them, but this time disappearing all in line towards the east. That left Menzies to pick up the metal bowl. He took a long time over his task, glancing all the time furtively at the figure still erect and motionless at the intersection. Till finally he, too, vanished into the night.

When everyone had gone, Todd walked away from the intersection. Lampeter saw him thrust out his hand to look at his watch. Then he disappeared behind a gorse clump at the other side of the runway. Lampeter thought at first he had lost sight of him altogether, and was just about to stand up when Todd reappeared. Gone were the white robe and the hunched back and the gliding gait. Now there was the brisk sound of footsteps leaving the tarmac and approaching uncomfortably close.

The steps stopped. Todd was standing about fifteen yards from him, looking carefully behind him. Then, satisfied apparently that no one was following, he began to walk quickly towards the south-west.

Lampeter eased himself up as the shepherd had done and stooping low in that strange hare lope followed after him, keeping close to the bushes for cover, and ready immediately to drop flat on the ground.

It was marshy along this quadrant. He walked lightly but still his feet sank to his ankles in the green-covered bog. They made a sucking noise as he freed them. He half expected Todd to turn.

But Todd had reached the perimeter track. There was the sharper sound of shoes on tarmac. The only shelter along here was a derelict dispersal hut. Lampeter glided into its shadow, and paused. But Todd seemed satisfied he wasn't being followed. He looked at his watch again, and hurried off the perimeter track over some rough dry ground. Noisy ground, covered with scree. Lampeter walked on his toes, treading carefully.

He could hear the booming of the sea. Rain rattled somewhere on an old metal roof. A hundred yards or so away to the left was the beginning of the crevasse Crowther had fallen down. Todd was keeping well away from it, walking due south, past an old Nissen hut, along a broken concrete path. The rectangular shape of the southerly hangar loomed. Todd made straight for it. Paused for a moment before he crossed the tarmac apron, let out a churring night-jar call, and then, hurrying into its shadow, disappeared.

Moving quickly himself now, Lampeter followed. Out in the unsheltered open in front of the hangar, a dozen eyes seemed to watch him. There was no sign of Todd. The big front sliding door was tightly closed. But down the far side there were six high windows and at the far end a small door. He heard voices, thrown up and amplified by the hollow metal building.

'So it went smoothly?'

'Fine.' A short bark of laughter – Todd's, certainly. 'I'm

beginning to get a kick out of it.'

A small prim laugh – Dundas's. 'A good general uses the local customs. He doesn't acquire a taste for them.' And then more sharply, 'Where's the flame-thrower?'

'I took it off.'

'Why?'

'Bloody heavy, that's why. If you'd had it on for a couple of hours . . .'

'Damned good one, that! Came out of the Tin Arat consignment. Where did you put it?'

'It's perfectly safe. No one saw. It half skinned my back. I bet those bloody Arabs –'

'I asked *where*?'

'Behind the old rock, just off the intersection. We'll pick it up later.'

'And our guests?'

'Still at the inn.'

'All of them?'

'All.'

'Including the captain?'

'So Menzies told me.'

'Take off is at seven-fifteen. And we don't want any more nosing around here.'

'Oh, they're not all as daft as yon engineer. And after moving his aircraft off the runway for him at that, I could have bashed him.'

'You did,' Dundas said drily, and they both laughed.

'Well, the Starbomber had to get in.'

'All the same, that started everything.'

'He should have minded his own bloody business instead of rooting around while we were refuelling at the underground tanker. Jamie and I had to. There are things I have to do on my own initiative, you know. Like feeding that girl magazines and candy.'

Dundas grunted. 'And then the bomb bay idea . . . that was a boomerang. The pilot might have guessed the tide would bring him back. Without a body we'd have got them away.'

'Well, we *are* getting them away.' Todd's short laugh again. '*Far* away.'

'Thanks to me.'

'Foolproof?'

'Absolutely. *My* plans don't boomerang.'

'Won't there be questions?'

'Who from? The outside world has given them up.'

More respectfully Todd asked, 'When do we start preparing?'

'Two hours before the balloon goes up.' There was the sound of a yawn. 'Come on. You might as well come back for a bite and some sleep. I don't want you making excuses that your back hurts.' Almost aggrievedly: 'Those were specially designed for desert strikes. They should be perfectly comfortable.'

'It's the last one I've got in stock. We're almost down to bloody barley. When's the next lot coming in?'

'Tomorrow night.'

'Same time?'

'Yes. Same time.'

'Going to the same lot?'

'Ben Yussef, yes. Then there's a trawler coming into the harbour from Murmansk next week.'

'Hope you're not flooding the market.'

'Only making hay while the sun shines.'

'And while it doesn't,' Todd said.

They both laughed.

Beyond the window, footsteps echoed over the concrete floor of the hangar, coming towards the small door further up from where Lampeter stood. He cast around quickly for somewhere to hide himself. There was an old broken equipment trolley leaning against the wall. He crouched down behind it. It gave him little shelter, but he could see clearly through its rusted slats.

The door opened quietly on oiled hinges.

'What about further supplies?'

'Quite safe. Ryan's organized that in Leningrad.'

'And the lolly?'

'Quite safe, too. My man in Zürich is beyond suspicion.'

'What if Ben Yussef is in danger of winning?'

'That's the whole point of supplying both sides simultaneously.'

Dundas shone his torch casually around. 'Still raining.' The beam did not quite reach the trolley.

'Does it matter? Will it make it less effective?'

'Not a bit.' Dundas stepped carefully over the puddles on the tarmac. The distillery manager sloshed through beside him. 'They'll never see it.'

Lampeter listened carefully to their footsteps as they disappeared into the mist. He heard them stop. He heard the sound of a car's doors opening and shutting, and engine starting up. Just before he left the shelter of the trolley, car headlights swung past the front of the hangar, going towards the coast road.

Lampeter gave them thirty seconds before beginning to run.

1st November   FRIGEDÆG

The Day of Frigg, wife of Woden, mother of Thor

A thin crack of light showed up at the bar-room window and at first he thought that Menzies had got back before him. He walked softly up to the front door, not sure what his tactics would be if he had returned. But when he turned the handle, it was Claire not the landlord who appeared in the doorway.

Behind her Spence was sitting at the bar counter with the Astroliner operations manual open in front of him.

'We couldn't sleep,' Claire said apologetically, and then, seeing his expression, 'Are you all right? What happened?'

'Get the women up. Tell them to put on the first thing that comes to hand. Peter, wake the men. Keep them quiet and make them hurry. We're going *now*!'

She simply nodded.

Five minutes later, they were all shuffling downstairs.

'D'you think we're going to mek it, lad?' Mrs Crowther was still wearing a thick hairnet and there was the gleam of metal curlers underneath. Like the gleam of metal under the Druid's cloak, Lampeter thought, desperately herding them towards the Land-Rover.

'We'll have a good shot at it,' he said tersely.

'When are you reckoning to take off, sir?'

'Just as soon as we can get those engines lit.'

'But it's pitch black!'

'We'll use the landing lights.'

'Bad as that?'

'Yep.' And raising his voice, 'Is that everyone now? All right! Get moving! Into the Land-Rover. Claire and Peter, sit with me in the front.'

'Briefing.' Claire smiled wryly at Peter.

He smiled back at her. 'So long as he doesn't expect me to do the take-off while he takes on the islanders single-handed.'

Lampeter led the way out into the dark street. Mist was smoking round the inn sign. It swung creakily, moved by the light sea wind, the gaunt arms of the leafless oak stippled with waterdrops that glistened in the light, like an abundance of mistletoe berries. Aware now of its magical associations, the painted tree had taken on a new significance in Lampeter's mind, and the sight of it added impetus to his haste.

He pulled down the tailboard of the Land-Rover. 'Come on, Peter,' he said, taking hold of Mrs Crowther's arm. 'Give me a hand getting the ladies aboard!'

'No, not me you don't, lad!' Mrs Crowther shook off his helping hand indignantly. 'It's dozy articles like some big fellahs that'll need it.' She scrambled hastily up. Signor Borghese gripped Mrs Ewart round her waist and lifted her on board. He looked after her mournfully as if he recognized their time together might be all too short.

'Now who's going to lift me?' Jerry Ainsworth asked, manfully trying to assume the role of jester.

'Actually,' Dawn said, putting a hand on his shoulder and following Frau Hagedorn up, 'the Captain told me he was leaving you behind as a hostage.'

'Now the men! And sharp about it!' Lampeter said. 'Come on! Two at a time!'

'God, it's worse than the Piccadilly line,' Ainsworth said.

'How are we going to stop falling out?'

'Might it not be safer if the men sit and hold the ladies?' Signor Borghese asked, again taking hold of Mrs Ewart.

'I'm not sure –' Ainsworth pretended to groan under Dawn's weight – 'that I wouldn't rather fall off.'

They shuffled themselves into as comfortable positions as they could. The wind flapped at the canvas cover, showering them with raindrops.

'Isn't that everyone?' Lampeter called sharply, swivelling round. Behind him the door of the inn had softly opened. An ample figure clad from shoulder to toe in Dawn's magnificent mink coat stood in the lamplight. A smell of expensive perfume wafted towards them.

'Maiyrat.'

'I'm after coming wi' ye.'

Peter Spence was standing beside Lampeter slotting in the pegs of the tailboard, 'Well, you can't.'

'It's not for you to say,' Claire said. 'Captain Lampeter?'

'Let her, lad. That lass is right scared of her dad when he gets his rag out.' Mrs Crowther shook her head. The curlers glittered. Memory of the nozzle of the flame-thrower and the zombies with Menzies came back to him.

'All right. But there's no room at the back. Best pile up at the front with us. And be quick.'

Thirty seconds later everyone was on board and Lampeter had the engine running. He let the clutch out and the Land-Rover rolled forward into the driving rain, the headlights reflecting on the lightless windows of the cottages. Wraiths of incoming sea mist trailed in front of them as they crossed the harbour slope from the direction of the distillery. Lampeter's heart quickened.

'That your father, Maiyrat?'

The furry shape wedged between Claire and Peter wriggled forward, pressed her nose against the windscreen. She shook her head.

' 'Tis Jamie.'

'The ghillie?'

'Aye. The head one.' She spat out the words.

The figure shrank into the shelter of the cottages, hurrying forward.

'Did he see who it was?'

'I mind he did.'

Lampeter pressed his foot harder on the accelerator. The Land-Rover rocketed forward, left the shelter of the handful of cottages and started bumping over the narrow winding road to the cliffs. There was not a sound behind from the passengers as they hung on desperately. In the cabin, Claire was almost suffocated with the smell of mingled *Je Reviens* and *Diorissima*. The soft fur tickled her nose every time they negotiated a bend. She kept her eyes on Captain Lampeter's grim profile as he concentrated all his attention on the road. The lights picked out the sodden heather, the droplets glittered on the bracken fronds. At the headland curve she closed her eyes. Lampeter hardly slackened. The Land-Rover lurched. There was a frightened cry from behind as the passengers caught a glimpse of the creamy curl of the breakers. The tyres squealed. Lampeter straightened up.

'Tell them to look behind and see if anyone's following.'

'Yes, sir.' Dry-mouthed, Spence gabbled the message through the flap.

'And keep a look-out yourself!'

'Yes, sir.' He thrust his head out of the side window, feeling the wicked little spirals of wet wind clawing at his hair. Then another turn cut off the vision from behind.

'Might there be someone following, sir?'

Lampeter swung the wheel round the last bend and as they came into the stretch that led past the old airfield, trod harder on the accelerator. 'Yep. Now we're on the straight I'll put you in the picture.' He spoke softly and very rapidly, hoping that Maiyrat would hardly understand. 'So you see, if he warns Dundas, that might be it.'

Spence once more wound down the side window, as much to steady his nerves as to look out. The misty air felt bland on his sweating forehead.

They were past the old guard-room now. Another three hundred yards and they had reached the old MT Section.

'Anything, Peter?'

'No, sir.'

A pair of green lights bobbing over the grass turned his

stomach over. 'Just sheep,' he said shakily.

The old stores hut whipped past. A sudden shower of rain rattled on the canvas hood like muted machine-gun fire, and died away again. The outline of the hangar loomed up.

'Get them out fast,' Lampeter snapped at Claire, coming to an abrupt halt and jumping down. 'Keep them over to the right while we pull her out. Mr Spence, get the rope! Tie it to the nose wheel towing-point! Come on! Fast! Maiyrat can get herself out.'

He ran over to the hangar and rolled back the big door. The reassuring white shape of Tango Foxtrot glowed softly through the darkness. There was still no sound of any following vehicle. The airfield was quiet. Except that the damned night-jar, disturbed by their arrival, had started its weird high-pitched calling again.

While the passengers got out and huddled in the shadows to the right of the apron, Spence took the rope and attached it to the nose wheel towing-point. He tested it, and then flung the other end to Lampeter, who tied it to the tail bar of the Land-Rover.

'OK. Seems firm enough.' Lampeter looked up at the nose of the aircraft just inside the hangar. 'Mr Spence, get up into the seat and let the brakes off! Give me a couple of blinks for ready.'

'OK.'

Spence pulled down the rope ladder at the cockpit outside door and clambered aboard. Two minutes later, when Lampeter was again behind the wheel of the Land-Rover, he held up his torch at the pilot's window and flashed it twice.

Very gently, Lampeter let out the clutch and moved forward. Weirdly, silently, behind him Tango Foxtrot moved too, nosing out of the hangar and on to the sodden apron, and then on to the tarmac apron. Leaning out of the side window, he took one hand off the wheel, cupped his mouth and shouted, 'Brakes on,' simultaneously easing his foot right off the accelerator.

A slight squeaking sound mixed with the wet whisper of

the sliding tyres and then Tango Foxtrot shuddered to a stop.

Lampeter got out of the Land-Rover, and called up. 'Stay where you are, Mr Spence. I'll undo the rope.'

Gently herded by Claire, the small knot of people moved forward out of the shadows.

'Claire!'

She came over towards him. 'Sir?'

'Before they actually get on –' Lampeter put his hand on her arm, moving her away from them; he lowered his voice – 'you and Pete have a quick look everywhere. Someone might have . . .'

'Put something on?'

He smiled bitterly. 'They've enough to choose from.' He paused. 'If you do see anything *don't touch it!* Come to me. Spence and I will go over the flight deck and the forward baggage compartment. Hurry . . . but be careful!'

'Sure.' She smiled and swung herself up. She switched on her torch, and moved down the passenger cabin, shielding her torch with her hand. The blood glowed in her flesh. Blood, fire, danger. She shivered, directing the beam under the seats, along the racks. Everything remained undisturbed. Not a head-rest was altered, not a piece of hand luggage had been moved. There was even the loose strap hanging down from Herr Hagedorn's camera, the pile of sick bags Dawn had dropped last time on the floor. Behind the duralumin panel, she could hear Peter searching the rest compartment. She walked slowly back towards the tail. I am like an usherette, she thought, in a theatre, waiting for the show to begin. She repressed the thought of what that show would be when the curtains did go up. She reached the hanging cupboard. Most of the coats had been taken. She swished them aside, looked on the floor, felt in the pockets.

Nothing.

Neither was there anything different in the galley. No one had touched the tins she had left out, or opened a cupboard. In the ladies' powder room, the tell-tale soap had hardened, there was no footprint in the spilled talc.

She opened the trapdoor to the cargo compartment, and jumped lightly in. Down here it was like being in the belly of the whale. She could feel the movements of the two pilots, even hear the nervous murmur of the passengers waiting outside.

The torchlight glimmered on the four packing cases and one mailbag. The cases were still nailed down and metal bound. There was no sign of any interference. There were no footprints on the thin dust on the floor. Certainly no one had been down here. Heaving herself back up into the cabin, she walked forward.

'Anything?' she asked Spence.

'No. So far so good.'

'Same here.' She went over to the open cockpit door and called down softly to the ring of pale upturned faces. 'You can come up now.'

Quietly, not a joke, not a word between them, the silence broken only by their heavy breathing, they clambered up the rope ladder with varying degrees of awkwardness.

Maiyrat and Herr Hagedorn were the last to board. At the bottom of the rope ladder, the girl hesitated. For a moment Claire feared she was, at this critical stage, going to change her mind. But suddenly the girl's face cleared. She unbuttoned the coat, rolled it, tossed it up to Claire, and then stepped sprightly up the ladder, followed quickly by Hagedorn.

Before she slid the door shut, Claire took a long look out over the dark and sodden field. Faintly beyond the curtain of the mist, twin lamps seemed to glow with a distant muffled incandescence – and as quickly died away.

'All's well at the back, sir! Everyone strapped in.'

Lampeter grunted. Neither of the pilots turned round. Bill Barrett's seat seemed to shriek at her.

'I thought I saw headlights, sir.'

Lampeter's head swivelled round. 'When?'

'Just now.'

'Moving?'

'Yes, sir.'

'Which way?'

'Hard to tell with the mist.'

'Mmm.' Lampeter turned his head back.

'Before Starting Engines Check complete, sir!' Spence called.

'Could it be them?'

Lampeter shrugged. 'Energize number two!'

Spence pushed forward the right-hand red button on the instrument panel. 'Energizing two.'

'Light two!'

Spence fingered down the switch below the button. 'Lighting two.'

There was an immediate bang reverberating from the overcast like a crack of thunder, followed by a flash like lightning.

'Energize one!'

'Energizing one.'

'Light one!'

'Lighting one.'

Ahead of them, the perimeter track glistened damply. The raincloud was rolling away seaward. Lampeter taxied forward very slowly over the rough tarmac and weathered potholes, smoke either side trailed behind them as if someone were making a charcoal plot of their movements.

'So far so good,' Peter Spence said more cheerfully.

Lampeter was leaning forward, his eyes scanning ahead.

'It's all too empty. I don't like it. Jamie would have given the alarm. There should have been some sign of them by now.'

Spence was flashing his torch ahead, every now and then giving warnings that the edge of the perimeter track was too close. The beam showed up nothing except heather and bracken and rough stones and scree.

Lampeter pulled open his side window and peered out, still looking for following lights. He put his left hand outside and ran his fingers along the side of the fuselage, touching its cold silver wetness and the bumps of the rivets, feeling it as someone might run their fingers along the neck of a horse before a tough and dangerous ride. Everything depended on Tango Foxtrot now. Without her, they would all certainly be dead.

Even with her, there was danger. What had Dundas meant in the hangar? That they were all to follow the fate of

Barrett was clear, but how was it going to be done? He had been turning *that* question over in his mind endlessly at the same time as he had made his preparations to go. He was at least certain it had some connection with time. It was planned to take place at seven-fifteen, first light, the time he had told Dundas he would be taking off. Dundas and Todd were coming down two hours beforehand to make the preparations.

There was still complete darkness. No sign of lights behind. With any luck, they would be all right. The plot would misfire because he had advanced take-off time.

Lampeter screwed up his eyes and looked ahead. The overcast was higher now, and it had stopped raining. He could just see the edge of the perimeter track.

'Peter . . . shine your torch over the wings . . . see we're not losing any fuel.'

Spence reported, 'No leaks, sir.'

There was an eerie calm over everything. The wind had dropped, and there was no sound except the whine of the engines and the slight hiss of the tyres on the wet tarmac. There was no horizon, nothing visible except a deeper mound of darkness that was Begh, solid against the melting cloudy night.

'I don't like it,' Lampeter said. 'It's a bit too good to be true.'

'Maybe we're in luck, sir.'

'If we are, let's hope it lasts. Claire! Stay up front. Sit in Bill's seat. You won't know what the hell it's about, but you'll be another pair of eyes.'

'Yes, sir.' Obediently she glided forward, sat down and strapped herself in. Something about it gave her a kind of grim determination.

Slowly round the perimeter track they went, the engines gently muttering, the wheels bumping over the uneven track. At least there appeared to be no sign of the Bentley or of Dundas. At the front, the three of them kept watch tensely out of the windows, with Spence's torch flitting like an illuminated blind man's stick tapping along both edges of the perimeter track to keep them on the middle of the way. Every now and again the First Officer called out like a watcher calling soundings, 'A little left, sir, *left*!' Or, 'Lots of room this side!' or, 'Right, sir, *quickly* . . . dirty great hole!'

Yard by yard, they inched nearer to the end of the east-west runway. Watching Lampeter, Claire saw how grimly his mouth was set, how whitely the knuckles of his hand on the throttles gleamed through the taut skin.

'Peter, I'll be using the landing lights for take-off. By that time, it won't matter.'

His voice trailed away. How, he asked himself, did he know whether lights mattered or not? He knew nothing of Dundas's plan except that it was foolproof. Was there, despite his search, some explosive on board? Creeping out as they were under cover of darkness, did they already carry within themselves the means of their own destruction?

Just before he reached the runway, Lampeter turned and glanced first at Spence and then at Claire. The look was a baffling mixture, comradely and yet warning, disciplining and yet affectionate. It seemed to apologize in advance that all might not go as they hoped – yet demanded their co-operation nevertheless. By the time the look rested on her, it had acquired something else, something that made the possibility of disaster more heartbreaking still.

Then, abruptly, he looked away. His hand eased the throttles forward as he swung Tango Foxtrot round to starboard, off the perimeter track and on to the runway facing west.

'Landing lights!'

Two long spears of light thrust themselves forward into the black belly of the night. Bracken, stumpy heather, and the pock-marked runway surface fired yellow under the bright illumination.

Lampeter pushed both throttles hard against the stops. Tango Foxtrot began to move.

Slowly at first, then faster. Grass, whin-bushes, misty wrecks of buildings began rushing past the flight deck windows.

A hundred yards of runway went by. Then a second hundred yards.

And then suddenly, staring out into the night, Claire was sure that her eyes were bewitched.

The black runway ahead was moving, snaking, shimmering in silky rainbow colours.

'Look out!'

Lampeter slammed the engines into reverse thrust. The brakes shrieked like stuck pigs. The three on the flight deck were flung forward on their straps by the sudden shudder of stopping. Tyres squealed. A collective groaning and shouting went up from the aircraft. But whether from the protesting frame, the joints or the frightened passengers, Claire didn't know. Then right into the quivering cone of the landing lights rushed three terrified sheep. Not away from the bright dazzle. Fleeing from something worse – the shimmering runway that still gleamed in the arc of the swerving lamps. Lampeter was wheeling Tango Foxtrot over to the right. She watched his face blanched and lit by the backwash of light. The muscles on his jaw were working. Sweat poured down his forehead. Shock had stunned her mind, printed the scene black and white and static on her memory for ever. But for the moment she was unable to interpret it. All she recognized was that their lives depended on not reaching that moving stream.

She gritted her teeth, as still the aircraft did not stop.

'Christ! Peter, see that?' Lampeter gasped.

With a last screech and jerk Tango Foxtrot came to a stop. Lampeter wiped the sweat out of his eyes and leaned forward. In the long accusing fingers of light, he could see the silky river of kerosene relentlessly moving down the runway towards them, sliding and slithering over the uneven bumps and holes. And at the western end he could just make out three long pipes, grey as elephants' trunks, out of which the oil was pouring. The landing lights picked out the path of the hoses, tracing them across the night right to the underground fuel tank installation that Dundas had dismissed as last war and ancient.

'Christ, Peter!' Lampeter shouted. 'D'you see them?'

The white illumination silhouetted three figures standing by the pump controls and connection on the fuel tank. Under the glaring light they could quite clearly be recognized – Dundas, Todd and Jamie. Then Lampeter pushed the throttles forward, straightened the nosewheel steering and hell for leather made away from the lethal tide of kerosene.

'The bastards . . . the bastards,' Spence was saying over and over again. 'Get our jets on that kerosene and . . .'

'Dundas was quite right. There *wouldn't* have been any trace.'

They reached the end of the runway and wheeled off on to the perimeter track again. Lampeter was thinking how totally in character with everything that had gone before it was, this final plot of Dundas's. In that last huge conflagration would have been to the laird's mind the fitting climax, the right sacrifice and ceremony, utterly in keeping with the mask of black magic under which he operated for his own nefarious ends.

'Open the window, Peter.'

'Yes, sir.'

A wave of moist air, sickly sweet with the scent of kerosene came on to the flight deck.

Nobody said anything more as they taxied away, landing lights still blazing, back towards the hangar. Lampeter was trying to think of what he would say to the passengers, of some new plans to get away safely, when, as the aircraft curved round, he saw there was yet another figure now in the sidewash of the landing lights, over by the intersection.

A huge figure – unmistakable – running, lurching, shouting, bearing on his back that now familiar lump.

Menzies.

In horror, he saw the grotesque black silhouette lift its arms, stretch itself up to an immense tallness. Then a tiny spark glittered like a star at the end of a wand.

There was a whooshing sound like the beginnings of a storm. A swift red arch of flame spanned across to the intersection. Immediately the runway turned into a river of ragged, tossing flames.

Then Lampeter saw something else. Pieces of fire were running up one hosepipe, then the other, then the third – all three racing each other at breakneck speed. He saw the three figures – Dundas, Todd and Jamie – frozen a moment in terror, then turn, leave the pumps, begin to jump away . . .

Closer and closer came the three racing flames.

The next second, the night exploded. The three black silhouettes were swallowed up in red and yellow that tore a flaming hole out of the night sky with a noise like thunder. The airfield, the ruined buildings, the granite slopes of Begh, were bathed in an awesome transfiguring light. Now at last were the runways a fiery cross. It was as if the sun itself had risen out of the bowels of the earth.

Thick black smoke rose out of the tank like the trunk of a giant tree, and spread out to form a low overcast. Through it all the soft rain came down and dissolved into immediate steam.

The echoes of the exploding tanks reverberated through the metal bones of Tango Foxtrot, and the aircraft shivered as though trembling at the sight of her own fate.

Now well away from the flames, Lampeter switched off the engines. There was nothing they could do but watch.

'See how the passengers are,' Lampeter said to Claire without turning his head, his eyes still on the dark figure of Menzies now silhouetted against the holocaust he had lit.

The innkeeper looked down at the nozzle in his hand, then up at the big branching tree of smoke. He looked as if he was going to stay there for ever. Then suddenly he seemed to remember something. He slowly turned his head in their direction. Lampeter could see the pale disc of his face. He stood gazing at them for a few seconds.

Then still clutching the nozzle of the flame-thrower, he began half running, half staggering up the runway towards them.

Maiyrat was out of her seat before Claire could stop her. The aircraft shook as she stomped up the aisle, face crumpled like a child's. Light from the flames flickering through the portholes touched her heavy tear-stained cheeks. Claire just managed to grab her arm as Maiyrat burst into the flight deck.

'That iss my father out there. He iss not in his right mind. I must go to . . .'

'Shut up and stay where you are.' A grim-faced Lampeter was already half way down the crew exit ladder. Spence was still in his seat, indignation at being told to stay where he was obviously swamping his fright.

Lampeter lifted an impatient hand to wave the girls back and then he disappeared. They heard the sound of his feet as he dropped on to the tarmac, and then his steps echoing under the wing.

'No.' Claire shook her head as Maiyrat made to follow him. She still had hold of her arm. 'He knows best.' To herself she added, 'I hope.'

Through the flight deck windscreen, they saw Lampeter emerge from under the wing and walk down the beam of the landing light, going briskly but unhurriedly towards Menzies.

'Does he have to make himself such a target?' Claire said angrily.

'He'll want Menzies to recognize him.'

Claire bit her lips but said nothing. Her mouth was dry. Her heart was banging against her ribs.

'He will not hurt him, he is a douce man when he is himself.' But as if Maiyrat doubted her own words, she held Claire's hand in a crushing grip.

Menzies had slowed his pace. They saw him pause, and examine the nozzle in his hand, brooding over it as if he saw it for the first time. Or seeing how to work it again.

'He simply has to pull the trigger,' Spence said bitterly as if Claire had asked the question aloud.

'A douce man in his right mind, that iss so,' Maiyrat said like an incantation.

'How many times does it fire?'

'About six, I think.' And still in that bitter helpless voice, 'Once'd be enough. Burn him to a crisp.'

Sixty yards, fifty yards. The gap between the two men closed. The sky ahead now was pink with the false dawn of fire glowing on raincloud. It silhouetted the two men approaching each other like ancient combatants. The smoke rose and spread. On the flight deck they could smell it, feel it in their throats.

Their eyes glued to the two men nearing each other, they hardly heard other footsteps, or hearing them, dismissed them as their own heart-beats. Whoever made them kept well out of the landing lights, till suddenly he stepped into the glow of the fires.

Lampeter glimpsed him out of the corner of his eye. Step by step the innkeeper came nearer him. But he kept his gaze on Menzies's pallid face. There was no recognition of Lampeter there. The innkeeper's face was blank, loose-mouthed, stamped with horror.

Then suddenly a voice echoed across the tarmac. 'So ye found the secret of the fire, Angus Menzies, ye great soft bairn?' The shepherd, head high, shoulders squared, apocryphal in his scorn, came striding between them. 'Ye found your fire, so. Then let it clean. And ye found your tree –' he pointed to the great trunk of smoke, the wavering dissolving branches, and spat. With a fine theatrical gesture he held out one hand and motioned with the other for Menzies to unclip the harness. Like a man sleep-walking, the innkeeper obeyed.

'Ach, ye didnae mean a' that, I ken fine.' The shepherd's tone softened.

'Here, let me,' Lampeter said, as Menzies struggled clumsily to slide off the fuel container.

'No. No indeed.' The shepherd waved him fiercely back. Between them, they lifted the container, unscrewed the nozzle, and swinging the dismembered flame-thrower together, flung it into the marsh beyond the tarmac.

Lampeter recognized that the act to both of them was solemn and symbolic. He looked at the shepherd's face. This time, he remembered thinking, the magnificence was not illusion. With or without the sun, the island would come alive again.

Gradually the flames flickered lower, died down, burned themselves out. The pillar of smoke was dispersed by the wind. The hot tarmac cooled.

And again Tango Foxtrot quivered at the end of the runway, poised for take-off.

But now there was a difference. The clouds above had changed from black to grey. The real dawn had broken. Darkness had gone. In the light of day, not in the glare of the landing lights, the runway looked scoured out, curiously cleaned by the fire, stretching in front of them clear of all obstructions now Menzies and the shepherd had removed the fuel pipes – a long straight springboard up into the sky.

'Quarter flap.'

'Quarter flap, sir!'

'Booster pumps on.'

'Booster pumps on, sir!'

The litany of the Before Take-Off Check continued, the pilots' hands touching the controls and switches, their eyes moving over the instruments. Out of his left-hand window Lampeter could see a little band of three – the shepherd, Menzies, and Maiyrat waiting on the burned turf, watching the aircraft.

'Any fuel leaks, Mr Spence?'

The First Officer craned his neck to scrutinize the wings. 'None, sir.'

'If the repairs held after that abort, they'll hold the trip home.'

'So Dundas had it nicely worked out.' Spence adjusted his straps. 'If there were any questions why we went up in the kerosene, it was our own bad repairs that had done it.'

'Yes. He was clever.' Lampeter paused, his eyes scanning the circle of visibility through the windscreen. 'Ardnabegh, the island at the joining of the worlds,' he went on softly. 'How convenient for the laird. Illegal arms from all over the world . . . China, Russia, America . . . via the White Sea route, the North Atlantic, over the polar cap, coming to this deserted staging-post for transmission to all sides in the Middle East, and keep that war on the boil. And doing it literally under the white cloak of Ancient Druidism.'

Spence screwed one eye and tried to assess the depth of the cloud. 'Cunning!'

'Superstition,' Lampeter said, turning round and smiling faintly at Claire, 'is a powerful thing.'

She smiled her little lop-sided smile back. 'The island will probably be back on the map again after all this. Odd how things work out.' She didn't seem to be talking just about the island.

Lampeter nodded. Then in a brisk tone, 'See if the passengers are strapped in and ready.'

Back in the cabin, she was greeted with the soft sound of Philby's guitar and his deep voice singing what he pronounced to be *The Eriskay Love Lilt,* but which Ainsworth said was *Over the Sea to Skye.*

'Nay, lad, no more islands! I thought we'd all copped us clogs in that one. It's Glasgow, then Yeadon airport where we want to go.'

'I belong to Glasgee,' Mrs Ewart began to sing, when Signor Borghese shook his head protestingly and pointed to himself.

'Is there summat we ought to know, then?' Mrs Crowther peered round her seat and fixed her glittering spectacles on their two clasped hands. 'I know a right grand recipe for wedding-cake.'

'Pity we couldn't fix up Maiyrat with young Spence or Philby,' Ainsworth said.

'They could've done a lot worse.' Mrs Crowther strapped herself in vigorously. 'She's not a bad lass. She did right to stay with her dad.'

'Oh, she's not staying here all the time, honey. She is coming to see us in Lombardy. Signor Borghese has three nephews all as handsome as their uncle . . .' The rest of Mrs Ewart's plans were drowned in the shattering crescendo as Tango Foxtrot's engines roared up to take-off power.

'Thor-rr,' said Herr Hagedorn and smiled at his wife.

As Claire slipped back into the engineer's seat, Lampeter released the brakes. Lifting up his left hand, he saluted, then waved to the little party of three standing on the grass. Vigorously they waved back. Slowly the aircraft moved. The oleo legs bumped up and down on the rough ground as the aircraft accelerated. The control tower, the old hangars and buildings, the gorse bushes went flashing past in a blur of speed.

'Hundred and twenty knots, sir!'

Lampeter gently eased the control column back. The wheels left the ground.

'Undercarriage up!'

The engine note softened. The island fell away. Lampeter pulled Tango Foxtrot up into a gentle climb. Dark smoke chalked their twin track on the grey sky. Wraiths of cloud fled past. Far below the shadow of her wings lay the airfield of Crann-Tara, now hidden in mist, now visible like a pewter cross in the cold northern light.

Suddenly there was a white explosion of light. The droplets of the leading edges of the wings turned into dozens of little suns.

'Queer!' said Lampeter. He put his hand on Claire's and pointed. Far below and slipping behind them, the island lay bathed in golden light. Even the black cone of Begh was clear of cloud. 'The sun has come back to Ardnabegh.'

Fontana Books

Fontana is a leading paperback publisher of fiction and non-fiction, with authors ranging from Alistair MacLean, Agatha Christie and Desmond Bagley to Solzhenitsyn and Pasternak, from Gerald Durrell and Joy Adamson to the famous Modern Masters series.

In addition to a wide-ranging collection of internationally popular writers of fiction, Fontana also has an outstanding reputation for history, natural history, military history, psychology, psychiatry, politics, economics, religion and the social sciences.

All Fontana books are available at your bookshop or newsagent; or can be ordered direct. Just fill in the form and list the titles you want.

FONTANA BOOKS, Cash Sales Department, G.P.O. Box 29, Douglas, Isle of Man, British Isles. Please send purchase price, plus 8p per book. Customers outside the U.K. send purchase price, plus 10p per book. Cheque, postal or money order. No currency.

NAME (Block letters)

ADDRESS